SELLING MY SOUL

SELLING MY SOUL

SHERRI L. LEWIS

URBAN
CHRISTIAN

www.urbanchristianonline.net

Urban Books, LLC
1199 Straight Path
West Babylon, NY 11704

ISBN-13: 978-1-60162-848-0
ISBN-10: 1-60162-848-X

First Printing March 2010
Printed in the United States of America

10 9 8 7 6 5 4 3 2

Distributed by Kensington Corp.
Submit Wholesale Orders to:
Kensington Publishing Corp.
C/O Penguin Group (USA) Inc.
Attention: Order Processing
405 Murray Hill Parkway
East Rutherford, NJ 07073-2316
Phone: 1-800-526-0275
Fax: 1-800-227-9604

Dedication

To my write-or-die chick, Rhonda McKnight (*Secrets and Lies, Dec 2009*). Thanks for your invaluable help, advice, encouragement, and everything else you've always done for me as a sistawriterfriend.

Acknowledgments

Here I go again, thanking the same people since it hasn't been that long since my last book came out and not much in my life has changed. This will be short.

I thank God that He's helping me day by day to realize my dream of being a full-time writer. Thanks for the ideas, the favor, the connections, and the faith to continue pressing into destiny.

To my family—thanks for all you do to support my career as a writer. Words cannot express my gratitude.

To Rhonda and Dee—thanks for the plotting session that birthed this book. I couldn't have done it without you!

To Grace—thanks so much for your help with the facts and feelings from your trip to Mozambique. You made me feel like I was there! I pray God hastens the day of your return.

To Claire Hollywell—thanks so much for all the info you shared about Mozambique as well by email and through your blog. May God bless your work there.

To my literary godmother, Victoria Christopher Murray. Thanks for all you do. I mean everything!

To Mel Burns and Attorney Alesia Hilliard-Smith. Thanks so much for all your help with the legal information.

To my Bethel Atlanta family—thanks for all your love and support and for pushing me towards destiny.

To all the wonderful book clubs, reviewers, MySpace, Facebook, and blogtalkradio friends that have done so much to make my previous titles a success. I appreciate your support!

To my readers, I've been greatly moved by reports from missionary friends of the awesome move of God happening in various places all over the world. This book was based on info gained from a ministry I greatly admire in Mozambique. For more information, please check out Heidi and Rolland Baker of Iris Ministries at www.irismin.org.

one

The door to Flight 1748 from Johannesburg, South Africa to Washington DC's Reagan National airport opened, and for the first time in over two years, I stepped onto American soil. I couldn't believe I was back.

What I really couldn't believe was that I didn't want to be back. After such a long time away, I was excited about seeing my mom, my best friend, Monica, and *maybe* my baby sister. Other than that, I wanted to go back to Africa.

I had actually thought about it. Come back, head up to Baltimore to spend a week or so with Moms, fly down to Atlanta to visit Monnie, and then book another flight back to what felt more like home to me than anywhere I had ever lived. And back to the man I had tried so hard not to fall in love with.

The two years I spent in Mozambique had changed my life forever. What started out as a mission trip became an incredible life journey, and I wasn't sure I could go back to life as usual in the States.

Attention in the terminal, flight 1423 is now boarding for . . .

The first thing I noticed when I walked off the plane was

how fast everyone moved. The tangible sense of frenzied, chaotic, hurriedness unnerved me. While I walked at what felt like a normal pace, it seemed like everyone raced by me, bumping into me, giving me dirty looks for getting in their way. It was weird to hear everyone speaking English. I had gotten used to hearing Portuguese and tribal dialects.

As I strolled toward customs, I couldn't help but glance at the placard advertisements on the wall. Every ad seemed to have sexual undertones. What did a woman with long, sexy legs in a short, red dress with pouty lips have to do with life insurance? People whizzed by me dressed in designer suits that cost enough to feed an entire village for a month. They were talking on cell phones and not even taking the time to acknowledge the people they walked past. Rushing toward nothing.

After a long trek from the gate, I sat on the floor in customs, exhausted from more than thirty hours of travel. It was taking forever, but I was excited that in a few minutes, I would finally get to lay eyes on my mom. She waited just a few hundred yards away, on the other side of the stupid customs gate. Monica, unfortunately, was much farther away. She had moved to Atlanta while I was gone, so I wouldn't get to see her until one of us could plan a trip.

Two weeks before I left for Africa, Monica's life fell apart. I remembered the day she called me, hysterical after catching her husband in bed with his best friend. His best *male* friend. She got depressed, as anyone would, and had to get away from her life, so she moved to Atlanta. I couldn't imagine my life here without her. We had been best friends for the past seven years, and before I left for Africa, talked to each other daily and hung out every weekend.

When I finally cleared customs and came through the little gate, I scanned the crowd looking for my mom. For the last month, I dreamed about getting one of her hugs. My mother gave the kind of hugs that could melt all your problems away. The more nervous I got about the re-entry process—that culture shock of coming back to the States after having lived in another country and culture for two years—the more I knew my mom's hugs would make everything all right.

My eyes finally landed on my baby sister, Tiffany. I looked all around her, but didn't see my mother.

"Trina!" She smiled and waved at me. "Over here."

I was glad to feel happy to see her. We didn't always get along and rarely saw things eye to eye, but seeing her face comforted me.

"Tiffy!" I ran over and grabbed her. We hugged, and I held on to her for a few seconds.

We pulled apart, and I pinched her cheeks. "How's my baby girl?"

She rolled her eyes at my calling her that. I couldn't help it. All during her pregnancy with Tiffany, my mother told me she was bringing me home a baby girl to take care of. I guess she was trying to avoid sibling rivalry or something. It worked. I was the devoted big sister that had always taken care of my baby sister. Me and mom probably spoiled her too much, because now, she was a grown adult, thirty years old, and still thought she should be taken care of.

"Look at you, girl." Tiffany studied me from head to toe. I was wearing a classic Mozambiquan *capelana* skirt tied around my waist, a T-shirt, and sandals. She studied my hair. Of course I couldn't be bothered with perming my hair while I was in Africa. After being there six months, I cut off the damaged, straight ends, and let it go natural. Tiffany stuck her fingers in my afro. "I guess they ain't got no perm or pressing combs in Africa, huh?" She looked down at my unshaven legs. "I guess they ain't got no razors either."

I had to laugh and hugged her again.

Tiffany was her usual fashionable self. She'd had an obsession with clothes, make-up, and hair since she was a teenager. She had chopped off all her hair and wore a short, spiky cut that looked frozen into sharp, geometrical points with some kind of shiny varnish. She sported flared jeans with high heels and a red, cleavage-bearing top. At five-nine, she stood only two inches shorter than me and looked model perfect in whatever clothes she put on. It amazed me that she was always broke, but always looked like a million bucks.

"Where's Moms? She in the car?"

"She couldn't make it." Tiffany glanced downward and to the right, a gesture which surfaced when she lied or felt guilty about something. Which unfortunately happened quite often. "She's a little sick and stayed home. I'm gonna drive you up there later."

"A little sick? What do you mean?" I couldn't imagine any kind of sickness keeping Moms from greeting me at the airport after not seeing me for so long. Every time I had talked to her over the past month, that's all she talked about. How she couldn't wait to see me the second I stepped off the plane.

"Just a little sick." Tiffany's eyes did the down and to the right routine, and I got worried. If Moms was sick enough not to meet me and Tiffany was lying, something had to be wrong.

"Tiffy, don't play with me. What's going on?"

"Just come on, girl. We'll see her in a little while." Tiffany grabbed one of my huge suitcases and walked ahead of me toward the exit. I wasn't gonna press her because whenever she was evasive about something and I kept questioning her, we ended up in an argument. It was usually about her owing me money, or something stupid she did with some guy, or some bad life decision she had made. What could she possibly be keeping from me about Moms?

She turned around to look at me. "Why is this bag so light?" She lifted it in the air with ease.

"I gave everything away before I left. I only brought back a few things I bought over there for you and Moms and a couple of souvenirs for me."

She looked at me like I was crazy. "You gave all your clothes away? Why?" She looked me up and down. "You'll gain your weight back in a few weeks. Then you gon' be mad that you left all them clothes over there." She continued on ahead of me, mumbling under her breath, "Went over to Africa and lost her mind . . . giving all them clothes away. If you wanted to give clothes away, you could have brought them back and given them to me."

I shook my head, not even caring to explain that unlike her—with her endless wardrobe of high fashion—I had left my clothes with people who barely had anything.

"Tiffy, slow down." The difficulty of maneuvering through the thronging crowd made me a little dizzy. The air here even felt different.

"Sorry, girl." When we got closer to the entrance, she stood my bag next to me and said, "Why don't you wait here? I'll go get the car."

I nodded and watched her model walk, sashaying her hips toward the door. She turned back and looked at me, biting her lip. "I forgot to tell you. I've been driving your car for a while."

I let out a deep breath. "What happened, and how long is awhile?"

Her eyes flickered down and to the right.

"Never mind. Just go get it."

I couldn't believe how quickly tension crept back into my shoulders. I had been warned that after about a week or so of being back, I would start to feel the stress of life in America, but I had only been back fifteen minutes, and my peace was draining by the second.

Undoubtedly, Tiffany's car had been repossessed, and she was driving mine. Hopefully it hadn't been too long because Tiffany didn't believe in car maintenance. Oil changes, tire rotation, spark plugs; all that necessary stuff. Tiffany must have thought cars ran on magic. Every car that she had ever owned had either been repossessed or had died on the side of the road from lack of maintenance. I could only pray that she hadn't been driving my car so long that her neglect had damaged it.

While I waited for her, I glanced at a newsstand filled with fashion magazines, celebrity gossip rags, and sports magazines. Everything seemed so trivial and superficial. Where was the real news about the millions of AIDS-orphaned children all over Africa, the genocide in Darfur, and kids getting their arms chopped off for blood diamonds in Senegal? Who in the world was Rihanna, and why did she seem to be so important?

My eyes fell on *The Washington Times*. My heart dropped as I read the large front-page headline: CHURCH SEX SCANDAL. Americans only cared about gossip and drama. I hated it. Especially when it involved the church.

I glanced down at the picture of two men in handcuffs, being led away by policemen. One guy had turned his head to shield his face, but the other had been captured dead on.

I gasped. It was the head deacon at Love and Faith Christian Center, the church where I had gotten saved, and the church that Monica had been a member of before she moved to Atlanta. Her husband, Kevin, had been the minister of music there for years, but after everything that happened with them, he had moved to Atlanta about a year after she went.

I'd had limited phone and Internet access while in my remote little village in Mozambique, but from the little Monica had told me, Kevin had gotten involved in a ministry in Atlanta that helped people get delivered from homosexuality, and their marriage had been restored. Before going to Africa, that might have sounded strange and honestly, unbelievable to me. But after seeing miracles there like blind people seeing, deaf people hearing, and dead people coming back to life, I knew anything was possible with God.

I pulled out some money to purchase the newspaper so I

could get a better idea of what was going on. I scanned the article. The head deacon at Love and Faith and the pastor of their daughter church in Alexandria, Virginia had been arrested the day before. The men were accused of molesting little boys in the church for as long as twenty years. I remembered Monica telling me that Kevin had been molested at the church when he was ten years old. I was sure that it had been by one of those men. The article said the arrest came after the ministry council governing the churches received a letter from a man who had been molested there as a child. He had finally spoken out after God had begun taking him through a healing process.

Monica had told me that as part of his therapy, Kevin had mailed a letter to the Bishop's council overseeing Love and Faith Christian Center. In spite of his fears that his celebrity status as a gospel artist would be affected by the admission, he couldn't stand the thought of any more boys being molested. He felt guilty that he had kept the secret for so long. I was glad they kept the source of the letter confidential in the article. Monica would die if the truth about Kevin's past life got out.

I read the article further. Since the ministry council had begun their investigation, they discovered that several boys at Love and Faith DC and Alexandria had been molested. They expected that as the investigation continued, more would come forward.

My stomach churned. Twenty years? How had they gotten away with it that long? How come no one came forward before Kevin had? How many other men's lives had been affected like Kevin's? How could their pastor, Bishop Walker, not have known what was going on?

Did Monica know that the men had been arrested? How was she going to handle it when she found out? Was it possible to keep Kevin's past out of the press or would he be exposed and affected by this as well? If he were exposed, how would Monica handle it?

I tucked the newspaper into the front pocket of my suitcase, grabbed both bags and ambled slowly toward the front door to look for my sister and my car.

I was ready to go home. I had hoped to be able to relax for a few days when I got back, but already I had issues to take care of. First order of business was getting up to Baltimore to see how my mother was doing. Second, I had to call Monica to find out what was really going on.

two

If I weren't already stressed by the culture shock of reentry, wondering what was wrong with my mother, and worrying about what was about to happen with Monica, Tiffany finished me off when she drove up in my car. As I expected, when I peeked into the backseat, it was filled with junk. Papers, magazines, clothes, and dirty dishes. I peered into the front seat and saw stains on my upholstery. When Tiffany popped the trunk, boxes and trash bags left little room for anything else.

I clenched my teeth. "What is all this? Where am I supposed to fit my suitcases?"

"I'm sorry, Big Sissy." Tiffany used her usual term of endearment for when she was trying to butter me up to beg, or calm me down from whatever trouble she'd caused. "I forgot to take them out before I came, and didn't want to be late picking you up. I could only imagine how tired you were and didn't want you waiting at the airport."

Since logic didn't make sense to Tiffany, I didn't bother to mention that I'd emailed my flight information a month ago and that she'd had plenty of time to not only remove her junk, but get the car cleaned too. "Just how long have you been driving it, Tiffany?"

When she smiled a weak smile and did her eye deflection thing, I realized I didn't want to know. I let out a deep breath and got into the front seat, leaving her to fight to get the suitcases into the trunk. I tried not to imagine what my house would look like when I got there. When Moms had begged me to let Tiffany rent my house while I was gone, she promised to have a housekeeper come in once a month to keep it clean. She also said she'd check it on a regular basis to make sure Tiffany's packrat habits weren't getting out of control.

When Tiffany finally got the bags in the trunk and got in the car, I looked over at her. "Is my house a wreck too?"

"Of course not, Trina." She rolled her eyes like I was crazy for asking. "Moms had that cleaning lady come yesterday. She said she wanted it perfect when you walked in the door."

I lay back on the headrest. That was Moms. Always thinking of the details. Maybe she wasn't really sick. Maybe she was just at my house with my favorite foods on the stove, a "Welcome Home" banner in the foyer, waiting to yell surprise when I walked in the door. I smiled, hoping that was the truth Tiffany was hiding.

When Tiffany pulled out of the airport onto the freeway, I grabbed the door handle. "Hey, why so fast?"

She frowned and glanced over at me. "I'm not going that fast."

I looked out the window and it felt like we and all the cars around us were flying. Each time someone changed lanes in front of us or beside us, it seemed like they were going to slam into us. My stomach tumbled and my knuckles turned white from gripping the door handle.

"What is wrong with you? They don't drive in Africa?" Tiffany stared at me then back at the road.

They had talked about this in my re-entry class, but I didn't imagine it would be this bad. "I think I'm gonna be sick. I'm just gonna close my eyes until we get home."

It felt like Tiffany zigzagged all over the road at a hundred miles an hour. I prayed silently until I felt her slow down and pull off the freeway.

"You okay?" she asked.

"Yeah. Sorry. Thanks for coming to get me by the way."

"Of course, Big Sissy. I missed you and couldn't wait to see you. I never thought I would miss you so much when you were gone. Made me realize how much I love your ol' tail."

I hoped she was being genuine, but growing up with Tiffany had taught me that any niceties always came with a price. I'd find out what her verbal affection would cost me later. "I love you and missed you too, Tiffy. You know you my baby girl forever." I rubbed her arm, and we shared a smile.

I jumped when her cell phone rang.

"Dang, girl. You ain't ever heard a phone before?" She pulled it out and her face lit up when she looked down at the caller ID. She flipped it open. "Yeah, I got her. Wait 'til you see her. She look a trip. Nappy afro, no make-up, hairy legs, wearing some homemade-looking clothes with Jesus sandals. She ain't funky, though. I'm glad she didn't give up her deodorant."

I laughed and smacked Tiffany's arm. "Is that Moms? Give me the phone." I wrestled it out of her hand. "Moms?"

"Hey, Tree. How's my world traveler?"

Moms had called me Tree since my adolescent growth spurt. She said it was the perfect name for me because it was short for Trina and also accurately described my tall stature. She said I got the tall genes from my dad. I couldn't remember him being exceptionally tall. He left when I was five and Tiffany was three.

"Wonderful, Moms. What's wrong? Are you okay?"

The few seconds of hesitation before she answered said more than Tiffany's eyes had. "Of course I'm okay. I just wanted you and Tiffany to have some time to bond."

For Tiffany to lie to me was the norm, but for my mother to lie? My stomach churned and not from Tiffany's driving. "Time to bond? Moms, you know I wanted to see you the minute I got off the plane. Why—?"

I stopped myself. Whatever was so bad that had kept her from coming to the airport didn't need my guilt trip added to it. "You're right, Moms. It was good to see my baby girl when I got here." I knew that would warm her heart. It stressed her out that me and Tiffany didn't get along. "We'll be up to Baltimore as soon as I drop off my bags and get a shower. I can't wait to see you."

"Me too, Tree. I missed you bad. You know you girls mean the world to me. Have always meant the world to me." Her voice broke like she was about to cry.

Oh, God, what is it?

"See you in a little while, Moms. As soon as we can get there." I hung up the phone. My heart raced as fast as the car had on the freeway.

I made myself calm down. There was nothing that could possibly be wrong with my mother that God couldn't fix. I had seen Him come through in too many impossible situations while I was in Mozambique to even begin to worry. If it was sickness, He could heal it. Financial problems, He could provide. We had overcome mountains of problems there that I could have never dreamed of living through. There was nothing going on in America that could be as bad as contaminated water, babies sick with malaria, hundreds of orphans who'd lost their parents to AIDS, extreme poverty worse than I could have ever imagined. Whatever it was, we would pray, and He would fix it.

I jumped when the phone rang again.

"Okay, you gon' have to stop all this jumping and door handle clutching." Tiffany flipped open the phone again. "Got her, girl, and she is all tripped out. I'll just let you see for yourself. We're almost at the house. You on your way?" She glanced over at me with a huge smile on her face. "Okay, see you in about an hour." Tiffany hung up the phone.

"Who was that?"

"One of your friends from church. She insisted on seeing you the minute you got back to town."

"Who?" I let out a deep breath and lay back on the headrest, massaging my temples. "Tiffy, I don't want to see anybody right now. I'm tired and sweaty from traveling all night and day, and I just want to get a shower and go see Moms. Why would you invite someone to the house?"

"Don't be getting all mad at me. She called and wanted to see you. I thought you'd be glad to see her to. I'm just trying to make your homecoming nice." Tiffany pouted like I'd hurt her feelings.

I didn't need us getting off to a bad start so soon. "Sorry, baby girl. I'm just tired. I appreciate you trying to do something nice for me. Who is it?"

I could see her pressing her lips together to try to keep from grinning. I felt bad.

"It's a surprise. Dang, can't you let me do something nice for you for a change?"

"Sorry, Tiffy." I leaned across the seat and kissed her cheek.

"Oooh, yuck. Cooties." She wiped her face. We both laughed at her bringing up one of our favorite childhood games. I'd chase her around the house and kiss her, and she'd wipe off all my kisses, accusing me of infecting her with my love cooties.

She reached over and squeezed my leg. "I love you, Sissy."

"I love you too, baby girl."

We finally pulled into my driveway. My house looked so big. I thought of the small mud brick shack I'd spent some of the last two years in, or the huts or tents I slept in when we went to minister in the more remote areas. Compared to them, I lived in a castle. Gratitude and guilt fought to dominate my emotions.

"Here we are. Home, sweet home," Tiffany announced.

For the first time, I wondered exactly how long she planned to stay in my house now that I was back. Knowing Tiffany, she didn't have anywhere to go. I didn't have the strength for that conversation.

I got out of the car and walked in the house through the garage door.

Mmmm, my home. The warmth of it instantly enveloped me when I walked in. I left the suitcases at the kitchen door and walked through the house almost in awe. I opened the refrigerator and freezer and played with the knobs on the stove. I went to the kitchen sink and turned on the water, but quickly shut it off. Almost as if I thought that it would run out or something.

Everything smelled so . . . clean.

I remembered my first few days in Africa; I walked around covering my nose. The putrid smells overwhelmed my senses, and I always felt nauseous. For a while, I dabbed a drop of lavender oil under my nose several times a day, so I wouldn't throw up from all the odors. Then one day, I remembered waking up and realizing the smell didn't bother me anymore. Probably because I had a little odor of my own going on.

I wandered into the living room and sat down on my butter-soft, brown leather couch and relaxed back into the cushions. It felt so good . . . cushy comfortable. I wanted to stay there for the rest of the day. I got up and fingered through my massive DVD collection. I hadn't remembered my television screen being so large. I stepped into my office and looked at my computer, printer, fax machine, and scanner. I looked at my bookshelves and marveled at my extensive book collection.

When I got upstairs, the door to the guest room where Tiffany was staying was closed. I imagined the room looked like a tornado had hit it and focused on being grateful that the rest of the house was clean and intact. I went into my bedroom and stared at the huge, queen size bed. I looked into my bathroom at the Jacuzzi tub and glass shower. It all seemed so luxurious.

I was torn between running a warm comforting bath with aromatherapy salts and jumping in the shower real quick so I could go see Moms. As I peeled my clothes off, slightly tart from being worn for the tiring hours of travel, I remembered I had company coming, so I decided to take a shower.

I rummaged through my drawer and found a pair of jeans and a T-shirt to put on. I knew they'd be a little big on me since I had lost about twenty pounds, but they'd have to do for now.

I took a quick but soothing shower. The sheets of hot water pelting the length of my body felt like a heavenly massage. It was weird not to be washing up with water in a bucket, heated up over the fire. I could have stayed in there forever if I weren't overly conscious about how much water ran down the drain for every second I stood there. I finally stepped out and pulled a large Egyptian cotton towel around me, relishing the feel of the soft silkiness against my skin.

After I pulled a T-shirt and some underwear on, I walked out to the top of the steps. I hollered down to Tiffany that I was going to lie down for a minute until my surprise guest arrived.

I sank into my bed and felt like I had gone to heaven. The pillow-top mattress, fluffy down pillows, and silk sheets felt like paradise on earth. Tears filled my eyes as I thought of my pallet on the floor or rope slat bed in Africa.

God, I thank you for everything you've provided for me. Please forgive me for ever taking anything for granted that you've ever done. That you've always done.

I must have fallen asleep because I jolted awake when the doorbell rang. Tiffany's voice called out, "Trina, she's here."

I was suddenly aggravated with her again. I was exhausted, and all I wanted to do was see my mother. Who could she possibly think was so important? I pried myself from under the covers and out of my bed and pulled on the jeans. They were a size too big. I tramped down the stairs and saw Tiffany standing at the door.

She looked at me, her eyes bright with excitement. "Go 'head. Open it."

I forced myself to smile at her as I turned the knob. My jaw dropped when I saw who stood there. "Monica?"

three

I let out an ear-piercing African screech. "Monnie!" I grabbed her and hugged her. I pulled away, and then hugged her again. I held on to her crying for a few minutes. When we pulled apart, her face was covered with tears too.

"Oh my goodness, look at you. You've lost so much weight, Monica." My eyes traveled downward from her thinned face, to her muscular shoulders, to her sculpted arms, down to her round, swollen belly. I screeched again. "Oh my God! Oh my . . ." I put my hands to my face, then touched her belly, then back to my face again. "You're . . . you're . . . oh my God . . ."

Monica and Tiffany laughed at me. I grabbed Monica again and hugged her. Gentler this time so as not to squash her belly. I finally got the words out. "You're pregnant. I can't believe you didn't tell me. I mean, this didn't just happen yesterday."

Monica laughed and rubbed her belly. I stepped back and gestured for her to come into the house. "No, girl, it wasn't yesterday, but I wanted to surprise you. Me and Kevin went to the beach with some friends one weekend and next thing you know . . ." She beamed. "I'm six months along. I had to come see you now before Daddy Kevin refuses to let me travel anymore. He is so overprotective."

"I can't believe you came to see me. I'm so glad to see you."

Tiffany sucked her teeth. "Oh no; you didn't want no company, remember?"

I turned to give Tiffany a hug. "I'm sorry, baby girl. This is the best welcome home surprise I could have ever asked for."

I led Monica into the living room and gestured for her to sit down on the couch. "You want anything? Water? Juice?" I offered like I knew what was in the house.

"Water's fine."

"I'll get it." Tiffany bounced into the kitchen.

"I don't even know where to start." I sat down in the leather armchair next to her. "I don't even know what to ask. I guess I don't have to ask how you and Kevin are. Last time I talked to you, you guys were about to close on a house."

"Girl, Kevin bought us the most fabulous house out in the suburbs of Atlanta. It's a six bedroom, four and a half bath with a pool, a gourmet kitchen, and a home theatre and music studio in the basement. It's about 5,000 square feet and just wonderful . . . what's wrong?"

I must have been frowning. "Nothing. Wow. Sounds really huge just for the two of you." I looked down at her belly. "Well, three of you." I reached over and lovingly smoothed my hand across her belly, but I was thinking about how many orphaned kids could live in such a mansion.

Tiffany brought me and Monica a bottle of water and a glass of ice each and quietly slipped up the steps. Monica twisted her bottle open and poured half a glass. "I can't wait for you to come down and see it. I have the guest room all ready for your first visit."

I opened my bottle of water and drank almost the whole thing all at once, without taking a breath. Another guilty pleasure.

Monica stared at me downing the water. "Thirsty?"

I nodded. "So finish telling me about you and Kevin and how everything came back together."

"Where do I even start?" She twisted the cap back on her bottle of water and set it down on the coffee table. "When I moved to Atlanta after catching Kevin with Trey, my intent was to file for divorce, remember?"

"Yeah, girl. I remember from one of the last conversations we had before I left, you were psyching yourself up to contact a lawyer."

"It still seems so crazy. You couldn't have told me that I would have gone from consulting a divorce lawyer to six months pregnant before you got back. You know that had to be God."

Monica stopped talking and reached down to rub her belly, and I saw her stomach make a rippling motion beneath her hand. My eyes widened. I couldn't imagine what it was like to feel a baby kicking inside.

She continued, "I met this guy who let me borrow this book he had about people who had lived as homosexuals in their past. With prayer and therapy and classes, they got delivered and were able to live a heterosexual life, get married, and have children and everything. The man who wrote the book had a story similar to Kevin's. He was molested in the church when he was a young boy. After a horrible life 'in the life,' so to speak, he finally cried out to God and got delivered.

"When I read the book, I realized how much I still loved Kevin. He came to visit Atlanta on his concert tour, and I told him about the book. Long story short, he moved to Atlanta, and we actually met the pastor who wrote the book. He's a part of a nationwide group of ministries that helps people get delivered from a lifestyle of homosexuality. Kevin joined his class and also saw a psychotherapist. At that point, he was living with a friend of ours down there while we were figuring things out."

Monica took a deep breath and a little sip of water and went right back to talking fast. "I know it sounds crazy, Trina, but he changed right before my eyes. I saw God deliver him. You should see him now. He's not the man he used to be. Ten times better. Confident, strong, really walking in authority as a man of God."

She slid her shoes off and propped her slightly swollen feet up on the coffee table. "So anyway, one weekend, me and a group of our friends went to the beach. Kevin and my best friend—well my other best friend—Alaysia, got baptized. Later that day, everybody left the house and me and Kevin . . . well you know . . . and wouldn't you know, the first time we did it, I ended up pregnant. Goes to show that my birth control those first couple of years of marriage were a worthwhile investment."

We both laughed.

"We had planned to take things slower, you know. Let Kevin finish therapy, do some couples therapy together, maybe even do some counseling with the ministers at the church, and then have a marriage rededication ceremony and all that." Her belly rippled again, and she reached down to rub it. "Apparently God had other plans. For whatever reason, He decided to put a rush on things."

I laughed and reached over to rub her belly.

"So tell me about Africa. Girl, even with all that's happened, my life is boring compared to everything you've been through the last two years."

I looked at Monica's water bottle and wondered if she planned on finishing the other half. "I don't even know where to start. Later we'll have to get on my computer so I can show you all the pictures because you have to see it to really understand it."

I barely breathed as I tried to describe my time in the village of Mieze. The difficulty of caring for sick and orphaned children, the lack of decent drinking water, the poverty. And yet the beauty of a community crying out to God for revival. Seeing people get healed and give their lives to the Lord.

"Girl, I don't see how you lived like that. No running water?" She held up her Deer Springs bottle. "I can't imagine walking three miles just to get water to drink or wash with. And having to go to the bathroom in a hole? I can't imagine how it smelled over there."

I laughed. Monica obviously missed everything I had said about people getting healed and saved. "You get used to it after awhile."

"What was the food like? What did you eat?"

"Mostly beans and rice. Sometimes fruit and vegetables. Every once in awhile, someone would kill a pig or a chicken and everyone would share. Sometimes we would find fish in the lake. That was the best treat."

Monica scrunched her face up. "Oh my Lord. You're a better woman than me. I couldn't have done it. Where did you sleep? What was the house like?"

"House?" I laughed. "Hut or tent is more like it. They did have a mud brick house that I rotated in sometimes."

"Okay, I can't take anymore. Get to the good part." Monica's eyes lit up. "Tell me about the guy."

I laughed and shook my head. "The guy . . . yeah . . . what can I say?"

She leaned forward on the edge of her seat.

I shrugged. "He's a nice guy. Real heart for missions. In love with God. He's cool."

"Don't even try it. When you were emailing me and on those brief phone calls you made, it sounded like you were head over heels in love about to get married at any minute."

I rolled my eyes. "You're tripping. I did not, Monnie."

Her eyes widened. "I can't believe you. You made him sound perfect, almost like Jesus Himself came back to earth."

I shrugged and laughed. "He's cool."

She narrowed her eyes at me. "Are you doing it again? That fear of commitment, fear of giving your heart away, fear that it won't end up right so you do whatever you can do to sabotage it before it can go anywhere thing again?"

I stood and walked into the kitchen to get another bottle of water out of the pantry. It seemed crazy to see rows and rows of bottled water lined up on the bottom shelf. I looked at the rows of food—junk food with absolutely no nutritional value that Tiffany insisted on eating.

I came back into the den and sat back on the chair, pouring my water over the ice this time. I couldn't believe how good the ice cold water tasted. It wasn't like we had ice in Mieze. I looked down at my watch. "How long are you staying in town? Much as I'm enjoying catching up with you, I gotta get up the road to see my mom. I think something might be really wrong and she and Tiffany won't tell me."

Monica pressed her lips together and looked down at the floor.

"You know something? What is it?"

She looked up at me and bit her lip.

I stood up, towering over her. "What is going on? Why won't anybody tell me anything? I can't believe you know and won't tell me what's going on." Tears started flowing down my face. I knew I was overly emotional from being jet-lagged, but still, they were all wrong for keeping the truth from me.

Monica reached up for my hand and pulled me back into the chair. She reached over and took my other hand and squeezed them both tight. "When I called Tiffany a week ago to let her know I wanted to be here for your homecoming, she burst into tears and told me she was glad I was coming because she didn't know how to handle this all by herself. Your mother wouldn't let Tiffany tell you what was going on because she knew you were coming home soon anyway and didn't want you to end your trip early."

The sad, serious expression on Monica's face and the somber

tone in her voice had my stomach churning in knots. "What . . . what is it?"

"About three months ago . . ." Monica hesitated for a second and took a deep breath, ". . . your mother was diagnosed with cancer."

four

I let out a gushing breath like someone had let the air out of me. I felt like Monica had just kicked me in the gut. "Cancer? What kind? Oh, God, I can't believe this."

Monica squeezed my hands. "Lung cancer."

I put my hand on my chest. "Lung cancer. Oh, God. That's bad, huh?"

Monica looked at the floor again. She was a nurse, so I knew she understood more than she would probably tell me. "I'm not sure how bad it is. If it just stayed in the lung and didn't travel anywhere else, she could do pretty okay. It depends on the kind, how large it is, how aggressive it is, whether it's spread . . . all sorts of stuff. If it's localized and they can cut it out and maybe do radiation and chemo . . ." Monica shrugged, not making me feel any better.

I stared at Monica like she was speaking Swahili. "What are you saying? Or not saying? Just tell me the truth. Don't try to protect my feelings. I need to know what's going on."

Monica reached over and took my hand again. "I don't know yet, Trina. I don't want to say too much until I get more information. Okay?"

I nodded and sat still for a few minutes. Then I got up and marched over to the bottom of the steps. "Tiffany, get down here now," I yelled as loud as I could.

Monica rose and waddled over to me. "Don't get mad at her, Trina. She's been a wreck handling this all by herself."

"Well, she didn't have to. She should have called me the minute she found out." I called up the steps again. "Tiffany, I know you hear me. Get your butt down here."

Monica put a hand on my arm. "Trina, please don't give her a hard time. Your mother threatened her and made her swear not to tell. She was scared to death when she talked to me. You know how your mom can be."

I softened. I did know how Moms could be. As much as she was loving, she could be stubborn, mean, and downright scary at times. Even at thirty, Tiffany was still scared of her and would do anything to please her.

When Tiffany finally emerged from her room and came down the steps, her eyes were bloodshot red and swollen. She must have been crying in anticipation of Monica telling me about Moms's diagnosis. Instead of yelling at her, I took her in my arms. "Come here, baby girl." I squeezed her tight, and she sobbed.

"I was so scared Moms was gonna die before you got home. And that she'd be mad at me if I told and that you'd be mad at me if I didn't. She looks so sick, Sissy. I can't handle it anymore." She melted into a puddle of tears.

I led her over to the couch and sat her down beside me. I cradled her in my arms and rocked her until she stopped crying. I was sorry she'd had to go through this without me.

"Everything's gonna be fine, Tiffy. Moms isn't gonna die. She's gonna be just fine. Okay? Don't worry. And I'm not mad at you. I know how Moms can be. Stop crying, okay?"

She nodded and sniffled on my shoulder. "Everything's gonna be okay?"

"Of course, baby girl. Everything will be fine." Instantly we were transformed back to years ago, after Daddy left. Nights when Moms worked late, and we were home by ourselves huddled in my bed, afraid of thunder and lightning or the boogeyman, or the bad men on our Baltimore row-house block. Or like the time when Moms was in a car accident, and our stupid Aunt Penny told us she was almost dead when all she had was a broken wrist. Or when one of Moms's awful boyfriends would come over drunk. We'd hear them arguing and Moms getting slapped around before she could get to the kitchen to get her skillet or knife.

I held Tiffany now like I had all those times to try to protect her from the pain of the world. No matter what was going on, I had always wanted to make sure she felt safe.

"Come on, let's go see her." Monica brought Tiffany some tissue, and she blew her nose. She took both of our glasses into the kitchen, then came back and picked up my two empty water bottles and her still half-filled one.

I watched her take them to the trash can. "Wait! You're not gonna throw that away, are you?"

She stopped with the bottles hanging midair over the trash can. "What?"

"That water. The bottle is still half full."

Monica looked down at the water bottle and back at me like I was making a big deal out of nothing. I reached out for it. She brought it to me and I drained the rest, then gave her the bottle to throw away. Both her and Tiffany stared at me like I was crazy.

"What, they don't have water in Africa?"

I narrowed my eyes at Tiffany. "You have no idea."

"I don't know why you drank all that water. You're gonna have to stop and pee at least three times on the way to Baltimore," Tiffany said.

I chuckled at the thought of shocking them by stopping on the side of the freeway and digging a hole behind the bushes to use the bathroom. "I'll be fine. Just let me grab some toilet paper to take."

They both stared at me again.

"Oh. I guess they'll have it wherever we go . . . never mind. Tiffy, you ready? Monica, I'll get to see you tomorrow, right?"

Tiffany bit her lip. "Well, actually I was hoping Monica would take you. I need to stay here and clean out your car since you'll probably need it back now." She looked down and to the right.

My eyes widened. "What? You need to . . . what?"

She burst into tears again. "I can't do it, Sissy. I can't go see her today. I've seen her every day this week. Every time I see her, it makes me more sad and depressed. And I can't handle being there the first time you see her." She looked up at me, her doll eyes wide open. "I have a job interview tomorrow. I need to be ready. I know you want me to get this job so I can get my own car and get my own place so you can have your life back. Right?" She blinked her long lashes a few times.

I couldn't look at her. I just turned to Monica and said, "Do you mind driving me?"

"Of course not. That's what I'm here for. And we have so much more to catch up on anyway." She winked, and I knew I wasn't off the hook with telling her about my uninvited romance.

I thought about the newspaper tucked in my suitcase, wondering if she even knew what was going on. "Yeah, you're right. We do."

five

I'd thought my carsickness on the way home from the airport was because of Tiffany's crazy driving, but once we got on 495 headed to Baltimore, it felt like Monica was zooming at a hundred miles an hour too. I gritted my teeth and clutched the door handle.

Monica looked over at me. "You okay?"

I nodded, then shook my head. "I think I just need to get used to being in a car again."

"Well, I assure you I'm a safe driver. Kevin would kill me if I let anything happen to me or his baby." She grinned.

It made me happy to see her so happy. When she dropped me off at the airport two years ago, I never imagined that when I got back, she and Kevin would still be married, and she'd be pregnant with his child.

Almost as if she heard my thoughts, she said, "Remember when you were about to get on the plane to leave for Africa, and you gave me that scripture that says what Satan meant for evil, God was gonna turn it around for good and that somehow, my life would end up being better than it ever had been before?"

I nodded.

"Isn't God awesome? He did just what you said. Even more than I could have imagined."

I decided it was a good time to broach the subject. "So, what ever happened to Bishop Walker and the guy that molested Kevin?"

Her face clouded over a little. She gestured her head toward the backseat. "Grab that newspaper back there. You'll see. A bunch of drama just broke. I was afraid this would happen."

"I read the article while I was in the airport waiting for Tiffany," I admitted. "I was trying to see if you knew."

She nodded. "Yeah, I know. Kevin mailed off the letters to the Bishop's council last July. I guess it took them this long to do their investigation and find out that what he said was true. What saddens me is that a couple of the boys that came forward have been molested in the last year. I wonder what would have happened if Kevin had come forward sooner. I wonder how many other boys there were in the last twenty years. It's scary when you think about it. How many men's lives were potentially destroyed like Kevin's would have been if we hadn't come across Exodus ministries?"

"What if . . ." I didn't want to mention the unthinkable.

"What?" She glanced over at my face. "What if during the investigation Kevin's past gets leaked out?" She shook her head. "I don't know what I'd do. Our life has been great for the past nine months. Our marriage is better than I could have ever imagined. His first album has been off the charts since it debuted. He and our friend, David, are working on a new project with a group they've started down there. We just moved into our new house. And we're gonna have a beautiful, healthy baby boy. I don't want it to get leaked. I'm happy now, and I don't want anything to mess that up."

I pried my fingers from their death grip on the seatbelt to rub Monica's arm. "I hear you, Monnie. It's gonna be okay. God didn't work all this stuff out to let things go bad now. He's gonna take good care of you guys."

She smiled and took my hand. I wanted to tell her to put it back on the steering wheel, but reminded myself that Monnie was the safest driver I knew, in spite of being a little heavy on the gas.

"You're right, God has been too faithful for me to even worry." She put her hand back on the steering wheel. "You know the craziest part? Kevin says he wouldn't mind. Since he finished his classes, Kevin's worked closely with Pastor Ford, the head of the deliverance ministry who wrote the book I told you about. Kevin feels like if his story came out, he would use the platform to minister to people who have experienced sexual abuse and are struggling with their sexual identity. He says that since God sent people into his life to help him get delivered, he should reach back and do the same. He says he'd be able to represent as a successful gospel artist with a strong healthy marriage and children—that if he could overcome, so could they."

I considered it. "He may be right."

Monica gripped the steering wheel tight and squeezed her eyes shut for a second, almost causing me to have a fit. "No, I can't handle that. I have to admit, sometimes it's still a little embarrassing to me. And what if the gospel world rejects him and they don't buy his albums or go to his concerts? What would he do? This might sound bad, but I've gotten used to being the kept wife. Other than spending a few hours a week doing personal training and step classes at me and Alaysia's gym, I like not having to work. And when the baby comes, I definitely don't want to work."

"Girl, you know that's where me and you differ. I wouldn't ever depend on a man to support me. I would never trust a man that much."

"Yeah, girl, we're still praying for your deliverance in that area."

"I don't need deliverance. I'm happy being just how I am."

"What, untrusting and lonely?"

"No, independent and self-sufficient. And I'm not lonely."

"Girl, I don't see how you do it. I thought I would die in the eighteen months without Kevin. I like having a man in my life."

I shook my head. "Naw, girl. I ain't like that."

Monica snuck a peek at me. "Come on. You don't ever get lonely?"

I shrugged. "I always got something to do. I ain't got time to be worried about no man. I don't need anybody slowing me down or distracting me from my purpose."

Monica sucked her teeth. "I ain't got that anointing. Maybe you're one of those women who's called to be single. I never realized you were like that. I just thought you were taking a break because of your battle with the fornication demon. I didn't know you planned to stay alone forever."

I had to laugh. I didn't grow up in church and before I got saved, I had my share of sexual encounters with more than a few men. Even after I gave my life to Christ, it was awhile before I could give it up. It took many days of crying out at the altar, immersing myself deep in the Word, and being mentored by an awesome women's ministry at my new church to get free. I wasn't ever trying to get entangled like that again.

In spite of the number of men I had slept with in the past, I had never been in a committed relationship. On my introspective days, I had to admit that I was afraid to give my heart to a man. I never wanted to experience the heartbreak and devastation I had seen my mom go through when my father left and in the few relationships she'd had after. I don't think she ever recovered, and I wasn't trying to let any man mess me up for life.

"So what about the guy in Africa then?" Monica brought me out of my thoughts.

"Huh?"

"Yeah, what's his name anyway? How old is he? What does he look like? Give me some details. You know a girl needs details."

"There's really nothing to tell. We got close while I was over there and ministered a lot together. But now he's there and I'm back here and that's all there is to it."

I wished that was all there was to it. Because as much as I had tried to prevent it, Gabriel Woods had maneuvered his way into a place in my heart where no man had ever been allowed before.

"Dang, Trina. Humor me. Just give me a few details."

I exhaled to let her know I was annoyed by this conversation. She grinned to let me know she didn't care nothing about me being aggravated with her relentless questions.

"His name is Gabriel Woods. He's thirty-nine years old. He grew up poor in Detroit, and that made him want to become an urban community developer. He transformed some neighborhoods in the inner city there and made a huge amount of money in the process. And then God turned his heart to Africa. He's been instrumental in building houses, roads, wells, and hospitals in the area where I was stationed. He pours most of the money his businesses in the States make into Africa. He's lived back and forth between Mozambique and the States for the past ten years. There. Is that enough details for you? Not that any of this matters."

"Wow . . . he sounds intriguing and worldly and smart . . . and rich. You sure you don't feel anything for him?"

I rolled my eyes. "Can you stop at the nearest rest stop? I have to pee."

"We just passed an exit. Why didn't you say anything sooner?"

"Because you were grilling me about Gabe."

"Gabe? So he has a nickname. That's a good sign."

I exhaled loudly. "Monnie, just pull over and let me pee in the bushes." I opened the glove compartment to her rental car to see if there were any napkins in there. I should have brought my roll of toilet paper like I'd planned.

"Eeeeww, no way. You're back home now. Like the Bible says,

when in Rome, do as the Romans do. In America, we use toilets."

"Fine, Monnnie. I need you to stop somewhere soon, then."
I chuckled. "Do as the Romans do? Where is that in the Bible?
I thought you told me you'd been studying the Word more since
you started going to your new church."

"I have. That's in the Bible . . . somewhere."

We both laughed.

After about five more minutes, we pulled off the freeway and
into a gas station. We both got out and hurried through the little convenience store to the restrooms like we were afraid we
wouldn't make it. Me from all the water I drank, Monica probably from just being pregnant. Monica walked in first. She
turned back around quickly and bumped into me. "Oh gross, it
stinks in there and it's dirty."

I rolled my eyes and walked around her into the restroom.
After I finished and washed my hands, I came back outside to
the car where she stood, holding her stomach with one hand
and fanning with the other. "That was so disgusting. I don't see
how you could stand the smell."

I shook my head. "You have no idea."

"Girl, listening to you, I might never go to Africa."

"You'd be fine if you went to the city. We just happened to be
in a remote area, that's all."

"Yeah, girl. You'll never find me in the bush."

"Don't call it that, Monnie."

"Why not?" She frowned.

I got in the car. It had to be because I was tired. My absolute
best friend in the whole world was getting on my very last nerve
being all prissy and entitled. I rolled my eyes. Americans . . .

"So what are you going to do now that you're home?" Monica maneuvered her way back onto the freeway.

I reached out to grab the door handle. My fingers were sore
from clutching it. "Well, I have enough money saved to live for
about six months while I look for the right job. I want to take

my time and make sure it's something I love." There was no way I was going to tell her that in my heart of hearts I really wanted to go back to Africa. Although with Moms sick, I didn't think I'd get to do that anytime soon.

"You're not going back to PR? I thought you loved public relations. You're so good at it." Monica looked down at my hand gripping the door handle and slowed down some.

I shook my head. "I don't want to do PR anymore. It was starting to get on my nerves before I left, and I can't imagine going back to it now. I want to find something in the non-profit sector. I'd love something working with kids or women in transition or something. If I did anything remotely close to PR, it would be to raise awareness about what's going on in Africa. There's been a lot more of that lately with the Red campaign and Bono and Madonna and all those folks. But if people really knew, this country and other developed countries would be doing so much more to help. Maybe I would use my PR experience and fundraising skills for that."

Monica looked over at me. "I really admire you, Trina. You're really like a real Christian is supposed to be. I ain't gon' lie. I don't think I could give up my life and comforts over here and live the way you did for the past two years. You make me feel selfish. All I want out of life is a happy family." She rubbed her belly. "A good marriage, one or two more children, and a peaceful life in suburbia. I enjoy teaching Sunday School and volunteering with the kids at church from time to time, but that's about it. I'd never even dream of going to Africa. Makes me feel like I'm not really saved, or that maybe I don't have enough of the love of God in my heart." She saw me grab the dashboard when it looked like a huge truck was going to ram into the side of the car, and she slowed down some more.

"It's definitely a call, Monica. God put it in me. That doesn't mean I'm any more of a Christian than you are. We have different callings, and no one is better than another. You're called to

support Kevin's music ministry and to be an awesome wife and
mother. Don't take that for granted. That's a beautiful thing."

"And you're called to sleep in huts and pee in holes in the
ground in Africa." She laughed at her own joke. "Girl, God
knew better. I can't live without my bed and down comforter
and the mall and my hair products and razors. And toilets. And
bottled water. And good food."

I laughed with her. "Girl, it's amazing what becomes not important to you anymore. All the things we think are essential . . .
you learn to live without them. It's a fair trade-off for a much
simpler and more meaningful life." I added, "For me, anyway."
Not wanting to make her feel bad.

I looked at the clock on the dashboard panel. "Gosh, I didn't
remember Baltimore being this far away. Why is it taking us so
long to get there?"

Monica's mouth dropped open. "You've got to be joking. I've
had to drive 60 miles an hour to get your hand off the door
handle, and then 55 to keep you from pushing that imaginary
brake you got on the floor down there. You know me. If you
want me to get you there, I can. I was just trying to keep you
from putting a hole in the floor of the car."

I laughed. "Sorry, girl. You have no idea." I leaned back
against the headrest. "Go ahead and do your usual eighty. I'll
just close my eyes and plead the blood."

She laughed, and I felt the car shift into high speed.

I must have drifted off to sleep because next thing I knew,
Monica was jostling me. "Trina, wake up, girl. We're here."

I sat up and blinked, trying to orient myself to where I was.
Instead of trees and mud huts and swarms of African children
running around, I saw brick buildings and concrete. And the
kids running around on this street didn't make me feel like
bending to embrace them. They made me want to lock the car
door.

"You okay?" Monica rubbed my arm.

"Yeah. I'm good. Just jet-lagged. Let's go on in."

We locked the car and rushed up the walk to my mother's brick row house. I noticed the mailbox was overflowing and opened it and pulled the mail out. Without meaning to, I noticed several of the letters had pink envelopes. A couple said, "final notice." My heart sank. One thing my mom never did was get behind in her bills. She had worked two jobs the entire time me and Tiffany were growing up. It was important to her that even though we were dirt poor, we could wear designer clothes like the rest of the kids. I never cared, but Tiffany, the fashion maven, took full advantage.

Moms also put large sums of money aside from her paychecks for us to go to college. I had gotten a full scholarship and told her to keep it for herself for everything she had done for us growing up. Tiffany had wasted the money going on and off to college for many years. She never finished a degree because of her frequent major changes. Moms was probably still Tiffany's primary means of financial support. Or at least until now. Looked like she needed some support herself now.

I rang the doorbell and stepped back. Nothing could have prepared me for what I saw when the door opened.

I gasped. "Moms."

six

"Tree!" My mom reached out for me.

I was so shocked by how she looked that I just stood there. Her face fell, and I shook myself out of my stupor to hug her.

"Moms! It's so great to see you. I missed you so much." Hugging her felt like hugging a skeleton. My arms could have wrapped around her twice. I pulled away from the hug and looked at her closely.

Her eyes were sunken, and her skin was pale gray rather than peachy brown. Her usually plump, round cheeks were sickeningly thin. I reached up to touch her head covered with a scarf. I rubbed my fingers over it and realized it was flat on her scalp. Her beautiful, thick hair was gone. She had always been much shorter than both me and Tiffany at 5'5", but now she seemed even shorter, smaller. My mother had always been "a looker" as they called her back in the day. It hurt me to see how much the sickness had stolen her beauty.

She forced a weak smile, but I knew my inspection of her was making her feel awful. Somehow I'd have to find a way to act like nothing was wrong.

"Come in, girl. Look at you. Your crazy sister said you looked like . . . Monica! Is that you?" My mom's eyes traveled downward to Monica's belly. "Oh my word. Look who done swallowed a watermelon seed."

Monica laughed, and we both followed her into the house. The house smelled like sickness—the same smell I had experienced on the few trips I made to the hospital to sit with some of the children from the village.

Moms's usually immaculate house was cluttered and messy. Hers was the kind of house where you could stand in the front door and see pretty much everything there was to the first floor. The small kitchen crowded by a large breakfast table. The living room with the old floor model television serving as a stand for the new television. The worn couch that Moms had re-upholstered every few years for as long as I could remember.

Upstairs, there were three small bedrooms. Unless something had changed since I left, me and Tiffany's rooms looked like we never left. Still had the same beds, dressers, and little school desks. Tiffany's room probably still had her New Edition posters all over the walls. As always, pictures of me and Tiffany graced the walls everywhere throughout the house.

As I followed Moms, I realized how slow she was walking, like moving through the house took all her strength. I looked at Monica with a million questions in my eyes. She squeezed my arm and tried to smile.

This was one of those times it was good for my best friend to be a nurse. I would be sure to have her help me ask Moms about her condition, and then I would grill Monica with more questions later. Maybe she could help me talk to the doctors tomorrow. I was sure I wouldn't get the straight truth from Moms. In spite of how bad she looked, I knew she'd try to gloss it over and assure me that she would be fine.

"Tree, you hungry?"

I started to say no until I felt the grumbling in my stomach. I realized it had probably been a good eight hours since I had eaten.

Moms looked at my droopy jeans. "They ain't got no food over in Africa? Girl, you skin and bones."

Look who's talking. "The food is different over there, Moms. Plus we walked almost everywhere we went. Got a lot of exercise."

"Well, I knew my baby was coming home, so I had Aunt Penny come over and cook. We got a real welcome home feast for you."

She started taking covered dishes out of the refrigerator. It pained me to see her get short of breath as she carried the dishes to the counter. I knew it would hurt her feelings if I offered to help.

Monica walked over to the refrigerator. "Let me get that, Ms. Michaels. You sit down and visit with Trina. You guys have a lot of catching up to do."

I could have kissed Monica. She winked at me when Moms turned her head.

Moms came over to sit down with me at the kitchen table. I remembered the bills I had been clutching since I came in the door. "I got the mail. It looked like it was about to spill out the box."

My mother looked down at the pink envelopes and late notices and grabbed them out of my hands. "Thanks, Tree. I'll just put them in the drawer over there." Her eyes didn't meet mine. When she sat back down, she reached across the table and grabbed my hands. "So tell me about Africa."

My heart warmed a little at the sparkle still in her eyes. Typical Moms. We weren't going to talk about the big, stinky elephant in the middle of the room. Her question made me know I wasn't to ask about her health or the bills. I was to tell her about my journey, and we were all supposed to act like nothing was wrong.

As I recounted some of my experiences in Mozambique, she stared at me, eyes wide with wonder. A few times she reached over and pulled her fingers through my afro. She smoothed her hand across my cheeks and squeezed my leg. She kept touching me like she couldn't believe I was sitting in front of her. At one point, I could see tears forming in the corners of her eyes.

"What's wrong, Moms? Are you in pain?"

She sat back and waved away my fears. "Of course not, Tree. I'm just so proud of you. I can't believe everything you did. You sacrificed so much to help those people over there. Our people. You make a mother's heart proud." Her voice choked up, and tears spilled from her eyes. "You make me feel like I'm leaving an awesome legacy."

I felt a knot rise in my throat. "Eventually you will, Moms. But you're not going anywhere anytime soon. I'm not gonna let that happen."

She chuckled. "How you figure? They got cures for cancer over in Africa?"

"As a matter of fact, they do."

The microwave dinged and Monica opened it and pulled out a plate heaped with food. The smell of down home, southern cooking filled the room. Even before she brought the plate over, my nose told me there were collards seasoned with pork, candied yams, sweet corn, and fried chicken on that plate. "Goodness, Monica. That's enough to feed a tribe."

She looked down at the plate. "I figured you must be hungry." She brought it over to the table.

I pushed the plate over between me and my mother. "You guys have to eat some of this with me."

Monica shook her head. "I pretty much eat only organic food."

I stopped myself from rolling my eyes. I respected her wanting to be healthy, but it seemed crazy to be picky about food when people were starving in other parts of the world.

Moms pushed the plate back over to me. "Ain't got much appetite these days. Chemo done messed up my taste buds."

I pushed the plate back toward her. "Please try to eat a little bit. For me?"

Moms smiled and picked up the fork Monica had set on the table. I wished I had brought enough clothes with me to stay for a month. Maybe if I lived here and made her eat and encouraged her spirit, she'd get better. I knew people with positive attitudes fared better with illnesses like cancer.

Monica walked toward the kitchen door. "I think I'm gonna step out to the grocery store and see if I can find something I can eat." I knew she was giving me and Moms some time to talk. "I'll be back in a bit."

I walked her to the front door. "Be careful."

"Girl, I know these streets. I'll be fine." She lowered her voice. "You okay?"

I nodded my lie, and she gave me a hug before walking out the door.

I went back and sat down at the table with my mom, leaning over to kiss her on the forehead.

"So tell me about this cure, Tree." My mother looked skeptical already. "Some tree bark or roots they got over there?"

"No, actually it's the power of God. You wouldn't believe—"

She put the fork down, pursed her lips, and rolled her eyes. "Tree, don't come in here talking that Jesus stuff. You know I ain't trying to hear it."

"But Moms, you wouldn't believe all the miracles I saw in Africa. Tumors dissolving, deaf people hearing, blind eyes opened. There was this baby that had been dead for hours, and we laid hands on it and prayed for it, and it woke up crying. Cancer is no big thing to God."

She shook her head and got up from the table. "Girl, you know I don't believe in all that Jesus stuff. If it's my time to go, it's my time to go. God left this house a long time ago."

I knew she was referring to when my dad walked out on us twenty something years ago. She walked over to her purse and took out a pack of cigarettes and her slim gold lighter she'd had for as long as I could remember.

My mouth fell open. "You're still smoking?" I could barely say the words.

She shrugged. "I got the cancer already. What difference would quitting make now? I might as well enjoy myself."

She clicked the lighter and put it to the end of the cigarette. She inhaled, and then blew out a puff of smoke.

Without thinking, I rose and snatched the cigarette out of her mouth. "Are you crazy?"

My mother's eyes blazed, and she looked at me like I had lost my mind. "Am I crazy? You the one crazy. Girl, I don't care nothin' 'bout you going to Africa. You ain't that grown to be steppin' to me like that. Asking me if I'm crazy."

I stood there, towering over her. She pulled another cigarette out of the pack. I snatched it from her before she could get it to her mouth. I snatched the pack, crumpled it and threw it in the trash. "I can't believe you're still smoking. I've been telling you about this since I was a little girl, and you still insisted on smoking. Now look what happened."

My mother stood there staring at me. She looked like she wanted to smack me. I had only gotten a beating once growing up. Tiffany, on the other hand, acted like she couldn't make it a week without feeling the sting of the belt or switch.

I stood my ground, daring her to pull out the other pack of cigarettes I knew were in her purse. Instead, her shoulders slumped and tears streamed down her face. She leaned into my chest and wept. "I'm dying, Tree. Dying. Durn cancer done spread all over my body. Doctors say I ain't got much longer to live. The chemo can't save me. It's just enough to shrink it a little, but there's too much to get rid of. The chemo can only push the time away. If it don't kill me first."

I took her in my arms and held her while she shook. "You're not gonna die, Moms. I'm not gonna let that happen."

It felt weird to be comforting my mother. She had always been my rock and strength. Had inspired me that there was nothing in life I couldn't conquer. Now here she was, skin and bones. A shell of her usual strong, feisty self. I refused to look at the situation in the natural. The God I had come to know in the last two years was awesomely supernatural. There was nothing impossible for Him. Not even terminal cancer.

I led my mother back to the table and sat her down. I smoothed my fingers across her cheeks, wiping away her tears. "You're going to be fine, Moms. Even if you don't believe in Jesus, I have enough faith for the both of us. He's not gonna let you die. He knows I couldn't handle that. So if for no other reason, He's gonna heal you just for me. And for Tiffany. Who's gonna take care of her lazy tail if you die?"

We both laughed. I grabbed both of her hands and squeezed them tight, then leaned over and kissed her forehead.

"Speaking of . . ." I got up and walked over to the mail drawer where she had stuffed all the overdue bills. I pulled them out and brought them over to the table, spreading them out in front of her. "What's going on?"

She looked down at the table, then back up at me. "I had to leave work three months ago. You know the COBRA on my insurance is crazy high. Plus . . ." She looked down and to the right and I knew I didn't want to hear what was coming next. Moms rarely did the eye thing because she rarely lied. She was one of those straight up people that always told the truth no matter how much it hurt. In fact, the only time she lied seemed to be when it had something to do with my father.

"Plus what, Moms?" I gently lifted her chin so she'd have to look me in the eye.

"Well . . . Tiffany ain't worked steady in about three months. Since I was the one that begged you to let her stay in your house instead of renting it to somebody reliable who would pay the rent on time, I . . ."

My heart sank. "Oh, Jesus. Moms, tell me you haven't been—"

She nodded and looked down at the table again. "I've been covering your mortgage and bills and helping Tiffany out with other stuff."

I let out a deep breath. "When are you going to let her grow up? The longer you take care of her, the longer she's gonna need to be taken care of."

"I know, Tree. But I couldn't let your house go under. I shouldn't have talked you into renting to her. Just shoulda let her be on her own. Or stay here."

We looked at each other and cracked up.

"Yeah, right," I said. "Like you and Tiffy could stay in the same house for more than a week without killing each other."

"I know, chile. I don't know what we gon' do now that you're back. I know you're gonna be ready to put her out soon." A worried look filled her eyes.

"Don't worry, Moms. We'll work something out." I didn't need her concerned about Tiffany being homeless right now. I'd find a way to deal with her just to give my mother some peace.

I fingered through the bills one by one and groaned. "Moms, why didn't you tell me sooner? I would have come home and taken care of you and the bills and everything."

"And what would have happened to all those kids in Africa?" She stacked the bills and pulled them away from me. "I'm not your responsibility. I'm the mother, you're the daughter. It's not your job to take care of me."

I pulled the bills back toward me. "If I took care of you for the rest of your life, which will be years and years, I could never repay all you've done for me. Everything I've ever done, anything I've ever accomplished, I owe it all to you. The best mother in the world."

She held up her hand. "Stop with all that, girl. I ain't done nothing but raise y'all in the ghetto and make sure you didn't starve."

"Whatever, Moms. You know you're the greatest." I rubbed my hand over her scarved, bald head, trying to make myself get used to it. "I wished you had called me. Or at least when I called you to let you know I was staying an extra three months, you should have let me know what was going on then. Why would you let me stay longer?"

"I figured whatever was going on was important if you decided to stay." Her eyes twinkled. She picked up my left hand and held it. "I was hoping you were staying longer because of that man you told me about. Thought sure you'd be coming home with a ring on your finger."

I pulled back my hand and swatted her. "Now I know you're sick. You encouraging me to get married? What happened to 'men ain't no good' and 'you can't trust them for nothing but to be untrustworthy?' 'Give them your heart and they'll break it for sure.' 'If you let a man—"

She held up a hand to stop me. "Was I that bad?"

My eyes bugged out. "Yeah, Moms. Worse."

She chuckled, shaking her head. "I'm sorry, baby. I guess that's why neither one of y'all can keep a good man. I done filled your heads with all that poison." She let out a slow deep breath and intertwined her fingers with mine. "I guess staring death in the face makes you think. I've been thinking about my life and the mistakes I made. Thinking about you girls and what I want for you. I want you to be able to get married and have a family and live a good happy life. I don't want you to end up lonely and bitter like me. You don't want to die alone, Tree." Her voice cracked and her eyes teared up again. "Ain't nothing worse than dying alone."

I rubbed her back and wiped her tears away. "You're not going to die anytime soon. And when you do die, years and years from now, you won't be alone. You'll be surrounded by all the people in your life that love you."

She grabbed my shoulders and made me look at her. "Promise that will include a son-in-law and some grandchildren. And from you—not Tiffany. I'm scared of what man she might bring home. And God knows she doesn't need to bring any kids of her own into this world."

I laughed and rubbed her arm, hoping she wouldn't force me to make that promise.

There was a knock at the door. "Monica got back quick. I didn't know there was a health food store close to here."

I opened the door and couldn't believe what I saw. There were about six kids standing there.

"Where Miss Michaels at?" one of the smaller boys said.

"You gotta be kidding me." I muttered under my breath. I stepped back and let the kids in. They flooded into the kitchen and gathered around my mom.

Two of the girls walked over to the table and hugged her and kissed her sunken cheeks. The boys didn't waste any time opening the refrigerator. "What you got to eat?"

I stood in the kitchen doorway with my hands on my hips. "I can't believe this. Moms, these kids don't need to be hanging around here still."

Moms scowled at me. "Leave my babies alone. They keep me happy."

I didn't fuss too much because I knew she was right. As I watched the kids swarming around her, eating Aunt Penny's soul food and talking animatedly about their day and the goings on in the neighborhood, I saw my kids in my village in Mieze gathered around me eating beans and rice. I guessed I came by it honestly.

I smiled and leaned against the counter watching them. "Make sure you guys wash these dishes when you're done." I pointed a threatening finger at each one of the kids. "Y'all better not be bringing Ms. Michaels no cigarettes. You hear me? If I catch any one of you bringing her a pack of cigarettes, you'll have to deal with me. Understand?"

Each one of them nodded at me with wide open eyes, probably terrified of the scary giant with the big afro.

While Moms was distracted by one of the little boys showing her the latest dance, I picked the bills up off the table and took them into the living room and put them in my bag. Hopefully, she wouldn't notice they were missing. I would go through them later and see how bad things were.

I called Monica to say I was too exhausted to go back to Silver Spring and that I wanted to spend some more time with Moms. She was glad to be able to spend the night at her parents' house, about twenty minutes away. I had thrown a couple of things in an overnight bag before leaving my house, knowing I would want to stay.

After an hour or so, I chased the kids out of the house and told my mother it was time to go to bed.

"You just get back and you bossing me around already?" Moms kissed my cheek and gave me the biggest smile to let me know how glad she was to have me home.

As I sunk into my twin bed in my old bedroom, gratitude washed over me again. It wasn't as comfortable as mine at home, but it wasn't a hard hut floor or a luxurious rope bed. After tossing and turning for about half an hour, I realized that it was too comfortable. My body was used to sleeping on a hard surface.

I also couldn't believe how alone I felt. In Africa, I either slept in a small hut with several other missionaries or surrounded by clusters of African children who wanted to be close to Auntie Trina. And it was weird sleeping without my mosquito net. I felt exposed and almost . . . naked. The sounds of the cars and buses passing by and people talking and arguing on the street outside were strangely disturbing.

After another half hour, I could hardly stand it. I took the comforter off the bed and tipped into my mother's room. I laid on the floor next to her bed, right up under her.

"Tree, baby, you okay?"

"Yeah, Moms. Just weird sleeping in a bed by myself."

She reached down and rubbed my back and I almost cried. The exhaustion of the trip, Mom's illness, and her financial problems weighed heavy on me. The culture shock of being home had hardly started.

I took a deep breath and imagined myself lying on the beach on one of my visits to the mission base in Pemba, looking up at the expansive, clear sky with low hanging clouds, serenaded by the swelling waves of the Indian Ocean. In a place where everything displayed God's beauty and splendor.

Right before I drifted off to sleep, I thought of the bills downstairs in my purse. I might have to take a job sooner than I'd planned. Whatever it took, I was gonna make sure Moms was well taken care of.

seven

The next day, I woke up with the sun as I had for the past two years. When I lived in the remote village areas, we had no electricity, so we woke up with the sun and ended most activity at sunset. That meant most of our days went from five A.M. to five P.M. When I cracked my eyes open, it took me awhile to figure out I was back home. As soon as I did, I turned over on my pallet on the floor and forced myself to go back to sleep.

I didn't awaken again until hours later, when I heard the doorbell ring and Monica's voice shortly thereafter. I got up and quickly got dressed, brushed my teeth, and went down the steps.

"Well, she's alive." Moms hugged me and ran a thin hand over my afro. "Tree, I thought you was gon' sleep all day." I could tell she was trying to get used to my hair.

I hugged Monica. "You sleep well?"

She stared at my eyes. "I should be asking you that."

I shrugged. "It's gonna take me awhile to catch up."

Moms said, "You didn't bring no clothes? You can put on something of mine if you want to."

I looked down at the same jeans and T-shirt I'd put on yesterday after my shower. "No, these are fine." I walked over to the stove and found leftover pancakes and eggs. I realized I hadn't eaten much the night before and fixed a plate and sat down to eat.

"Ain't you gonna warm it up?" My mother frowned.

I shook my head and tore off a piece of pancake, picked up some eggs with it, and gulped it down. Moms stared at me like I had no home training. "They ain't got forks in Africa?"

I shook my head and gulped down another bite of pancakes and eggs. Moms and Monica looked at each other, then looked at me. They finally sat down at the table with me.

"Have y'all heard about this?" Moms looked past me at the small television on the kitchen counter. I winced when I saw what was on the screen. It was the 12:00 news, showing Deacon Barnes and Pastor Hines being carted off in handcuffs. Moms got up to turn up the volume.

"According to their church leadership council, these men are accused of molesting boys in their congregations for over twenty years. Since this story has broken, eight more families have come forward with similar allegations. We can only expect many more . . ."

Moms sucked her teeth. "And you want to know why I don't go to church. They a bunch of hypocrites, that's why. Young boys supposed to be in church learning about Jesus, but instead, they get raped. That's why it's so many gay men in the church now. Foolishness like that."

Monica went pale and bit her lip. I knew she was bracing herself because Moms was just getting started.

Bishop Walker appeared on the screen next, holding up his hand, refusing to answer the questions of several reporters nearly chasing him into the church.

My mother stood. "Ain't that y'all's old church?" She put her hands on her hips. "You mean to tell me the church you was trying to get me to go to was full of all that hell? I knew there was a reason I didn't want to go. There's more sin and hell in the church than us regular folk who ain't got time to be bothered with a bunch of holy rollers telling us we going to hell. Who you think going to hell now? That's why I know all I need to do is live right and love people. Not do nobody no harm. I'll be living better than half the so-called Christians."

"Moms, please." I picked up the last bit of egg on my plate with the last chunk of pancake. "Can we not talk about this right now?" The sick feeling in my stomach had me wanting to not eat that last bite of food, but there was no way I was going to waste it. Moms stopped fussing in time for us to hear the next bit of news.

"The investigation began when a letter was received from a former member of Love and Faith Christian Center reporting that he had been molested by both individuals starting twenty years ago. Love and Faith's church council refused to release the identity of the individual who wrote the letters alleging the sexual abuse. One has to wonder what made the individual finally come forward. We will continue to try to get further information as this story unfolds . . ."

Monica let out a little gasp and laid her head on the table.

I instantly arose and went to her, rubbing her back. "You okay?"

She lifted her head and nodded, apparently trying to keep herself together for my mother's sake. "I'm okay. Just ate something at my parents' that didn't agree with me. You know my stomach is only used to organic, healthy stuff." I took her hand and gave it a squeeze. I walked over and turned off the television.

"Hey, I was watching that," Moms said.

"Don't you want to see what I brought you back from Africa?" I walked over to my bag and pulled out a *capelana* skirt I had brought her. "This is the first of many gifts. I left the rest at home." I stood her up to tie it around her waist but couldn't bear how thin she had gotten. The skirt wrapped around her twice. I sat her back down in the chair. "I have a better idea."

I removed her head scarf, maintaining my composure at the

pitiful sight of her bald head. I smoothed my hands over it, fingering the last bit of peach fuzz that hadn't fallen out yet. I tied the *capelana* skirt around her head and made an elaborate wrap. The vibrant colors in the skirt brightened her face. "Beautiful," I said.

She walked over to the microwave and studied her dim reflection. Her face lit up, and she walked down the hall into the bathroom. I followed her. She fingered the head wrap, turning from side to side and finally smiled at herself in the mirror. "Don't I look like an African queen?"

"Absolutely, Moms." I squeezed her shoulders.

She turned around to hug me. "Thanks, Tree. I'm so sorry about all this."

"Shhh. Everything's gonna be fine." I held her for a few minutes, hoping I could impart faith and strength to her.

Later, after Monica went back to her parents' and Moms lay down for a nap, I pulled her bills out of my purse and sat down at the kitchen table. The more bills I opened, the heavier I got. By the time I had tabulated all her expenses, I was even more upset at Moms and Tiffany for not telling me what was going on so I could have come home sooner. I calculated the cost of getting everything current, and then her monthly expenses for the next few months. It would take more than half of the money I had saved.

I decided to count it a blessing that I still had money and that I could take care of her. I realized that now, instead of having six months to find a job, I only had two or three. Still plenty of time to find what I wanted. When I thought about the fact that I would now have to pay Moms's bills and mine indefinitely, I shortened the time to a month. Which meant I needed to start looking right away.

I would still leave my "invisible" chunk of money in my savings account. I kept about five thousand dollars stashed away in a high interest account and vowed never to touch it except for life and death situations. I forced away the thought that Moms's situation was that critical.

One thing was for certain. Tiffany was going to have to get a job and keep it. No way her grown behind was gonna be living in my house, eating my food, using my electricity and water, and not paying nothing. Doing whatever it was she did with her time while I worked all day. She was going to have to pull her own weight. I knew Tiffany thought she could float easy over the next few months because I would never put her butt out on the street with Moms sick. She was about to find out how different I was.

eight

After spending another night on the floor next to Moms, I got up earlier the next day. I was restless with nothing to do. I realized that in Mozambique, by nine in the morning, I would have gotten up and cooked for thirty children and walked the three mile trek with the other women of the village to get water. After two years, I had just begun to master the art of carrying the large water jug on my head, swaying my hips.

I got up and got dressed, and then went downstairs.

Moms turned around from the stove and stared at me. "Tree, you've had those same clothes on for the past two days. They may be a little short, but I still have some of my old clothes that will fit you. Why don't you go up to my closet and find something?"

I looked down at my jeans and T-shirt. "These are fine. They're still clean." I realized she would have more of a fit if she knew I hadn't bathed since I had taken that first shower at my house. I had just washed in the sink. Daily showers and clothing changes hadn't been a part of my life for the past two years.

Monica came over, and I begged her to take me to a park somewhere so I could see some grass and trees. I tried to make Moms go with us so she could get some fresh air, but she said she didn't want to be bothered by no bugs. I checked her purse and nightstand drawers for cigarettes before I left. As we were walking out the door, I took a deep breath and scrunched my nose, sniffing. "I better not smell no cigarette smoke when I get back. You hear me, Moms?"

"Chile, you ain't nobody's mother, so don't be trying to tell me what to do."

"Try me, Moms. I still know how to pick a switch off a tree."

She laughed and swatted my behind. "Get some fresh air for me. Y'all be careful."

When we got to the park, I took off my shoes and relished the feel of the earth beneath my feet.

"How long are you staying?" I asked Monica. We started walking through the park, Monica walking on a concrete path, me walking next to her in the grass.

"I had planned to stay the whole week, but Kevin is getting nervous and wants me to come home." She looked at me, and I could tell she wanted me to encourage her to go on back to Atlanta.

"You should get back. I know he misses rubbing your belly." I reached over and gave her tummy a rub. "I'll be fine. I promise. Are you gonna be okay? I thought you were going to pass out watching the news yesterday."

Monica was silent for a second, and then her face turned angry. "Kevin should have never signed his name to that stupid letter. What the . . . what in the world was he thinking? He should have just sent it anonymously. With such serious accusations, the council would have started the investigation whether his name was on it or not. But no . . . his therapist convinced him that it was part of his healing process to 'own' what happened to him. Stupid psychology . . . junk."

I could tell Monica was trying not to cuss.

She continued, "You know how reporters are. They just want a juicy story. And what a juicy one this would be. Star gospel artist molested as a child. Secret past life of homosexuality. Story at eleven. And my life would be ruined. For the sake of a good story."

She stopped walking and turned to me, tears forming in the corners of her eyes. "I can't handle this right now, Trina. Please pray with me that this doesn't come out." She grabbed my hands. "Please, pray to the God that raises babies from the dead and opens blind eyes that I get to keep my new life."

I squeezed her hands. "I'll pray, Monnie. But you can't let yourself get all upset and worried about this. You have a baby to think about. You can't get all emotional and stressed out."

She pondered my words for a second, then rubbed her hands over her belly, her jaw now set in determination. "You're right. I have to think of the baby." She looked up at me, less anxiety in her eyes. "I miss you so much, Trina. I'm grateful for my new friends in Atlanta, but no one has been a spiritual strength to me like you always were. Sure you don't want to move down South?"

I smiled. "Can't. Gotta stay here with Moms." I didn't tell her that if I moved anywhere, it would be back to Mozambique.

She nodded. "I know. If things get too stressful here, you know you always have a place to visit in Atlanta."

We walked a little farther, and she asked, "Are you gonna stay up here for a few more days? I'm sure Tiffany would be willing to come up and get you."

I shook my head. "I need to get back to my house and get some things together." I let out a deep breath. "I need to find a job."

"I thought you were going to take some time off to rest first."

"Moms' bills are pretty serious. I need to go ahead and start looking now. I still have a couple of months, but I want to take my time and find the right thing."

We walked along a little farther and came to a set of swings. Even though they were child sized, they were pretty sturdy looking. I sat down in one and rocked back and forth a little.

Monica steadied herself in the swing next to me. "So have you talked to Gabriel since you've been back?"

I shook my head. "He won't go back to the mission base for a week or so. I won't be able to talk to him until then."

"You miss him?"

I shrugged, not wanting to admit how much I did.

"How long did you guys date anyway?"

"Date?" I chuckled. "We didn't really date. I mean, it's not like we went out to dinner, or to the movies or to the theatre or anything. Unless you want to call digging wells and building huts dating."

Monica made a face, and I realized I'd never be able to convey my experiences in Mozambique to her. "Okay, so how long were you guys seeing each other . . . uh . . . when did you meet him?" she asked.

"I met him when I first got there. He's one of the leaders of the mission teams. We worked closely together the whole time I was there. We got closer over the second year I was there."

"What does closer mean? I mean, were you guys in a relationship or was there just this attraction you were trying to ignore?"

I pumped my legs on the swing a couple of times and sailed into the air. As I floated back toward her, I let the words slip out, "He asked me to marry him a week before I left."

Monica gasped and leaned forward. I was afraid she would fall out of the swing. I dragged my feet to stop and grabbed her to keep her from falling belly first onto the ground.

"Asked you to marry him? Trina! I can't believe you didn't tell me."

I looked down at my feet, now covered with dirt from stopping myself on the swing. "I guess I forgot."

Monica's mouth fell open. "A man proposes to you and you forget? No way, Trina. What did you tell him?"

I shrugged. "What could I tell him? I was on my way back here. He can't imagine moving back to the States. I'm sure a cross-continental marriage wouldn't work."

Monica nodded. "I guess not. And I'm not about to let you go moving to Africa."

I bit my lip.

"What?" Monica frowned. "You thought about it?"

I nodded. "Yeah. Some. Well . . . a lot."

"I'm trying to figure out a way to get you to move to Atlanta, and you're thinking about moving to Africa. How can you possibly think of moving to Mozambique?" She smiled. "That must be some kind of man."

"It's not the man. It's just . . . being over there changes you. I understand what he means about never moving back. I kind of felt the same way myself."

"You mean, you would trade toilets and showers, running water and clean clothes, cars and highways, television and a comfortable bed, air-conditioning and good food—"

I held up a hand to stop Monica's list of creature comforts she obviously couldn't imagine surviving without. "Yes. I would. For a much simpler life. A much more meaningful life. Where everything isn't superficial and materialistic. The way we live here feels ridiculous to me now. It's all an illusion."

"So it's just the simple lifestyle you want to go back to?"

"Not only that. It's my calling. What God put me on earth to do. I don't think I could be happy anywhere else doing anything else."

She nodded. "So it's the simple life and the calling. Not Gabriel? He has nothing to do with the longing I've seen in your eyes to jump on a plane to fly back to Mozambique ever since you got home?"

I bit my lip, then pumped my legs and started to swing again.

When I swung toward her, she said, "Yeah, that's what I thought."

When we got back to the house, I spent a little more time with Moms, and before it got dark, we decided to head back to Silver Spring. When she walked us to the door, she held me tight before I left. She was trembling, and I hugged her as hard as I could without hurting her.

She clasped my hand. "I have chemo on Monday. Tiffany or Aunt Penny usually takes me. Do you think . . . ?"

"Of course, Moms. I'll be here first thing Monday morning to get you. I'm gonna go home and take care of a few things, and as soon as I'm done, I'll be back. I'll stay the whole week, and we can go have some fun like we used to. Go to the movies and out to eat or something?"

My mother looked down at the ground. "I don't like going out that much anymore, Tree. I don't like the way I look." She put her hand up to her scarf and grabbed at her skirt that was hanging off her. "And I get tired real easy. Maybe—"

"Maybe I'll bring food, and we can rent movies. How's that?"

She forced a smile. "Sounds good, baby. Just like old times."

But that wasn't like old times. Tiffany had gotten her vanity from my mother. She loved to get dressed up—looking "all special" as she said it—to go out and have a good time. Ever since me and Tiffany left home and Moms could live on one job, we could hardly find her home. She and my Aunt Penny went to play bingo or go thrift store shopping and yard sale hunting. Me and Moms went out to eat and to the movies at least once a month.

She must be going crazy staying in the house all the time. I'd have to make sure I at least took her out to go driving. What I really needed to do was pray to God for a healing miracle.

And then it would be just like old times.

nine

I awoke early the next morning on the floor next to my bed. I had tried to sleep in it, but it was even cushier than my old bed at Moms's house. I went searching the kitchen cabinets for something to eat, but found them filled with non-nutritious junk. I'd have to go grocery shopping later. I settled on some eggs, bread and milk.

As I sat down to eat, I noticed Tiffany had left some mail on the table. I perused several letters and noticed a very official looking one from my mortgage company. When I opened it and read it, my head began to pound. Apparently, my adjustable rate mortgage had ballooned four months ago.

Tiffany obviously hadn't bothered to open any of their letters and had kept paying, or had Moms keep paying the same rate. I had it automatically withdrawn from my checking account, and they deposited the money each month. Now I was two thousand dollars behind on my mortgage.

Which meant I needed to get a job . . . yesterday.

I forced myself to go out on my back patio and lay on the hard concrete, determined to seek God. I prayed, praised and worshipped, but it felt so different here. Like even the spiritual atmosphere was different. In Africa, I felt like I could reach my arms upward and touch God. Here, the heavens literally felt like brass.

I thought about banging on Tiffany's door to confront her about it, but what was the point? She'd make up a bunch of excuses and lies, and I wouldn't be any closer to having the bill paid.

Instead, I went into my office and booted up the computer. I needed to update my resume, and then send it out to every possible opening in the non-profit sector. Two hours later, I was even more frustrated. The available jobs were slim to none, and nothing really seemed like what I wanted to do. It occurred to me that I might have to consider going back to PR for a short while, just to overcome this financial crisis. Just until Moms got healed and I got all our bills caught up.

As I checked online job databases, I was shocked to find my old company had an opening. They were one of the most prestigious public relations firms in the area and rarely had openings for long. In fact, most of the time when they posted openings, it was just a formality. They usually had already picked the new hire. The boss lady must be desperate for some fresh blood from the outside.

I put in a phone call to a friend that worked there with me.

"Well, well, well. I can't believe what I'm seeing on this caller ID. Is this Trina Michaels, back from Africa?"

I smiled. "Yes, Sonya dear. It's me."

"When did you get back? And did you bring a Mandingo warrior with you?"

I had to laugh. "Girl, you still crazy, huh?"

"Won't ever change."

Sonya used to be my *gurl* at work before I left. She was one of those sistahgirls that you loved to talk to because they were crazy and so much fun. The only thing that kept us from being closer and hanging out together outside of office hours was the fact that she wasn't saved and still living the life I fought so

hard to overcome. I didn't need to hear about all her different
lovers and her over-the-top experiences with them. Just wasn't
good for my walk.

We exchanged pleasantries for a while, and then I needed to
get down to the business at hand. "So, I noticed there's an
opening at Silver Public Relations Management. What's going
on?"

"You looking? When you left, you said it was for good."

"I know, but I miss doing PR. More than I thought. You
know once it gets in your blood, you can't let it go," I lied.

"Girl, Blanche will be too happy to hear from you. She's had
the worst time filling your spot."

Silver PR was a large firm in DC. I was the "church girl" that
handled most of their Christian businesses and clients and
many of their non-profit organizations.

"Really? What happened?"

"The first girl they hired was a super crazy religious fanatic.
She blasted gospel music and got mad when we played hip hop
or R&B, talking about how we was introducing spirits into her
holy atmosphere. And she screwed up accounts with the
clients. She was too churchy even for church people. Blanche
fired her after a couple of months."

"Oh dear. Sounds like a nutcase."

"Then she hired this other guy that was just weird. Didn't really
talk to anybody and didn't have much of a personality. He sat at
his desk with his hands folded and his eyes closed all the time. I
don't know if he were praying or casting spells on all of us. He
was just that strange, girl. I think Blanche was desperate, and
he had a decent resume and said he was a Christian."

I searched through my desk drawers for some fancy paper to
print out my resume on. It was starting to sound like that was
only a formality that I might not have to bother with.

Sonya continued, "Since then, they've been assigning
church clients evenly between all of us, but we ain't you. We
don't use the right churchy talk and can't connect well enough

with the churchy people to make them happy. Girl, ain't nobody like Trina Michaels."

"Dang. So Blanche ought to be happy to hear from me?"

"Yeah, but you know her. She ain't gonna let you know the position she's in. She'll probably make you feel like she's doing you a favor. Play hardball with her. Make her pay you what you're worth. Especially with this new big client they're trying to hook. Girl, it's some craziness, and they need a straight-up church girl to handle it. With you, it would almost be a guarantee. Otherwise, Blanche will probably try to dress me up in a long skirt and no cleavage top, make me wash off my makeup and send me in there trying to pretend I got Jesus. Can you imagine?"

I laughed, knowing Blanche would go that far for some money. "Thanks, Sonya girl. I appreciate you giving me the scoop."

"Girl, you know we got to stick together."

I hung up and sat still in my office chair for a minute. Did I really want to go back to public relations? Could I really stand to go back to my old job at my old company? The real question was, did I have a choice?

I would take the day to pray about it, and if I felt like God gave me the go ahead, I would give Blanche a call. Until then, I would continue to perfect my resume and search the computer for other opportunities.

I didn't get a chance to ask God about getting my old job back. Fifteen minutes later, the phone rang and the caller ID read *Blanche Silver*. Sonya must have gone directly to her office to tell her I was back and interested.

"Hello, Blanche. How are you?"

"Trina Michaels, welcome back to civilization. Great to hear your voice. How are ya?"

She was being friendly. Must be desperate. "I'm good. Tired, but adjusting to being home. How are you?"

"I'm good. Sonya tells me you're in need of a job."

"Not really in need. I just called to tell her I was back and to say hello, and she mentioned you were in need of a Christian liaison person." I wasn't about to let her think she was helping me out. I couldn't afford to give her the upper hand.

"Not really in need." Sonya was right. In spite of her being semi-pleasant, Blanche was prepared to play hardball.

"Oh. I must have misunderstood Sonya. I hope all is well. How are the kids?"

"They're fine. Look if you need a job, your old spot is available."

"Um, hmm. Actually Blanche, I was thinking of taking a month or so off, just to get re-acclimated and spend some time with my mother. Maybe go visit my friends down in Atlanta. I'll give you a call when I'm ready to go back to work, though. If it's still available, maybe we can talk then."

"Trina, you never know what this market is going to look like. That would be foolish. You should come in tomorrow. I have a great new client for you. Something you'd love."

"Tomorrow? My goodness, Blanche. I'm still jet-lagged and haven't even unpacked my suitcases. How about next week some time? That still wouldn't give me a chance to go to Atlanta though. How about two weeks from now? Give me a chance to get my bearings."

"I'm offering your job back with a fifteen percent raise. But I would need you here no later than the day after tomorrow. This client needs immediate attention. Immediate."

"Blanche, I wouldn't be any good to you this exhausted. I'll skip Atlanta, but at least give me a couple of days to rest."

"Twenty percent, Trina. Day after tomorrow." Her voice had escalated to a heated point that let me know I had pushed her as far she was gonna go.

"Oh dear. Well, if you need me, I guess I can come in day after tomorrow."

"I'll see you at ten, Trina." She hung up the phone.

I knew it just about killed her to give me a raise. God knew I needed it though. I hadn't even taken the time to pray, but I felt like God was taking care of me and Moms's need before I even asked Him to.

I had to get myself together. I didn't think any of my suits would look decent enough to wear to work. And I had to get some nutritious groceries in the house. I got up and got dressed to go shopping.

When I got out to the garage, I peered in my car and was surprised to find that Tiffany had gotten her junk out of the backseat. Maybe she was working hard to turn over a new leaf. A few moments later, I noticed a huge pile of junk in the corner of the garage. The same junk that had been in the backseat.

I had been willing to ignore the dirty dishes piled in the sink, her shoes in the middle of the kitchen floor and her clothes on the living room floor, but this was the final straw.

I marched up to the guest room and banged on the door. "Tiffany. Wake up."

No answer. I tried to turn the knob, but realized she had locked the door. I banged on the door several times, and there was still no answer. I went to hunt for an Allen wrench to jiggle the lock. When I finally got the door open, I had to call on the Lord not to run over to the bed and choke the life out of Tiffany.

Her room looked like an earthquake *and* a tsunami had hit it. There were piles of dirty clothes everywhere, including in the bed with Tiffany. There were dirty dishes lined up on the dresser, and the carpet looked like it hadn't been vacuumed in the last two years. And the smell . . . I couldn't even think of anything to describe it. And I had lived in Africa for the past two years.

"Tiffany!"

Even with me standing over her, yelling at the top of my lungs, she didn't stir. I was used to her sleeping like a coma patient, but this was a bit much. I reached over and jostled her, and she still didn't crack an eyelid. I went from being mad to scared. "Tiffy! Wake up."

I knelt down beside her to make sure she was breathing. Just as I put my face close to hers, she let out a deep breath that almost sent me reeling across the room. Her breath reeked of alcohol and something else I couldn't allow myself to believe. I bent and smelled her shirt, confirming my fears.

Weed. Tiffany was drinking alcohol and smoking marijuana.

I grabbed her firmly and sat her up in the bed, shaking her the whole while. "Wake up, Tiffany!" I shook her so hard, the thought of being arrested for shaken baby sister syndrome crossed my mind.

She finally scrunched her face and held up her arms, trying to push me away. "What? Leave me alone," she said without opening her eyes.

"Wake up. Look at me." I squeezed her shoulders so tight, I was sure she'd have bruises later.

"Owww, Sissy. You're hurting me." She finally opened her eyes, but kept them downward, refusing to look at me. "Let me go." She sounded like a little girl when she said it. My little baby girl I had tried so hard to raise and protect from the elements of the world.

"What is your problem? Do you really think you're gonna live in my house and carry on like this?" I let her go.

She rubbed her shoulders where my hands had been, studying them for marks I may have left on her.

I stood up. "Wash your face, brush your teeth and meet me downstairs in ten minutes."

She flopped back over on the bed and whined, "I'm tired, Sissy. I don't feel like getting up right now."

I grabbed her by the arm and snatched her back up into a sitting position. "You got two choices. You either get yourself downstairs to talk to me, or you pack your stuff and get out now. You hear me?" I let her arm go and pointed a long finger in her face. "I don't care nothing 'bout Moms being sick. I will put your nasty, trifling tail on the street in a heartbeat if you don't straighten up. Believe it."

Her eyes widened as if she finally realized I was serious. She hung her head, blinked a few times and scooted to the edge of the bed.

I stomped out of the room. I went down to the living room to wait for her, pacing and praying the whole time.

I had always known Tiffany to be between jobs. She never got fired, because she was usually a reliable, conscientious worker. She either ended up quitting a perfectly good job because someone offended her, she couldn't get along with her supervisor or because she "just didn't like it." Therefore, she was always in financial trouble, borrowing from me and Moms when she got into dire straits.

She had moved so many times in the last ten years, the post office probably refused to honor her changes of address anymore. She always picked the wrong men who were usually just as trifling and transient as she was. I even knew, although she and Moms had tried to keep it from me, that she'd had abortions on two different occasions. Maybe more.

As if that wasn't bad enough, now drugs and alcohol? That had never been a part of her routine. As I walked and prayed, I asked God for the best way to deal with her. Screaming and physically abusing her wouldn't do any good. I had to get to the bottom of what was going on. I knew she was depressed about what was going on with Moms. But still, to go that far? There had to be some man involved.

I finally heard her feet shuffling down the steps. I knew she was taking her time getting down to me and probably thinking of what lie she would tell to dig herself out of this. She finally emerged from the staircase and shuffled her feet over to the armchair. I almost expected her to stick her thumb in her mouth like she used to when she got in trouble as a little girl.

I sat down on the couch and clasped my hands together. We

both sat in silence for a few minutes, me staring at her and her playing with the tie strings on her sweatpants. I knew it was too much to expect her to act like a grownup and explain herself, so I decided to speak first. "What's going on, Tiffany?"

She shrugged, continuing to tie and untie knots in the strings.

I gently grabbed her chin and forced her to look at me. "Tiffany?"

Her eyes went down and to the right. "I'm just a little tired. I took some medicine last night because I felt like I was coming down with a cold." She pulled back from my hand and looked downward again. "Oh. Sorry about the room. I'll clean it today."

I could feel my blood turning hot. I took a few deep breaths, but couldn't seem to get control of the anger rising in me. "Do I look like a fool?" I ran two fingers across my forehead and got right up in her face. "Do I have stupid written on my forehead?"

She shrugged her shoulders and bit her lip.

I stood up and started pacing back and forth in front of her. "Do I? You have the smell of alcohol seeping out of your pores and your clothes and hair smelled like you slept at a rap concert last night. If you tell me one more lie, Tiffany, I swear, I'll . . . I . . ." My eyes searched around the room. I felt like my mother. When we made her mad when we were little she would search the room and grab the nearest thing she could find to beat us with. Well, usually Tiffany with. Wooden spoons, hairbrushes, shoes—anything she could get her hands on quickly.

Tiffany sunk back into the couch.

"Do you really think you're gonna live in my house and carry on like that? You know I don't roll like that, nor will I allow that in my home. You're supposed to be finding a job so you can help me and Moms out with the bills. Instead, you're out partying and getting high all night? I just had to accept a job I have no desire to take. You think you're gonna lay up in this house, in that *nasty* room, while I go to work everyday? Huh?"

Tiffany blinked her eyes and shook her head.

"You are thirty years old, Tiffany—a grown woman. You are too old for me and Moms to be taking care of you anymore. And she can't right now. Do you want to be a burden to her while she's fighting this illness? How do you think she would feel if she knew you were out smoking and drinking? Are you trying to kill her yourself? How do you sleep at night?"

"I can't." Tiffany bowed her head and her shoulders started shaking. She burst into loud sobs. "I can't sleep, Sissy. What if Moms dies? She's gonna die. Soon. You saw her."

I let out a disgusted breath, but went over to the couch to sit next to Tiffany. I took her in my arms and held her. She still smelled—bad, but I had held people who smelled far worse in Africa. Shoot, I smelled far worse the whole time I was in Africa.

When her sobs finally subsided, I said, "Baby girl, I understand you being upset about Moms. It was very difficult for me to see her like that. I have to rest on my faith that God is going to heal her. That's the only thing getting me through this. I'm sorry you've had to go through this by yourself. And even though Moms threatened you, I wish you had called me."

I gently turned her face to look at me. "But you have to understand that drinking and smoking isn't going to make it any better. It can only make it worse. How long have you been smoking weed?"

She shrugged and cast her eyes downward. I nudged her chin to make her look at me. "About a month," she finally answered.

"And the drinking?"

She let out a long, stinky breath, forcing me to let her face go. "A couple of weeks after Moms got diagnosed."

I made a face and fanned the air. "Anything stronger than that? Cocaine?"

"No! Of course not." She looked shocked and hurt that I would ask her that. "I'm sorry, Sissy."

I shook my head. "I don't want you to be sorry. I want you to do better."

"I will. I promise." She gave me that little girl look.

I stood up. "You're going to spend the rest of the day cleaning that room and the messes around the house you've made since I've been back, including the garage. Tomorrow, you're going to have to start searching for a job. I'm gonna be just like the unemployment office. Everyday, you have to report to me where you've looked for a job and what the outcome is. You need to have a job by the end of the week."

Her eyes flew open. "There's no way I can get a job that quick, Sissy. You know what the economy is like?"

"I don't care nothing about the economy. Get a job at Macy's, shoot, McDonald's if you have to. After you get your job, we'll decide on what your monthly payments will be." I planned to collect her money every two weeks until she had enough to get a good apartment on a METRO line. I would let her stay here until she had at least three months rent saved up.

"And no more alcohol or marijuana. If you need to go see somebody to talk about all this, we'll set something up."

"I ain't going to see no shrink." She folded her arms. "I'm not crazy, Trina."

"I didn't say you were crazy. I know Moms's condition is difficult to deal with. Especially if you don't have faith to know that God will make everything okay."

Tiffany narrowed her eyes, and I almost expected flames to shoot out of them. "You sound just like them crazy church people. Always talking about what God's going to do. When it's all said and done, you're gonna be standing right there at Moms's gravesite next to me, crying and wondering why God didn't show up. What you gonna say about God then?" She spat the words, sounding just like my mother.

"Tiffy . . ." I reached out to rub her back, but she snatched away and stood up. "I'll do everything you said, Trina. But don't try to drag me into some magical fantasyland and believe that God is gonna do some miracle and poof!—Moms will be fine. She's gonna die, and you need to get ready to deal with it. At least I'm trying. It might be the wrong way, but at least I'm facing the truth. Moms is gonna leave us. And all we'll have is each other, and crazy Aunt Penny. I don't want to hear none of that Jesus mess no more, Trina." She marched up the stairs to her room and shut the door.

I thought of the scripture where Jesus could work no miracles in His hometown because of the people's unbelief. A little fear rose in my heart.

What if Tiffany and Moms talked us out of the miracle we so desperately needed?

ten

I wished I could keep on the jeans and T-shirt I had been wearing since I got back, but instead, I stood in the mirror with a stupid pantsuit on. Who invented such an outfit? It hung off me, in spite of the safety pins I had carefully placed in the back to try to draw the waist in some.

After yelling at Tiffany the day before, I didn't think it would be cool to ask her to drive me to the grocery store. So I got in the car to fend for myself. Luckily, driving wasn't as difficult as I thought it would be, probably because I only drove on the local streets. I was in no way prepared for what would happen to me when I walked into the Giant Food store up the street from my house.

I did okay in the produce section, stocking up on plenty of fresh fruits and vegetables. I bought some fresh fish. I wasn't sure I could go back to eating meat after having watched chicken and pigs killed right in front of me and watching the villagers eating every imaginable part of the animals.

It was when I got to the aisles of food that it started to get to me. Looking at an entire aisle filled with a million different brands of cereal alarmed me. There were twenty-four different kinds of salad dressing. Eight different kinds of peanut butter. Ten different brands of syrup. Nine different types of mustard. Mustard? An entire aisle of different kinds of potato chips and sodas. My eyes trailed across rows and rows and aisles and aisles of food.

All I could think of was my babies. My little children, who barely had enough to eat on any given day of the week. Their swollen bellies, skin full of sores from poor nutrition, susceptible to every illness that came along because they were so malnourished.

I held it together until I got to the bottled water. I couldn't count the different kinds of water. Not only were there several types of spring water, there were flavored waters, vitamin waters, flavored sparkling waters, distilled water, it was endless. I thought of three-mile treks just to get to fresh enough water for us not to catch a fatal case of diarrhea. I remembered spacing my bucket baths farther and farther apart so as not to waste the precious resource because of my American obsession with daily showers.

And here was an unending supply of something so abundant, we took it for granted. In Mozambique, it was the difference between life, good health and death.

I quickly pushed my cart to check out, and then hurried to my car before the dam broke. Once inside, I cried until I had no more tears. I cried for all the babies we had buried while I was in Africa. I cried for the mothers who lost their children because they couldn't afford to feed them. I cried for orphans whose parents had died of diarrhea—something an American would whine and complain about, but would never imagine dying from.

So here I stood in my mirror, wearing a pantsuit that was way too big because I knew after my grocery store experience, there was no way I could survive a trip to the mall for new clothes.

I would need to put some clause in my new contract that I could wear whatever I wanted to on days I didn't have to meet with clients. Depending on how huge this client was and how desperate Blanche was for the money, I might even be able to negotiate working from home.

When I walked into the office, the first person I saw was Sonya. She gave me a big hug. "Dang, girl. Maybe I need to go to Africa so I can lose some of this weight." She patted her huge behind and rubbed her protruding belly. Sonya was one of those people that tried every crazy fad diet that came out. Maple syrup diet, lemonade diet, peanut butter diet, even a pig skin diet. I don't think she ever lost a pound.

"The Africa diet? Yeah, that might work for you, Sonya." We laughed.

She pointed me towards my old work area. I walked over to my old desk, now empty and clean, still not believing I was back in this place. I took a deep breath and thanked God that there was a job open quickly that I was familiar with. And that I'd be making more money than before. I'd have me and Moms out of debt in no time, and I'd be able to start saving to go back to Africa.

From the news, I had gathered that there was a housing crisis so it might not be the best time to put my house on the market. If I could find some reliable folks to lease it to, that would be another burden I could be free of, and I'd be one step closer to Mozambique.

"Trina. You're late." My nerves were instantly plucked by Blanche Silver's grating voice. When I'd left, I thought I was through hearing her bark my name. She walked up to my desk with her hands on her hips, her eyebrows knitted and lips pursed.

I looked down at my watch. "It's ten 'til ten." I refused to be moved by her. I made myself remember that she needed me as much as I needed her. And that she had no idea how desperately I needed her.

She gave me a plastic smile. "Good to see you, Trina. You look different. What'd you do?"

"Changed my hair and lost some weight."

"Um hmm." She nodded. "You look very different."

I wasn't sure whether to thank her or be insulted. Not that it mattered.

"I trust that your trip was a success?"

I nodded, knowing that she didn't really want to hear anything about it. She just knew it was the right thing to say.

She clasped her hands together. "Come into my office. Let's talk business." Obviously that was all the energy she had for small talk. Not that I minded. Exchanging pleasantries with Blanche Silver was never really pleasant.

"Have a seat." She gestured for me to sit in the office chair in front of her desk. Her walls were covered with her degrees and awards, pictures with some of our high profile clients, and newspaper articles on clients and the firm. She probably surrounded herself with constant reminders of her accomplishments to quiet the unfulfilled, unsatisfied gnawing that obviously haunted her.

"So I may have spoken too soon when I offered you a twenty percent raise yesterday. It looks more like it will be ten percent."

I rose from my seat. "I wish you had called me and saved me the trouble of coming in then." I started walking toward her office door. The problem with playing games with people for years was that after awhile, the game became familiar. I knew she just wanted to see if she could get me for cheaper.

She rose quickly, cursing under her breath. "Why are you giving me such a hard time?"

"I'm not giving you a hard time. It was not my intention to come back to work here. You have a new client that you want me to represent. In order to persuade me to do so, you made me an offer that piqued my interest. Now that I'm here, you want to rescind that offer. I don't have the time or patience for that. I'm still exhausted and don't need to play games with you."

She held up a hand to calm me down, surprise and what

even appeared to be respect in her eyes. "All right, Trina. You'll get your twenty percent." She opened a folder and took out an offer letter. It contained my job description and the promised salary increase. She probably had the exact same letter in that folder with a ten percent raise on it, had I been dumb enough to take it. Made me mad enough that I wanted to walk out of her office. I thought about all the bills I had to deal with, took the paper and sat back down in the chair.

After a few minutes of hesitation, I signed the letter. I felt like I was signing my life away. The letter required me to stay at least a year at that pay increase, otherwise I would have to pay the difference back. I reasoned to myself that it would give me plenty of time to get Moms set, and I could save tons for Africa. I would be able to stay a good long while and also make the kind of donations I wished I could have made on my last trip.

After I signed the paper, Blanche said, "I'd like to give you time to settle back in, but as I mentioned, this client requires immediate attention. I'll have Martin explain what's going on, and we'll have you set up an introductory meeting as soon as possible. There are a couple other clients we'll have you take over, but this particular one is top priority. I trust you'll give it your best. It's good to know I have someone I can count on with this kind of client."

Blanche stood and shook my hand. "Nice to have you back on board, Trina." She smiled, and I almost believed her. Her smile left almost immediately as she looked at me from head to toe. "You're going to need to get some new clothes, do something with your hair, and for God's sake, put on some make-up. You're not in Africa anymore." She sat back down at her desk and turned toward her computer, dismissing me.

I sucked in a breath and bit my tongue to keep from replying. I left quickly, wondering if I should have pushed for a six-month contract or working from home. Blanche wasn't the kind of person you could make any changes with after signing on the dotted line. I shrugged off the little concerns nagging me and walked to Martin's office.

A huge smile spread across his face when I walked in his door. "I am *so* glad you're back, Trina." He stood to shake my hand. It was weird for him to be so happy to see me. Not that we didn't get along or anything before I left. He was just one of those people I said hi and bye to without ever having much other conversation. I kinda thought he might have been threatened by me. I was one of the firm's top public relations specialists. Even though I specialized in Christian clients and non-profit organizations, I could serve regular businesses just as well. I couldn't quite put my finger on anything in particular, but there were a couple of subtle comments he made at group meetings that made me wonder if I were a threat to his male ego.

He gestured for me to take a seat across from him. "This client has your name written all over it. And honestly, I wouldn't touch it with a ten-foot pole."

I frowned. "Why not? Too churchy for you?"

Martin's eyes widened. "You mean Blanche didn't tell you about the client?"

I shook my head, starting to get a little nervous.

He half grimaced, half smiled. "Whoa boy. Wait 'til you see this one. You've got your work cut out for you."

He pulled a folder out of a stack on his desk and thumbed through it. "That's just like Blanche. She probably buttered you up with how great you are and how valued you are to the team to get you to take your old job back. Failing to mention that she's assigning you to work with the devil himself. What'd she promise you? A corner office?"

I wasn't about to tell him about my raise. I didn't want to add any tension by him knowing I made more money than he did. I smiled weakly. "No, I didn't even think to hold out for the corner office."

"Yeah, well, you'll learn. With Blanche, there's always a game. One day you'll be able to play it."

I nodded, content to let him think I was naïve and stupid.

He pulled a couple of sheets out of the folder. "Anyway, this is the client you'll be working with." He pulled out a newspaper article and chuckled. "Boy, Blanche really got you good." He shook his head in pity, like he was wondering how I could have been so stupid.

When he handed me the article, I sucked in a sharp breath. "You can't be serious." It was the very same article I had read in the newspaper at the airport. About Deacon Barnes and Pastor Hines being arrested.

I stood up. "There's no way I'm taking this client."

"You know them?"

I took a deep breath to get myself together. "I've been following the story on the news. It's awful. I think the last count was eighteen boys and young men coming forward so far. What PR could they possibly want?"

"Oh, it's not the men being accused. It's the pastor of the church they used to serve under."

My eyes flew open. "Bishop Walker?"

Martin squinted his eyes at me. "So you do know them."

No sense in lying. "I used to go to church there years ago. I left because . . ." I took the article from Martin and glanced at it again. "So why is he hiring a PR firm? As far as I've heard, no one's accused him of anything . . . yet."

"Trina, you know."

We said it together, "Damage control."

Martin passed me the whole folder. "I'm sure his first and foremost goal is to distance himself from these men as much as possible. He wants to make sure his name stays clear and that his image and his church's image isn't the least bit affected by all this. From what I understand, he's built quite an empire. You know those mega churches are huge money makers. He can't stand to lose the status, nor the money he's gained."

My first inclination was to argue with Martin about mega churches being money makers. Unfortunately, I knew that in Bishop Walker's case, it was the truth.

Martin continued, "Because of your legacy here, this firm still has the best reputation in the area for dealing with churches. He said we came highly recommended."

I put the article back in the folder and laid it on Martin's desk. "There's no way I can take this client."

"Did you sign an offer letter?"

I gulped and nodded. "But that doesn't mean I have to take this client. I accepted the job, not this particular client."

"Yeah, but you know as well as I do that accepting the job means you're willing to accept whatever client is assigned."

Blanche knew that as well. Here I was thinking I was getting over with a twenty percent raise. It was probably nothing compared to what Bishop was prepared to pay to keep his name from being dragged through the mud with his deacon and pastor. Blanche had played me, letting me think I was getting over on her.

And because I was so desperate for money, I had fallen right into her trap. The worst part was, I hadn't even taken the time to pray about the situation. I had just assumed it was God, meeting my immediate need.

I picked up the folder and started toward Martin's door.

"Wait, there are a couple of other clients I'll be passing over to you. Other church stuff. Nothing as juicy as this one, but you know pastors and church people have a way of getting themselves in trouble. Bunch of hypocrites and liars. You'd think—"

"I'll be back for the other clients, Martin. I need to talk to Blanche."

I forgot all about office protocol and Blanche's mean-spirited temper and barged into her office. "You can't possibly think I'm going to take this client." I dropped the folder on her desk.

She held up the offer letter and didn't say a word.

I stood towering over her desk. Maybe if I were completely

disrespectful and a bit threatening, she would fire me. "What would make you think I would accept this client? Remember the situation a few years back I refused to take on, with the pastor having babies by young women in the church? This is ten times worse than that. How could you possibly think I would take it?" I put my hands on my hips, realizing she knew full well what my reaction would be. "How convenient that you didn't mention who the client was while you were making your offer. You know me well enough to know I wouldn't want to have anything to do with this."

A calm smile spread across Blanche's face. "I also know you well enough to know that if you weren't desperate for a job right now, we wouldn't be having this conversation. You did a good job standing up to me and getting the raise you wanted. But don't think for a second your nonchalant act had me fooled. We need each other right now. You do the job. I'll pay the money. Everybody's happy."

"Happy? How can I be happy working with this kind of client?"

"Give me a break, Trina. You're so self-righteous. Traipsing off to Africa, sleeping in the jungle with the poor, sick, starving people of the third world so you can prove what an awesome Christian you are. Bottom line is, you had a price and could be bought. I might have had to pay you more had you known who the client was, but bottom line, money talks."

I started to open my mouth to tell her just what I thought about her, but she held up the offer letter and pointed to my signature at the bottom. "This conversation is over. Call the Bishop and set up an appointment."

I stood there for a minute with my mouth open. She dismissed me by turning back to her computer again. I had no choice, but to leave her office.

And to go to my desk to call Bishop Walker.

eleven

When I talked to Bishop Walker's secretary, she told me he was looking forward to meeting with me immediately and that Blanche had told her I would be available to meet that afternoon. I rubbed my temples and let out a deep breath. It wasn't even worth going back to Blanche's office to argue. I was stuck with Bishop and his scandal, and the sooner I moved forward with this thing, the sooner I could get it over with.

Two hours later, I found myself entering the administrative offices of Love and Faith Christian Center. When I introduced myself to Bishop Walker's secretary, she got up from her chair and almost ran over to shake my hand. It looked like she had to stop herself from hugging me. "I'm Nadine Turner. So glad to meet you. Trina, you said?"

I gently tried to pull my hand away from her tight squeeze. "Yes, Trina Michaels. Glad to meet you as well."

She still didn't let go of my hand. "I'm so glad you're here. Bishop will be glad to know you're here as well."

I could only imagine the stress she had been under since the news broke. I was sure reporters had chased her into the building the first couple of days, maybe even followed her home.

And I couldn't imagine the number of phone calls she'd had to field. I wondered how many times she had considered quitting. Looking in her eyes though, I knew she was one of those women who were hopelessly devoted to her pastor, no matter what he did.

She walked back over to her desk and picked up her phone. "Your public relations specialist is here. Yes, sir. Trina Michaels, sir." She hung up the phone and gestured toward a large door behind her desk. "He'll see you right now." Her face beamed like she thought I should be honored to be meeting with the Bishop and that he was willing to see me right away. Honored? She had no idea how much I really knew about him.

She opened the door for me and gestured for me to go in. I almost expected her to curtsy before closing the door.

"Ms. Michaels, please come in." Bishop Walker stood to shake my hand. He looked a lot older and more tired than he looked when I left the church seven years ago. Being evil had that kind of effect on a person.

He looked at me like he was trying to place my face. I wondered if he would remember me. He'd had about nine thousand members when I left, so it was doubtful. I probably looked familiar because Monica and I were best friends, and he knew her well because her husband was the minister of music. He had probably seen my face more than the average member, but it was never like he knew me by name. "Please have a seat, and make yourself comfortable."

I sat down in the chair across from his pretentiously large desk. I focused on the wall for a second, looking at his degrees, citations from the church council, and pictures with some city political officials. What stood out the most were the pictures of Martin Luther King Jr. and a black version of the typical picture of Jesus. I tried to keep from rolling my eyes. He didn't deserve to have either of them gracing his wall.

"I do appreciate you coming on such short notice. Ms. Silver let me know you were just coming back from a missionary jour-

ney in Africa and had just returned to work." He put on an admiring face. "So good to know that I'll be not only working with
a Christian, but one that obviously has the heart of God for His
people. I'm sure the strength you gained there will be a great
help to me in maneuvering such a difficult time in the life of
this church family."

He let out a deep, troubled sigh. "I still can't believe this is
happening. As a pastor, my life's quest has been to protect and
serve the sheep God has placed under my responsibility. To dis-
ciple them in the things of God and to help them reach their
greatest potential. To think that I may have failed any of my
sheep . . . that God would have entrusted them to my care and
that under my watch, they were . . . violated . . . I can hardly
bear it."

He truly deserved an Academy Award. I thought about
Monica crying at my kitchen table two years ago, telling me
how Bishop Walker had known that Kevin was involved in homosexual activity since he was in high school. He had sent his
lover away and taken away Kevin's responsibilities as a church
musician. When he believed that Kevin had gotten it "out of
his system", he put him back in charge of his choirs. With Kevin
as the minister of music, his church experienced steady growth.

When Kevin and Monica came to him about getting married, he had rushed them through premarital counseling and
married them off as quickly as he could. Somehow, during the
premarital counseling sessions, Bishop Walker conveniently
forgot to tell Monica what he knew about Kevin's past.

When she came to him after finding Kevin cheating with
that same lover who had moved back to town years later, he
swore them to secrecy, sent the lover away again, and tried to
sweep the enormity of the situation under the rug. He claimed
that he would counsel them and pray with them and everything would be all right.

He probably wore the same fake troubled and concerned
face talking to Monica that he was wearing for me right now.

I nodded and smiled, pretending to be equally troubled and concerned. I would let him keep talking and putting on his award-winning pious, pitiful act just so I could see where he was coming from. I would have to trust that God would keep me from throwing up all over his expensive, thick carpet.

"By the way, your work comes highly recommended. You handled a situation for a dear pastor friend of mine a few years ago. He and his wife were going through a divorce at the time, and you know how the Christian world frowns on divorce. Gives me such confidence in your ability to walk with me and my congregation through our current pain." He shook his head and pressed his lips together.

Did he really think there was any comparison? Yes, divorce and Christianity was controversial, especially for a pastor who's supposed to be able to keep his family life together as a qualification for being in a position of church leadership. But there were no criminal charges involved with a couple getting a divorce. And there weren't eighteen innocent boys' lives affected either.

I decided to put on a little act of my own. "It's my pleasure to serve fellow members of the body of Christ, especially pastors that put themselves on the front line of battle—caring for people's souls and making themselves direct targets of the enemy. I understand that sometimes difficulties occur and that even though people would put men of God on a pedestal, they're human just like everyone else. Susceptible to temptation and the flesh and regular human weaknesses. Or in other cases, willing to cover the sins of another in love, just as the Bible instructs, for the greater good of the body as a whole." Perhaps if I came across as understanding, even compassionate, he would admit that he knew. That would at least make him easier to work with.

He put on a shocked face, obviously taken aback by my implication. "Ms. Michaels, I assure you that's not the case in this situation. While I understand that love covers a multitude of sins, this is clearly not the kind of situation where that scripture would apply. I would never have covered the sins of these men if I had known. The number of lives they've affected is far too great. It's never for the greater good of the body when young boys are hurt."

I wanted to tell him he didn't have to convince me of his innocence. I was stuck with him whether he knew about the men's crimes or not. "Then that makes our campaign all the more important, Bishop Walker. You and your church are almost as much victims of these men's crimes as the boys." God would have to forgive me for pouring it on so thick.

He nodded, taking off his shocked face and assuming a new, victimized face, seeming to appreciate my level of understanding of his distress.

His office door opened, and his secretary entered with a cup of coffee on a tray with cream and sugar. She set it on a small table under the picture of black Jesus and carefully counted out two teaspoons of sugar. She poured some cream in it, stirred it and checked the color, and then added a couple more drops of cream. She brought the coffee cup over to his desk and set it down with a napkin. Bishop barely nodded his acknowledgement of her.

"Would you like anything, Ms. Michaels?" he offered.

"Water would be fine." I tried to hide my surprise when his secretary actually did a little bow and scurried off to get me some water. If he had enough members like her, he didn't have to worry about his church numbers decreasing too much.

Bishop picked up the cup of coffee and took a small sip. He frowned and set it back on its saucer. I was afraid his secretary would get chewed out for it being too hot or too sweet or too something when she came back.

"So Ms. Michaels, how would you suggest we begin?"

"I think the first thing you're obligated to do is hold a press conference to explain your position."

His eyes widened like that was the last thing he wanted to do.

I continued, "I've seen the news since I've been back. Every time you hold up your hand to a camera and walk away, it looks like you have something to hide. People will start to believe you knew. Even faithful members of your congregation will start to wonder. If you sit down and explain yourself to the press, just like you have to me, I'm sure people will understand that you knew nothing of what was happening over the last twenty years." I tried to keep the venom out of my voice when I said that. Did he really think me or anyone else would believe that he was completely ignorant to what was going on right under his nose for twenty whole years?

He frowned and drummed his fingers on his desk for a second. "Okay, if you think that's what's best. What else?"

There was a tiny knock at the door, and Ms. Turner came back with an ice cold bottle of water for me and a frosted glass that apparently just came out of the freezer.

"Thank you so much, Ms. Turner. How thoughtful of you to make sure it was nice and cold," I said. Bishop Walker could learn a thing or two about how to treat people nicely that worked so hard to serve him.

He held up his coffee cup. "This is too hot and the cream tastes a little sour." His voice tightened with irritation. "Get me another one."

Oh well.

She bowed her head. "Sorry, Bishop. I'll be right back with that." She tipped out the door.

I answered his question. "In addition to an immediate press conference, you'll have to be ready to answer the press every time more information comes out on the criminal investigation and court case—how ever long it takes. Whenever new news comes out, the press and the public will want to know your response."

He drummed on his desk a little harder and clenched his teeth. "I don't know, Ms. Michaels. I don't feel like we owe them an answer. Why should we have to give them an explanation for every little thing that happens? I should just be able to say that I'm innocent of any wrongdoing or knowledge of these men's behavior, and that should be sufficient."

I poured the water in the glass, watching the frost melt. "This is America, Bishop Walker. In this country, the press is king and image is everything. Americans are hungry for gossip, and if they're not given an answer, they come up with their own, and it's usually the most negative possibility. If you want to maintain your good name, then you have to answer. Every time you're asked." I took a sip of the water and marveled at how good the coldness felt rolling down my throat. "I know you understand that, otherwise I wouldn't be sitting here."

He clasped his fingers together and leaned toward me. "I guess you're right, Ms. Michaels. It's important to protect what we've worked so hard all these years to build. God has blessed us thus far, and I'm sure He'll continue to, even under such difficult circumstances. So you'll be handling the press conferences?"

"Of course, you won't need to worry about anything other than handling their questions. Which is no easy task." I took out a legal pad and pen I had slipped into my bag at the office. "We should move forward as quickly as possible and start our damage control campaign. Do you have time to go over some things now?"

"This is my top priority. I'm yours for as long as you need me." He smiled graciously.

I almost gagged. "Okay." I forced myself to smile. "Another thought, Bishop Walker. I think it would be wise to go beyond simply giving an explanation of your innocence. You're going to need to offer the victims some sort of help. Of course, you'll apologize at the press conference, but then you need to show how deeply you're concerned for their healing and well-being. I think it would be beneficial to offer the victims counseling."

He nodded. "That's an excellent idea. We can offer them counseling from any of the members of our ministry staff."

I shook my head. "I was thinking more of something on a professional level. Do you have any licensed counselors on staff?"

Bishop frowned. "You mean like a psychiatrist?"

"No, more like a psychologist or licensed social worker. A person trained in providing psychotherapy for people who have been sexually molested."

I could see the dollar signs clicking in Bishop's head. I said, "I'm sure cost is no object to you or your congregation in ensuring that these individuals' emotional needs are met. I'm sure you're aware that sexual abuse is one of the most damaging things that can happen to an individual, especially at a young age."

Bishop Walker stroked his goatee. "Well, I'm sure the victims would be much more comfortable with a member of our ministry staff than with a complete stranger."

"As comfortable as they were with Deacon Barnes and Pastor Hines?" I knew I was pushing him, but the worst thing that could happen was that he could fire me. Which would also be the best thing that could happen.

He pressed his lips together. "I do see your point. I'll have Ms. Turner to begin to look into that."

Almost as if on cue, she gave her tiny knock at the door and entered, coffee tray in hand, head bowed. "I'm so sorry this took so long, Bishop. I hope this is better. If not, let me know, and I'll run to the store for more cream." She mixed the coffee on the little tray table again and set it on the saucer in front of him. After another little bow, she quickly exited the room.

I took a long sip on my water, finishing it off. I wanted more, but wouldn't dream of asking Ms. Turner for another thing. "Bishop, if you would, answer a few questions for me. In watching the news casts over the past couple of days, there are some things I wanted cleared up."

He nodded, taking a slow sip on his coffee. He didn't frown

or smile, so I figured it must be okay. Guess Ms. Turner would keep her job for at least another day.

"How is it possible that over the course of twenty years, young boys were being molested in your church and you had no idea? These men were in positions of leadership, so obviously you worked closely with them. How could this go on right under your nose and you not know it? A couple of the boys even said that it happened in the church. Right here in your sanctuary. Really, how can you call yourself a man of God with things like that going on under your nose? It's really hard to believe that you didn't have any knowledge about it. One would even have to question if we went digging far enough, whether we'd find that you had participated in the same kind of behavior. Were you molesting little boys too, Bishop Walker?"

I could see the heat rising off his face. He looked like he was about to explode. He rose from his large chair and pointed at me. "Who do you think you are, making those kinds of accusations about me? You have no right to say those things to me. In fact, I'm calling your boss now." He picked up the phone then slammed it down. "How dare you! Get out of my office." His voice bellowed and echoed off the walls.

I stood with him, remaining completely calm. "Bishop Walker, is that the way you're going to react the first time you speak with the press?" I folded my arms, waiting for him to collect himself.

Ms. Turner opened the door. "Is everything okay, Bishop?" She glared at me like she was ready to pick me up and throw me out herself. All five feet two inches of her.

Bishop took a deep breath. "Everything's fine, Ms. Turner. Ms. Michaels and I . . . everything's fine." He gave a reassuring nod, and only then did she back off. She gave me one last warning glare before she left. Reminded me of a little toy Shiatsu dog barking its head off like it could really hurt somebody.

I sat back down in my chair indicating for Bishop to do so as well. "Please forgive me for catching you off guard, Bishop, but I wanted to see how you would respond. Compared to the press, what I just did was . . . friendly. You have to expect that and much worse. Your response has to be calm and contained. You can't afford to lose it like that on national television."

Bishop sat there almost trembling, recovering from my on-slaught of questions.

I sat quietly, giving him time to think. It was a trick I had been playing on clients for years to prepare them for press conferences. I had never enjoyed it as much as I just had with Bishop, though.

I couldn't wait to tell Monica about his reaction.

Monica . . .

Oh, dear God. How was I supposed to tell Monica that it was my job to make Bishop Walker look like an angel, completely innocent of ruining her husband's life and the lives of countless other men and boys? She'd never understand, and she'd never forgive me.

"Ms. Michaels, how do you suggest I respond to their questions then?"

I shook Monica out of my head and focused back on Bishop Walker. "The most important thing to do is practice." I pulled a sheet of paper from a folder in my bag. "I've prepared a list of questions I anticipate you being asked. I want you to spend the rest of the day thinking of an answer to them. I'll be back tomorrow for us to go over them. After I'm sure you're adequately prepared, I'll begin setting up things for the press conference. This needs to happen in the next couple of days, so I trust that you'll do your best to prepare as quickly as possible."

I stood to make my exit. "It would be good if you had the name of the psychotherapist you plan to refer the victims to before we do the press conference. It will show how committed you are to helping."

He frowned, but nodded. He had probably agreed earlier just to make me shut up about it, but really had no intention of covering the high cost of therapy for eighteen boys and young men. And how ever many more would come forward as things unfolded. I was going to force him into it. At least I could make sure something good would come of me being involved in this whole mess.

I couldn't prove that he knew anything about what had been going on all those years, and that was the only reason I was still there. Even if he didn't know, he was still responsible for the spiritual atmosphere of his church. If he were such a man of God, surely God would have pointed out to him that something was wrong.

One thing was for certain, Bishop Walker needed to pay one way or another.

twelve

After I left Bishop Walker, I went back to the office and got my other client assignments from Martin, reconnected with some of my media contacts, and worked a little to organize my office space. When I got home, I went through my closets to see which of my suits still looked half decent on me. After that, I surfed the Internet for a couple of hours. I ordered a few suits online from a couple of the stores I usually frequented. I didn't want to pay the extra money to overnight them. Blanche would just have to deal with my droopy suits until they arrived by standard mail.

I met with Tiffany who honestly made an effort to find a job that day. Her room was clean, and the kitchen was spotless. I knew I could expect things to stay clean for at least a week, then I'd have to stay on top of her to maintain things. It didn't make any sense to me that she was capable of keeping things clean, but just didn't. When I asked her to explain it, all she did was shrug and say she got busy and next thing she knew, things got out of hand. Busy doing what, God Himself only knew.

After I finished questioning her about her day, I sheepishly asked her to help me do something with my hair and to let me borrow some of her make-up. I didn't want to perm my hair again. She picked it out a little, but couldn't seem to get the afro tamed enough to look professional. We both agreed my head was shaped too funny for a short cut. We finally decided that she would press it, pull it back into a rubber band, then attach one of her fake hair buns to it. That would last me until the weekend when we would have time for her to braid it.

Sitting at the kitchen table smelling my hair frying and holding my ears so they wouldn't get burnt reminded me of days when we were growing up. Aunt Penny snatching Tiffany's head around, smacking her every once in awhile, telling her she ain't had no business trying to be tender headed with her nappy headed self. Moms would finally push Aunt Penny away from a crying Tiffany, which left Aunt Penny free to torture me.

I chuckled, and Tiffany didn't even ask what I was laughing about. "Girl, Aunt Penny was crazy, wasn't she?" We both laughed.

Tiffany stopped pressing my hair for a second, and put her hands on my shoulders. "Sissy, I'm sorry about . . . everything. I hate disappointing you. I promise I'm gon' do better. And I'm sorry about what I said about God. I wish I had your faith, Trina."

I reached up and squeezed Tiffany's hand. "You can, baby girl." *And you will.* It wasn't the time to preach to her, but I knew God was softening her heart for me to be able to minister to her.

When she finished with my hair, Tiffany told me to hold on for a second. She ran upstairs and came back with a tape measure. "I'ma get your measurements so I can fix some of your clothes. You can't be going to work looking like a homeless person."

I laughed. She took several measurements, jotting them down on a napkin. "Come pick out your favorite outfits, and I'm gonna start working on it tonight. I can go over Stacy's and borrow her sewing machine and stuff."

I looked at her with surprise on my face.

She answered my unasked question. "Stacy wants to be a fashion designer, and she's been teaching me to sew. That girl is fierce. She's going to New York and is gonna be rich and famous one day."

I smiled and shook my head. Stacy and Tiffany had been best friends since fourth grade. They were more alike than me and Tiffany. Stacy never kept a job, couldn't pay her bills, and had a thing for useless men. The only difference was that Stacy had two small children. Every six months or so, the two of them decided on a new career with which they would get rich and take the world by storm.

"I know what you're thinking, but this is for real this time. Stacy is gonna be a designer, and I'm going to do all her hair and make-up for her shows. Watch how we fix your clothes."

Tiffany disappeared up the stairs, and a few moments later, I heard her rummaging around in my closet. I guess it wouldn't hurt. It wasn't like I could wear any of them now anyway.

Finally, when I couldn't think of any other pressing things to occupy my evening, I had to pick up the phone. Procrastination time was over—I had to call Monica to tell her about my new assignment. I couldn't seem to come up with a way to frame things to make it the least bit acceptable to her. Even though she knew Moms was sick and that I'd do anything to help her, there was still no way Monica would understand.

I sat down at the kitchen table and dialed Monica's number. After the phone rang a few times, I thought I'd get away with leaving a message and maybe being able to put off the conversation until tomorrow. Just when I expected to hear the recording and the beep, she picked up the phone.

"Hey, Trina girl!"

"Hey, Monica. How are you? You had a safe trip back?"

"Yeah, girl. It's so crazy to see your cell number on my caller ID. I can't believe you're back. I can't believe I can talk to you on a regular now. You have got to come down here to visit soon.

I wish I had spent more time up there with you. God, I missed you."

"I missed you too, Monica." Her excitement drove the guilt like a knife into my heart. "I can't believe I can talk to you without a ride into the city to be able to use the phone. I can just pick up my cell, press number two on speed dial, and there you are." I gave a nervous laugh that I knew would give me away.

"You okay, Trina? Is everything all right with your mother?"

"Yeah, Moms is fine." I sighed. "I had to go back to work today." I fingered the stack of mail Tiffany had put on the kitchen table when she came in earlier. It was mostly bills.

"Already? Goodness Trina, you haven't even caught up on sleep yet. Why so soon?"

"Girl, not only do I have to take care of my mom's bills, when I got home, I realized Tiffany had let my house bills get way behind. I had no choice but to go back as soon as possible. I got my old job back with a raise. Which God knows I needed, desperately."

"Oh, good girl. God is so faithful. I'm glad that He came through for you. You'll be out of debt in no time."

"Yeah . . ." I let out a deep breath.

"Trina, what's wrong? Girl, please, whatever it is can't be that bad."

"Oh, but it can . . ." There was nothing to do but just tell her. "My first assignment was a damage control client. You'll never guess who."

"Okay, so don't make me try. Who is it?"

"Bishop Walker." I tore up a couple of credit card offer letters and stood to put them in the trash.

Silence. So long that it made me nervous. I sat back down at the table.

Monica finally spoke. "Bishop Walker? What do you mean?"

"I mean, I have to do damage control for Bishop Walker. He's trying to keep his image intact through this whole scandal. He needs to prove that he knew nothing of Deacon Barnes'

and Pastor Hines's activities and that he is completely committed to making sure they are brought to justice and that their
victims get whatever help they need."

Silence again.

"Monica?"

"Yeah, I'm here. So what did Blanche say when you refused
to take him on as a client?"

"That I had signed the contract and that I had no choice but
to take it."

"And so you quit?"

Now I was silent. I stood and put the rest of the bills in my
overflowing kitchen drawer. I would have to take the time to
sort through them soon to make sure there weren't any other
surprises Tiffany had ignored.

"Trina, you quit right?"

I let out another deep breath.

"Trina, you can't be serious. You're actually going to help
Bishop Walker? How could you even think of doing that?"

"I don't have a choice, Monnie. I signed a contract before I
knew about Bishop Walker."

"So get out of it."

"Monica, it doesn't work like that."

"Well, how does it work then?"

I didn't have an answer for her. I never stopped to think
about what would happen if I walked into Blanche's office, refused to take Bishop as a client and tore up the offer letter I
signed. I wouldn't have a job, that's what would happen. And
no way of paying my bills. And Moms's bills.

"Monica, you have no idea how bad Moms's bills are and
how bad my bills are." I looked over at the kitchen drawer and
felt my stomach sinking.

"I don't care. Trust God to make another way. Do you really
believe God wants you to represent Bishop Walker?"

I couldn't answer.

"Do you? I mean, when you prayed, God told you that this

was His plan for you? It's His will for you to help represent that . . . that . . ."

I knew Monica was fighting to keep her usually well-controlled cussing demon under raps.

"After what he did to us? After everything that happened to Kevin? I mean, multiply that by at least eighteen more times that we know of and God knows how many more. And you're going to help him come off free and clear. And I know you, Trina. You're the best at what you do. By the time you're finished doing your job, he'll look like a perfect angel. And instead of everyone leaving the church like they should, his church will probably grow. You want to be a part of that? Responsible for this man—who has no morals, no scruples and nothing of the spirit of God living in him—you want to be responsible for the growth of his ministry?"

I couldn't say anything to her.

"Trina, I'm listening."

I let out another deep breath. "Monica . . ."

"What, Trina?"

Her voice was escalating. I wanted to tell her to calm down for the baby's sake, but I was afraid that would make her even madder. I had to try my last possible defense. "Monica, I have to look at it this way. In spite of the way Bishop Walker handled everything with you and Kevin, that doesn't mean he knew. I know he's a liar, but what if he's being honest about this? What if he didn't actually know about Deacon Barnes and Pastor Hines?"

Silence. For too long this time. Tiffany came back downstairs with a couple of my suits and held them up for my approval. I gave her a thumbs-up and got up from the kitchen table.

"Monica?" I walked into my office and shut the door.

"Trina, you can't be serious. You mean he actually convinced you that he didn't know?"

"I'm not saying he convinced me. I'm just saying I don't have any proof that he knew."

"So you're saying if you had proof that he knew, you wouldn't represent him?"

"Of course, Monica. If I for one minute thought he had any knowledge about what was going on, I would tell Blanche that I couldn't take him as a client."

"You promise?"

"Of course, Monica."

"Okay, then let me tell you this. About nine months ago, Kevin was in a car accident because he couldn't sleep from the nightmares he was having about being molested. Bishop Walker came to see him in the hospital. Kevin told him about everything that happened when he was little. He specifically told him about both Deacon Barnes and Pastor Hines. Bishop Walker threatened that if Kevin came forward, he would release the whole story to the press, including Kevin's sexual history. He even threatened to spread lies that Kevin had molested boys in the church. So he knew. And did nothing about it."

I couldn't say anything. Just laid my head back against my office chair.

"And the worst part, two of the boys that have come forward were molested in the last nine months. If Bishop had done something the minute he found out, those two boys would have never been victimized."

I let out a slow, long breath.

"That's two boys who will never be the same again. They may end up being promiscuous, may never have a healthy love relationship, or may even struggle with their sexual identity. They may never trust God because men of God violated them. Who knows what will happen to their lives? And it could've been prevented, Trina. So I ask you again. Are you really going to help Bishop Walker and make it look like he's completely innocent?"

"No . . . you're right. There's no way I can do that. I didn't

know. He made me believe he had no knowledge of it. I'm
sorry, Monnie. Please forgive me."

"I will. As soon as you tell Blanche Silver that you're not
gonna represent Bishop Walker."

"I will, Monica. I promise. First thing tomorrow."

"Okay. I gotta go. Call me after you talk to Blanche." She
hung up.

I put the phone down on my desk and rubbed my hands
across my freshly pressed hair. I had expected her to be upset,
but hanging up on me? I guess I deserved that. I couldn't believe Bishop Walker lied to me. Actually, I couldn't believe I allowed myself to believe him. Maybe I needed to believe he
didn't know so I could live with having to do the job. Now that
Monica had told me the truth, there was no way I could do it.

But to tell Blanche I couldn't do it? I would lose my job. And
God knows I needed it.

There had to be another way. Maybe I could persuade
Bishop Walker to tell Blanche he didn't want me to represent
him. That way, she couldn't fire me for refusing to represent a
client as assigned. I had to do it in a way that Blanche wouldn't
be suspicious that I was the cause of it. Maybe if Bishop Walker
was concerned that I would leak the truth about him knowing
to the press, we could come to an agreement that he would tell
Blanche he was no longer interested in her firm taking him on
at all. He had decided to go a different route. I would be free of
him, but able to keep my job.

And Bishop Walker would do anything to save his image,
status and huge pastor salary, including letting me out of this
obligation.

thirteen

The next morning, I showed up to Bishop Walker's office at our scheduled time. Ms. Turner was all smiles when I got there and directed me to go right into Bishop Walker's office. When I walked in, he was sitting at his desk, sipping on what must have been a perfect cup of coffee.

I marched over to his desk. "You lied to me. You said you didn't know anything about what those men were doing. But you knew. And you did nothing to stop it. Do you know that since you found out, two boys were molested? Two young, innocent, pure boys whose lives will never be the same. If indeed you only found out then. I honestly believe you knew much earlier. How can you sleep at night? How can you look at yourself in the mirror?" I stood there with my hands on my hips, breathing hard.

"Very good, Ms. Michaels. But I'm ready for you this time. I spent the entire evening going over your questions, and I'm well prepared. There's nothing the press can say to shake me up. I have to thank you. Your questions were excellent and really made me think about what I need to say in our press conference. When will it be scheduled by the way? I feel like I'm ready."

I narrowed my eyes at him. "I'm not testing you this time, Bishop Walker. I'm serious. I know that you knew."

He took a sip of his coffee and set his cup down on its saucer slowly. "Ms. Michaels, what are you talking about? You know that I knew what?"

"I know that you've known for some time that Deacon Barnes and Pastor Hines had molested young boys under their care in your churches."

"Is that a fact, Ms. Michaels?" He leaned forward and stared me straight in the eye. "And how, exactly, do you know that?"

Here was the problem. I had been so angry at finding out the truth about Bishop and so concerned about saving my friendship with Monica and keeping my job that I hadn't thought past this moment.

I folded my arms. "I just know." Wonderful. I sounded like a ten-year-old.

"Ms. Michaels, for you to make such an accusation, I would hope that you have some proof." He studied my face again, like he had when we first met, like he was trying to place me. I knew he was racking his brain to figure out whether it was possible that I knew, and if so, how?

I stood there, trying to figure out what to do next. Just like in my dealings with Blanche, I was in over my head. I didn't know how to deal on the level of those gifted in the art of scheming, lying and cheating.

"Ms. Michaels?"

I stood there staring at him.

"What is it that you think you know?"

I would just have to go for it. "I know that nine months ago, Kevin Day told you that he was molested by both Deacon Barnes and Pastor Hines. And you did nothing about it. You pretended that it never happened. In the time between then and the time the ministry council responded to his letters and did their investigation, two other boys were molested. Like I said before, how can you live with yourself?"

For the first time since I had walked in the door, Bishop Walker looked concerned. His mouth opened then closed. He bit his lip, rubbed his goatee, then opened his mouth again. "Where did you . . . how do you . . ." He sucked in a deep breath. "I don't know what you're talking about."

"Kevin Day was in a car accident, and in his hospital room, he confessed to you what had happened to him as a child. You threatened that if he came forward, you would tell the press about his past . . . sexual history. Does that sound familiar?"

"How did you get this information? Who are you?"

I stood there, not sure whether I should tell him how I knew.

"There were only two people other than myself in that hospital room. So I'll ask you again. Who are you and how did you get your information?" Bishop Walker stood and stared at me. I guess he thought he could threaten the information out of me.

"I'm Monica's best friend."

He nodded and sat back down in his chair. "I see."

I had him right where I wanted him. "It's clear that there's a conflict of interest with me working for you. I think the best thing for all involved is for you to call Ms. Silver and tell her that you're no longer interested in having her firm represent you. I will keep this information confidential, as will Kevin and Monica. You're welcome to continue to do whatever your conscience will allow."

Bishop Walker rubbed his goatee, then picked up his phone. "Ms. Turner, please bring Ms. Michaels some water. We have a long meeting ahead of us." He gestured toward the chair in front of his large desk. "Please have a seat, Ms. Michaels. We have a press conference to prepare for."

I put my hands on his desk and leaned toward him. "You must have misunderstood me. I have no intention of working with you. I think it's in the best interest—"

"I heard everything you said, Ms. Michaels." He took a sip of coffee and picked up his phone again. "Ms. Turner, could you bring me a fresh cup of coffee? This one has gotten cold. And see if we have any Danishes or muffins for Ms. Michaels." He looked me up and down in a way that made me pull my droopy suit jacket tighter around me. "She looks like she must be hungry."

My mouth fell open. Had he lost his mind?

"Ms. Michaels, you may want to sit down. We could be here for a while, making sure I answer all my questions for the press conference correctly."

"As I said—"

"And as I said, I heard you." He sat back in his chair and drummed his fingers on his desk. "Now you hear me. As I said yesterday, I'm familiar with your work, and I think you're the best person to assist me in protecting my ministry from damage due to this current situation. I have no intention of letting you go."

"There's no way I can adequately represent you, knowing what I know. I have a conscience, and there's no way I can do this."

"Oh you can, and you will. Because if you don't, I'll have to make good on the promise I made Kevin and Monica in that hospital room."

I sank slowly into the chair. "What?"

"You heard me. Either you work with me until this situation blows over, or the next information leaked to the press will be the source of the letters sent to the Bishop's council. Along with the truth about Kevin's . . . history."

I clenched my teeth and gripped the arm of the chair. "You wouldn't do that."

"I wouldn't?" He smiled at me, and I could swear I had gone to hell and was sitting face to face with the devil. "Please believe that I would." He leaned forward and gave me a sinister grin. "So, Ms. Michaels, when is the press conference?"

fourteen

I should have never told Bishop Walker that Monica was my best friend . . .

I kicked myself for the fiftieth time. If I hadn't told him that, his threat of outing Kevin would have meant nothing to me. I should have let him think I had gotten the information through one of my media sources, and had no personal connection to Kevin and Monica. Now I was stuck. Really stuck.

I remembered the look on Monica's face in the car, and then in the park when she thought of the possibility of losing her wonderful new life if the truth about Kevin got out. There was no way that I could let that happen to her. I had to protect her at all costs. Even if it meant helping Bishop Walker lie to the world and maintain his ministry.

Could I live with that, though? Several times through the rest of our meeting the day before, I had to excuse myself to go to the bathroom. When he put on his sad victimized face and told his pitiful lies, I just knew I would throw up. Even though I hadn't been able to eat much since I talked to Monica.

During the meeting, I had thought of throwing him to the

wolves, letting him answer the questions wrong and inviting the most difficult reporters to the press conference. He must have heard my thoughts because he let me know he was paying Blanche top dollar for my work and expected that she'd be monitoring our progress carefully. If his answers weren't perfect or if certain reporters showed up at the conference, Blanche would know I was sabotaging things and would fire me. And if she fired me, Bishop would ruin Kevin and Monica's lives. And Blanche would blackball me so that I couldn't get a public relations job anywhere else in the city. And I didn't have enough experience in the non-profit sector to demand enough of a salary to take care of me and Moms's bills. I would lose my house. Moms would lose her medical insurance, and who knew what would happen then.

I had gone over it again and again in my mind all night and all morning, and I couldn't think of a way out. I kept coming to the same conclusion.

I had sold my soul to the devil, and there was no way I could get it back without somebody getting hurt.

And so, as always, I did my best work. I began making arrangements for the press conference, calling my more "church friendly" media contacts—if there was such a thing. We would hold it the next afternoon. Deacon Barnes and Pastor Hines were scheduled for arraignment, and it would be a perfect time for Bishop Walker to make his first statement. I spent the entire day on the phone. I had decided to work from home, in my office. Blanche could be mad if she wanted. I was getting the job done. It wasn't like she would fire me.

After making phone calls and last minute arrangements all day, I finally decided I had done my best to set things up and decided to go to bed early. I would need all the rest I could get for the next day. I was starting to feel less guilty about taking daily showers, and that night decided I even deserved a soak in my Jacuzzi tub, bubbles, bath salts, and the whole works. It was a heavenly treat, but wasn't enough to wash away the disgust-ing feeling I had about tomorrow's events.

I finally climbed into my bed to go to sleep. I had been trying to get back into the habit of sleeping there, hoping I would get a better night's rest. I was about to drift off to sleep when my cell phone rang. I didn't bother to open my eyes to look at the caller ID and just answered it. "Hello?"

"Hello, my beautiful angel."

"Gabe?" I sat up. "Is that you?"

"I better be the only one who calls you that."

Not too long after I met Gabriel, I remarked that he was named for the angel Gabriel. He said that I was the angel—a beautiful angel God sent to help him spread the gospel in Mozambique.

"What are you . . . how did you? I thought you wouldn't be back in Pemba until next week."

"I know." He was silent.

"What happened? Is everything okay? Did something hap-pen that you had to go to Pemba early? Is everything okay in the village?"

"Trina, everything's fine. Everybody's fine. Just as you left."

"Then what happened?"

"I . . . I had to . . ."

"Gabe?"

"I miss you, Trina." He exhaled slowly. "I needed to hear your voice."

It was only then I realized how badly I missed him. My heart melted. "Oh, that's so sweet." I pulled the comforter off the bed and spread it out on the floor and stretched out on it.

"Okay, this is the part where you're supposed to tell me you miss me too, and you're glad to hear my voice."

"I miss you too, and I'm glad to hear your voice." I let out a little chuckle.

"Woman, I think you take great pleasure in playing around with my heart."

I sucked in a breath, pretending to be shocked. "Why in the world would you say something like that? Play with your heart? I would never do such a thing." I laughed some more and pulled a pillow off the bed and propped it under my head.

"You have and you would. In fact, I think you packed my heart in your suitcase and took it back to America with you."

"Oh, Gabe." It was all I could take. The pressure of the last week surfaced, and I couldn't hold back the tears.

"Trina?"

"Yeah, I'm here." I couldn't keep the tears out of my voice.

"What's wrong?"

"Everything. You wouldn't believe everything that's happened since I've been back. It's been one thing after another."

"It's just re-entry. Culture shock and jet-lag."

"I wish that's all it was. That I could handle. I'm telling you everything's gone wrong." I realized how much I had come to depend on Gabriel. His strength had gotten me through so many difficulties in our little village. Gabriel helped me through my difficult adjustment period when I first arrived in Mozambique and couldn't handle the smells, sights, food and everything else that so was different from my life in America. He was the one that held me when I cried after my favorite baby I had gotten attached to died of malaria. He was the one that nursed me back to health when I caught an intestinal illness so bad, I thought I would die. Stinky mess and all, he was there the whole time.

"Trina, whatever it is can't be that bad."

"It is, Gabe. Believe me it is."

"Let me ask you this. Are you in good health with plenty of food to eat, clean water to drink, and a roof over your head?"

"Of course. It's not that, it's—"

"Is your life threatened in any way?

"No, but—"

"Is the God of heaven still reigning on the throne with our Savior at His right hand, ruling in dominion over all principalities, powers and might in this world and the world to come?"

I took in a deep breath and felt myself being strengthened by Gabe's words. "Yes."

"And are we still reigning and ruling with Him in heavenly places, with that same authority and dominion over all the works of the enemy? Do we still have full access to the throne room where we can bring all our petitions and trust that He hears them? Do we still have His creative power in our mouths that whatever we declare in His name must be manifest in the earth?"

"Yes, Gabe." I wiped the tears from my face and stopped crying.

"So none of that's changed since you've flown back home to Maryland? His sovereignty over all is still intact, even in America?"

"Yes." I smiled and remembered why it had been impossible for me to keep up the walls I had built around my heart to protect myself from falling in love with him or any other man.

"Okay, so now with these things in mind, tell me what's going on."

So I did. I told him about my mother's illness and how bad she looked. I told him about the prognosis she had been given. I told him about my mother's bills and how she was in danger of losing her health insurance. I told him about my mortgage and how behind I was. I told him about my savings being gone. I told him about Tiffany and her smoking and drinking. And then I told him about having to take my job back. He listened quietly the whole time while I laid it all out for him. I could feel his peace, the same peace we had lived under in Mieze where nothing could move us from our faith in God.

When I got to the part about Bishop Walker, I shut down. I was ashamed to tell him what I had agreed to do. Without telling him the worst part of everything that was going on, I knew it would make my tears seem trivial and overly emotional, but I was willing to take that risk.

"Is that all?" he finally said calmly when I had finished.

I sniffed. "Pretty much. I guess you're right. Maybe I'm just culture shocking and jet-lagging. I guess being tired is making me emotional."

"I can understand, Trina. It must be difficult seeing your mother so sick." I knew he could understand that part. His own mother had died of colon cancer about ten years ago. One night when we were sitting in front of the fire lighting the village after dark, he had told me how difficult it was to watch her suffer and die. "But my dear, have you so quickly forgotten the miracles?"

"No, I haven't forgotten. But she won't even let me pray for her. She doesn't want anything to do with my Jesus as she says it. If I can't pray for her, how can she be healed?"

"So you begin to pray for her heart. That God will soften it until she's willing to accept prayer. The king's heart is in His hands, yes?"

"Yes." I pulled the sheet off the bed and wrapped it around me. "Thank you, Gabriel. I'm so glad you called. I can't believe you went all the way into Pemba for me."

"You know I would go to the ends of the earth for you."

I sighed into the phone. "I miss you, Gabe. I wish you were here." I tried to catch the words, but they slipped out of my mouth before I could stop them. The man had just told me he would go to the ends of the earth for me and I knew he meant it. Silver Spring, Maryland was far short of the end of the earth, and I knew it would be nothing for Gabe to get on a plane if he thought I needed him to. "I mean, I wish I was there."

"I wish you were here too. In fact, that's part of the reason I called. To see if you had changed your mind and to find out if you were ready to come back."

"Gabe, we talked about this. I—"

"I know, Trina. And you can't come back now anyway with your mother in the state that she's in. As soon as she's healed, I trust you'll find your way back to me?"

I let out a deep, pained breath. "You know how badly I want to come back to Mozambique."

"I didn't say Mozambique. I said to me."

Silence hung in the air between us.

"Okay, Trina. I will be praying for your mother. Please, leave messages for me with Zembala here at the mission base. If you need me, I'll be there."

"I know. And I will."

"I will be leaving to return to Mieze in the morning. Remember God is on the throne. I love you, Trina. I trust that you know that."

"I know. And I love you too, Gabriel Woods." It had taken me six months, but I learned to say those words that I felt in the depths of my heart. I thought he would cry the first time I said them, about three months before I left. Even now, I could hear him smiling.

"Well, then all is well with the world."

I laughed with him. "Peace be with you."

"And peace be with you, my angel."

I laid back on the floor and pretended Gabe's arms were around me. I remembered the first time he held me. It was while we were standing over the grave of my little baby, Numpoto. They had placed her small body wrapped in cotton strips into the small hole in the ground, and I was overcome with tears. Gabe held my shoulders tightly until they covered her over with dirt. When they had finished, he turned me to him and took me in his arms. He explained that my little adopted child was now in heaven in the arms of God. A more blessed place than we could find anywhere in the world. Even in my sadness, I was strengthened. I felt the same calm, strong peace I felt now.

I would have to draw on that strength to get through the press conference the next day.

fifteen

The number of boys was up to twenty-three. That was the last count when morning broke. Twenty-three innocent lives now tainted. By so called men of God. Two of them in the last nine months. And here I stood in the back of the multipurpose room at Love and Faith Christian Center waiting to walk Bishop Walker through his latest, greatest performance.

I had refused to eat breakfast and even dinner the night before. I didn't think I'd be able to hold it down once he got started. Tiffany was wrong. If I kept working with Bishop Walker, I wouldn't be gaining my weight back any time soon.

All the major television stations were there, as well as the newspapers. The story was getting national coverage. If Bishop was a decent client, and if I were trying to make a career in public relations, this would be a dream come true for me. If I handled it well, Blanche's firm, and me in particular would be sought out. Which was why she was here as well. She knew how this coverage could catapult her firm to the next level. She kept glancing over at me, almost as if she were afraid I had something up my sleeve to sabotage things. She had nothing to worry about. Monica's peace and happiness were dependent on me doing my job right, so my best work was guaranteed.

A flurry of activity erupted when Ms. Turner opened the door to let Bishop Walker into the room. He walked, head bowed, over to the press podium we had set up.

He took a deep breath and put on his concerned face. "I want to thank all of you for coming here today. With everything that's been unfolding this past week, I thought it was expedient for me to make a statement, then take a few questions about what's been going on in my congregation."

He gripped the sides of the podium, as if he needed to hold on for strength. "First and foremost, I am overwhelmed and dismayed at the allegations that have come forth from so many past and present members of my church. It's difficult for me to know what to say. As we all saw at the arraignment, both men have pleaded innocent. Therefore, as is the foundation of our justice system, they are innocent until proven guilty. I have worked closely with these men for the last twenty years and nothing in their character would ever lead me to believe they could commit the heinous crimes they've been accused of."

Loud murmurs filled the room. Bishop held up a hand to quiet everyone so he could continue. "That being said, for this many individuals to come forward with the same allegations, I have to consider the possibility that it may be true. And that simply breaks my heart." Bishop's voice cracked and he stepped away from the microphone for a second.

Everyone was completely silent. If I didn't know the truth, I might actually halfway believe him.

He took a deep breath and came back to the microphone. "I think this is the most difficult thing that can happen to any pastor or shepherd of any congregation. We give our lives to protect and develop our sheep. To think that . . ." His voice cracked again, and he hung his head. He coughed and cleared his throat. "To think that young boys under my watch could have . . ." he hung his head and stepped away from the podium again. Ms. Turner brought him a bottle of water and a hand-kerchief.

God, he was good. It was scary how easily he could lie. The only thing he was sorry about was the possibility of losing his mega church. Or should I say mega church tithes . . .

"I am completely committed to getting to the bottom of all this. I will do anything I can to aid in the investigation because it is of the utmost importance that the truth is discovered. That is my only interest here. Truth and justice. If these men are innocent as they say they are, then I am committed to helping them clear their names and be fully restored to their lives. If, however, they are found guilty, then they should be punished to the fullest extent of the law."

He cleared his throat again. "And finally, for this many young men to come forward, *something* must have happened. Whether it was a misperception or misinterpretation of things or actual abuse, an event occurred that has hurt and forever changed the lives of alleged victims. And this is my utmost concern. The well-being of those who have in some way been affected by whatever has occurred. For whatever might have happened to these individuals while they were under my pastorate, I deeply apologize."

Bishop Walker looked down and shook his head like the pain he was experiencing at the thought of their pain was unbearable. "In whatever way you were hurt and in whatever way it has affected your lives, all I can say is that I am so sorry." His voice was thick with emotion. "More sorry than I can ever express."

He stopped again and took a deep breath. "Therefore, Love and Faith Christian Center will be providing professional counseling services for any of the alleged victims and their families who are interested in receiving it."

Murmurs arose again. I knew the press was buying it.

Blanche looked over at me and winked. I knew she appreciated that as my brainchild. I gave her a fake smile, but as soon as she looked away, I rolled my eyes.

Bishop continued, "As I said, this is all very shocking, overwhelming and disappointing for me. I assure you, I had no knowledge until the arrests were made that there was any possibility of any such activities going on in my congregation. I am committed to doing whatever is necessary to discover the truth. And finally and most importantly, to help the alleged victims get whatever help is needed to restore their emotional and mental health."

Bishop Walker gave one last dramatic pause, and then said, "I'm willing to answer any questions you may have."

The crowd erupted, each fighting for their chance to ask a question. The noise finally calmed down and clear questions came through. "Bishop Walker, you're telling us that your first knowledge of these men's alleged actions was when they were arrested?"

"Yes." Bishop Walker nodded calmly. "Well, to be exact, the Bishop's council that oversees our church called me the evening before the arrests occurred. I was made aware of the allegations and the pending arrests then. I was instructed not to have any contact with them or their families, and I have adhered to that instruction. I haven't spoken with any of them since this whole nightmare started."

Another reporter raised his pen. "Bishop Walker, you must understand how difficult it is to believe you knew nothing of this. No victims have ever come forward in the past making similar allegations? Nothing has ever occurred that made you suspicious of any wrongdoing? It's hard to believe this has gone on for twenty years and no one ever told."

For a split second, Bishop glared at me as if he feared I had ratted him out. He kept his composure. "I've asked myself that same question since all this started. I even did some research to make some sense of all this. What I discovered is this. The most unfortunate thing about sexual abuse, especially when the victims are males, is that there is such a high degree of shame involved, that the victims often do not tell anyone of their abuse, including their parents. Not only are they ashamed, there is also often guilt associated, and the victims think there is something they've done to invite the abuse. And so the secret is kept for years."

Blanche looked over at me and nodded her appreciation of my brilliance again. Made me feel sicker.

"Bishop Walker, why do you think the ministry council didn't notify you as soon as they received the letters? From what you're saying, they carried out the entire investigation without your knowledge. Do you think they feared that you might interfere in some way?"

I hadn't anticipated that question and therefore didn't get a chance to prepare Bishop for it. I froze, afraid of what he might say.

He didn't seem the least bit phased by the question. "I can't speak to the motivation for the ministry council's actions. I would think that they felt it necessary to carry out an independent investigation so that the families would be satisfied that they did their best to discover the truth without any possible interference or bias."

I let out a sigh of relief. I didn't know why I had worried. Bishop Walker was in the lying zone, and it looked like nothing could get to him.

"Bishop Walker, how is it that this type of activity could go on right under your nose without you suspecting anything? As a church leader, aren't you supposed to be able to judge the character of those that you work with?"

Bishop Walker nodded as if he had been waiting for that question. "As I said before, that's the most difficult thing about all of this. Because if it is discovered that the alleged activities of these men did occur, then . . ." Bishop's voice cracked. He wiped his hand across his face. ". . . then I have to accept full responsibility. I put them in places of leadership and therefore would be for all intents and purposes, guilty of every act of abuse. And that is a fact that I would have to live with for the rest of my life." Bishop Walker bent over the podium, as if overcome with grief. His assistant pastor hurried over to the podium and led him away, holding up a hand to indicate that the Q&A session was over.

Blanche gave me one last nod of approval. Bishop must have gotten nervous with that last question. He was only supposed to use the emotional breakdown/unable to answer further questions technique if it looked like things were going south.

Blanche came over to stand with me. "Very nice work, Trina. Well prepped, great answers, great emotion. Very nice work."

I gave her a wry smile. "I can only take partial credit. Bishop Walker is a natural born liar and only needed minimal coaching from me," I said under my breath for her ears only.

Sandra Jensen, one of the field reporters from Fox 5 News that I was pretty friendly with, came over to where we were standing. "Thanks for the call, Trina. I have to say until I heard from you, I was convinced that this Bishop Walker character had been covering for the men. But I knew that if you were representing him, he couldn't be dirty. I know your integrity and that you wouldn't be involved if you weren't certain he was telling the truth."

I couldn't say anything. Blanche interrupted before my hesitation gave away the obvious truth. "Thank you so much for coming. Ms. Michaels will continue to keep you abreast of information regarding this case as it unfolds. I have another press conference you'll be interested in that should be scheduled for early next week." She led Sandra away. She turned back over her shoulder and glared at me to get myself together.

I left immediately and walked to the bathroom. I went into a stall to take a few deep breaths. I knew I had to get back in there soon to make nice with my other media contacts, but I couldn't stomach anymore. I knew Sandy wasn't the only reporter who would believe Bishop Walker was innocent because of my representing him. Monica was right. I was about to make him come through this looking like a perfect angel.

I finally felt like my stomach had settled enough for me to go talk to some people and left the bathroom. I went around fake smiling and shaking hands, promising to call everyone when the next bit of info on the story came out. After most everyone left, Blanche included, I forced myself to go speak to Bishop Walker.

Ms. Turner indicated for me to go right in. Apparently I had reached the highest status and had open access to him whenever I wanted.

He smiled and rose when I entered, holding out a hand, inviting me to take a seat. "Ms. Michaels, I think that went rather well. I'm anxious to hear your thoughts."

"That went better than I could have imagined. It scares me how easily and brilliantly you lie." I sat in the chair across from him.

He didn't even seem phased by my comment. We were far beyond me feigning any undeserved respect for him. "I don't expect you to understand, Ms. Michaels."

"Understand? You mean you actually have some sort of explanation for your actions? Or inaction? I was there the day Monica caught Kevin with Trey. Do you know how devastated she was by that? That day would have never happened if you had bothered to tell her what you knew about Kevin before you married them. She told me about Kevin's lifelong struggle with homosexuality. Are you aware of how miserable he was for most of his life? Multiply their pain by twenty-three and counting, Bishop Walker. So, no. I don't understand how you can live with yourself or how you even consider yourself God's representative. Do you really think anything about your character represents God? You're a disgrace to everything He is."

"Everything God is? And what is that exactly, Ms. Michaels? You act as if He's real. God is simply a good idea. A code of ethics people choose to live by. You act as if He's truly a living being."

My mouth fell open. "What? You don't even believe . . ." I shook my head, staring at him. "You're not even a Christian."

He folded his hands together. "And what is that, except for another good idea? Don't get me wrong. Religion is quite effective in controlling people. Causing them to be good and keeping society from getting completely out of control. Can you imagine what this country would look like if all the people that ascribe to various religions lived like heathens, doing whatever they wanted, living by their own choices? Chaos. Complete chaos."

"And so if you don't believe in God, why would you even go into the ministry?" I wasn't sure I wanted to know the answer to the question. Or maybe I didn't want him to say what I already knew.

He gestured to his large office. "What other profession could a poor black boy from Mississippi with no athletic ability, no great opportunity for education, and no natural skills at any trade do and be this successful? All I ever had was the gift of gab, and I've made it work for me. Well. People throw money at my feet on any given Sunday. People slip large amounts of money to me in a brotherly handshake. And they worship the ground that I walk on. Will do anything I ask at a moment's notice. You've seen the way Ms. Turner waits on me hand and foot. Like I'm a king. I'm a man, just like her poor husband, but she treats me ten times better than him. Isn't that ridiculous? It's the American dream—money, power, respect."

"And it doesn't matter if people get hurt in the process? If little boys' lives are destroyed?" I could feel myself getting sick. And today I wouldn't mind if I threw up on his fancy carpet.

"Ms. Michaels, you act like I molested those boys. The only thing I did was to keep the church machine running. What do you think would happen to all my little sheep if some scandal were to come along that would destroy their image of me? Half of them would lose their religion if they figured out I'm not who they think I am. I'm really protecting all of them. What would they do without their religion?"

"You're sick. Disgustingly sick. I'm not going to do this anymore. Forget the money and forget Blanche. I don't want to spend another minute in your presence."

"You sure about that? How's Monica? I hear she's pregnant. It would be a shame for anything to emotionally upset her and make her go into premature labor or something. Don't you think?"

I stood and stormed toward the door. When I slammed into the door to make my exit, I heard a little scream, and then a thud. I opened the door quickly and saw Ms. Turner lying on the floor. "Oh dear. Ms. Turner, are you okay?"

Her eyes were wide open in horror. I was sure I hadn't hurt her that bad hitting her with the door for her to look as mortified as she did.

Bishop Walker hurried over to the door. "Ms. Turner, what are you doing on the floor?"

She recovered and bent over to pick up the coffee tray that she had obviously spilled when I bumped her with the door. She used the napkin to sop the coffee and cream that had flowed into a puddle on the floor. "I'm so sorry, Bishop Walker. I was just about to come in with the coffee when Ms. Michaels came through the door. I'm so sorry. I promise to make a fresh pot right away." She refused to look him in the eye, and her hands were trembling as she attempted to clean up the mess.

Bishop Walker reached down and thrust his finger into the small amount of remaining coffee left in the cup. "It's cold, Ms. Turner. Just how long were you standing outside the door, about to bring the coffee in?"

Her eyes widened.

Bishop turned to me. "That will be all for today, Ms. Michaels."

He gently grabbed my arm to stand me up from trying to help Ms. Turner clean up the items from the floor. "She'll get that. I'm sure you'll be in touch soon?"

I nodded.

He gestured toward the door. I was almost afraid to leave Ms. Turner alone with him. What would he do to her?

"Ms. Michaels?" Bishop's voice was firm.

I shook myself and hurried toward the door. "Good day, Bishop."

sixteen

My thoughts were still reeling when I got into my car and started it up. How could this man have one of the largest churches in the city and not even believe in God? I thought about the fact that I had gotten saved at his church and had built a foundation of my Christian knowledge there. My life had been changed by his ministry, and yet, he was practically an atheist. Being a pastor was a profession for him—a very lucrative one at that.

That explained how he could lie, scheme and not care about how lives were affected by his actions. All he cared about was the prestige and money. And he would do whatever it took to maintain them. How could God let him get away with that? Why didn't God strike him with lightning, or let him get hit by a bus, or be killed by an angry swarm of bees?

One last question drifted across my mind that did me in. Why did my mother have cancer and Bishop Walker was free and healthy to destroy people's lives? Where was the justice in that? My mother never hurt anyone. In fact, she'd devoted her life to helping people. She did everything she could to provide a good life for me and my sister and took care of every stray kid in the neighborhood. No child would ever starve, be unclothed or homeless as long as she was alive.

Part of what she said was right. She had lived all her life being good, but yet Bishop Walker, who had made a covenant with the devil, was prospering, and she was dying.

I felt like God stepped into my mind to save me from the perilous thought train I was allowing myself to ride on. Psalm 37 slipped into my spirit.

When I pulled up at the house, I walked into my living room and grabbed my Bible off the coffee table. I sat on the couch and turned to the scripture, reading it over and over. God assured me that I didn't need to fret about Bishop and his evil doings. One day he would get his due reward. I was actually afraid for him what that would look like.

As far as Moms was concerned, she had abused her body— pure and simple. She had smoked cigarettes all her life and lung cancer was a natural consequence of that. No amount of being good to kids could reverse that.

Even if it were breast cancer or some other cancer that nothing she did would cause it, sickness was just a consequence of man being fallen. When Adam was perfect and sinless, his body wasn't susceptible to sickness. Once sin entered, our bodies were fair game. Which was why Jesus went to the cross to reverse the curse so we could experience divine health again.

But how could I get my mother to accept and believe that? Healing was available to her, but she didn't want to have anything to do with it. And from everything I had learned in ministry training, bitterness and anger were major obstacles to God being able to heal someone. Worse than doubt and unbelief.

How could I get my mother to release and forgive so she could receive the healing she desperately needed?

God, please fix Moms's heart. You know I can't bear to lose her. Help her to forgive and release, then accept and believe. I can't handle it if she dies, God.

Before I could launch into a good intercessory session, my

phone rang. I was about to ignore it and go ahead and pray, but I saw Monica's number on the caller ID.

"Hey, Monnie."

"Don't 'hey Monnie' me. I can't believe you."

"What?"

"What? You know what. I just watched the press conference. That was your best work ever. Counseling for the victims, alleged this and alleged that, punishment to the fullest extent of the law. Even the bottled water and handkerchief and breaking down at the end and having to be carried away by Pastor Duncan. The whole thing had Trina Michaels written all over it. I know you, Trina. You're my best friend, or should I say, *were* my best friend."

"Monica . . ."

"I can't believe . . ." she started crying, and I could barely understand her next words. "I can't believe after everything this man put us through—put twenty-three families through—that you could do what you did."

She cleared her throat and sniffed. "You made him look completely innocent, Trina. I was watching in the office in the gym, and Talinda, one of my clients, was with me. After it was all over, you know what she said? 'That poor man. We'll have to pray for him and his church.' How can you do this? This is not the Trina I know."

She waited for me to explain myself. I was still stunned from her "*were* my best friend" comment. I put my Bible back on the coffee table.

"Trina, has your mother's health gotten you so stressed out that you can't think straight? Are you so worried about her dying that you're not able to hear from God?"

"No . . . it's just that—"

"Is it the finances then? Are you so worried about money that you're willing to sell your soul just to pay off some bills? If that's it, we can lend you the money. We can *give* you the money."

"I couldn't ask you to do that, Monica."

"I would rather do that than have you continue to help Bishop Walker. The money isn't a problem. The gym is doing great, and Kevin's album and tours even better. You know you have a pride problem and never want anyone to help you. Is your pride more important than you doing the right thing? Is money more important than you doing the right thing?"

"It's not that, Monica."

"Then what is it?" she shouted into the phone.

I held my phone away from my ear some. "You wouldn't understand."

"Then make me understand," she screamed.

I had to hold the phone even farther away. I remembered how Monica tore up their house after she caught Kevin in bed with his "friend." I wondered if she were that angry with me now.

"Monica, please calm down. Remember the baby."

I heard her taking some deep breaths. "Trina, I just need to understand why you're doing this. Please, tell me something to make this better."

I thought about telling her about Bishop's threat to out Kevin. That would change the whole course of this conversation. But if I told her, she'd be in the same conflicted state I was in. She'd have to ask me, her best friend, to do something she knew I didn't want to do, just to save Kevin's reputation and her wonderful life. As much as I didn't want her to hate me for what I was doing, I didn't want her to have to feel guilty about wanting me to do it for her sake. I didn't want to put her in the position to choose between keeping the life she loved and doing the right thing by exposing Bishop.

"Trina?"

"Yeah, Monnie. I don't know what to say. I can't explain myself in a way that I think you'd understand. You just have to believe that I love you with all my heart and would never do anything to hurt you. You have to trust what our friendship has been and who you know me to be, Monica. Like you said, you know me. You know the kind of person I am. That's all I can say. You know my heart."

Silence.

"Monica?"

"Okay, Trina. I gotta go." She hung up and I could feel the distance between us becoming much more than the seven hundred or so miles between Silver Spring and Atlanta.

I lay on the couch in the living room for a while. The day had given me a monster headache. The press conference, then the conversation with Lucifer's spawn, then finally the phone call from Monica. I needed to do something to unwind and feel better. The thought of a bath didn't do it for me. Visiting Moms, which normally would have been fun, would now be depressing and stressful.

I couldn't seem to remember what I did for fun before I left for Mozambique. Me and Monica used to hang a lot—going to the movies, out to eat, or having video night at my house. My monthly dates with Moms now weren't a possibility. I wasn't a big shopper and that would only make me feel worse right about now, anyway.

In Mozambique, fun was completely different from fun in America. Sometimes we sat around the fire late into the night, listening to people tell stories. Other times, we hiked into town and treated some of the children to a meal at a restaurant. Me and Gabriel used to go hiking by ourselves sometimes and had great conversations about life, our hopes and dreams. Sometimes we'd go back to the mission base and us and the other missionaries would cook a huge meal together and sit for hours, eating, laughing, and talking until the wee hours of the morning.

Fun in America involved some kind of mind numbing entertainment and food. In Mozambique, it was all about togetherness and a sense of community. Right now, I felt caught be-tween the two worlds and didn't know what to do with myself. My best friend now hated me, and even if she didn't, she was miles away in Atlanta.

I heard Tiffany's key in the front door. Maybe I'd see if she wanted to get into something. She walked into the living room, and then stopped, frozen, when she saw me sitting on the couch.

"Hey, Trina, what are you doing home?" She stood with an idiotic look on her face like I had caught her doing something she shouldn't.

"I had a rough morning and decided to finish the rest of my work from home today."

"Oh." She rushed past me into the kitchen, looking more suspicious by the minute. She opened the pantry and started stuffing some of her junk food into a plastic bag. "You had that press conference, huh?"

I nodded. "What's up, Tiffany. What's wrong?"

"Nothing." She closed the pantry door, but stayed in the kitchen. "I just stopped in for a second, but I'm about to head over to Stacy's house." She clutched her bag and gave a little nervous giggle that made me know something wasn't right.

"Come here, Tiffy. Have a seat and talk to your Big Sissy for a second."

Her eyes widened. "But Stacy's in the driveway waiting for me. I told her I'd be right there."

I patted the couch next to me. "Just for a second."

She dragged her feet over to the couch and plopped down. That's when I noticed. She had a brand new, varnish-frozen hairdo, a fresh, French manicure, and her clothes looked hot off the rack. "You look nice, Tiffy."

Her eyes went down and to the right. "Thanks, Sissy. Me and Stacy are going out later. But we're not going to drink or smoke or do anything. Just go to the club and hang out a little. You know."

I reached over and fingered the new jacket she had on. It had some fancy brand logo on it I recognized as being expensive. "This is a nice outfit. New?"

She nodded and bit her lip.

"Your hair and nails look nice too."

She looked down at the floor. She finally reached into her little Coach bag and pulled out a wad of cash and handed it to me. "Here. That should help out with catching up the bills and everything."

My mouth fell open. I reached for the wad and counted the bills. I could hardly speak. "Tiffy, where did you get a thousand dollars? And whatever else you got to be looking so good?"

She shrugged.

I closed my eyes and lay back on the couch. "Tiffany, I've had a rotten day. I don't have the energy to play twenty questions to pull some information out of you. Can you just save me the trouble, and tell me where you got this money?"

"My boyfriend."

"Your boyfriend?"

She nodded.

"He just reached into his wallet and pulled out a thousand dollars and gave it to you?"

"Yeah. A little more than that, actually. I was feeling down, and he asked what was wrong, and I told him about Moms and how I messed up so bad with your bills and everything. He didn't want me to be sad, so he gave me some money to help out."

"I'm not even gonna ask where he gets so much money to be able to give away a thousand dollars like it's nothing."

Tiffany did her eye thing, and I knew the truth. I let out a deep breath. "Tiffany, I honestly don't understand what goes on in that brain of yours. Do you honestly think I would accept money from a drug dealer to help with the bills?" I handed the stack of bills back to her.

She stood up. "I don't see why not. You're accepting it from a man who covers up child molesters. I'd say between the two, yours is worse."

My mouth fell open. "Wha . . ."

She dropped the money on the coffee table and walked out the front door.

seventeen

After going to my old church on Sunday morning, I decided to get on the road to head up to Moms's. With everything that had been going on, I hadn't had time to go early and spend some fun time with her. As late as it was, we'd only be able to have a nice dinner and get a movie from Blockbuster. I'd spend the night and would be ready to take her to chemotherapy first thing in the morning.

Church was okay, but as I expected, nothing like the presence-infested services I had gotten used to in Mozambique. The music was good, prayer was good, and Pastor Reynolds taught a great sermon on the joy of the Lord, but still . . . I was used to hours of worship where each person felt like God was sitting next to them. Where we literally sensed the presence of angels in our midst. Where miracles happened, often without someone even laying on hands and praying.

We had a saying that with the way the earth was rotated, Africa was much closer to heaven than America. Miracles were common and His presence thick.

I thought it was because the people were so desperate and dependent on God. There, He was their only option. They didn't have big hospitals, expensive medicine, or even clean water. If God didn't heal, then death was certain. In America, we had the best hospitals, the best research, and the best medicine. Therefore God really wasn't necessary, except as a last resort. And then it wasn't like anyone believed He would actually show up.

It was good to see some of my friends from church, but for some reason, I felt somewhat distant from them. Several of them promised to call and that we'd get together soon. Part of me hoped they would, so I wouldn't feel so bored and lonely, but another part of me thought I'd still be bored and lonely even if we spent time together.

When I called Moms to tell her I was on my way, she didn't sound right. It seemed like her breathing was really labored, and she could only say a few words before she had to take another breath. All my freeway fears dissipated, and I drove as fast as I could to get to her.

When I rang her doorbell, it took her forever to get to the door. I was about to go fish my key to her house out of my messy glove compartment when she finally opened the door.

"Hey, Tree . . . come on in . . . boy you got here . . . quick. You musta . . . been flying." She snatched a quick breath every few words.

"Moms, what in the world is wrong with you? You can't even breathe."

She waved a hand and tried to pretend like nothing was wrong, but we had to stop twice for her to catch her breath just to get to the kitchen table. "Just feeling a . . . .little winded for . . . some reason."

"Well, whatever the reason, it can't be good. I'm taking you to the hospital. Now."

"Aw, Tree. It ain't that serious."

I could tell she had tried to force out that whole sentence without taking a breath to prove to me that she was okay. It was apparently too much because she went into a coughing/choking/gasping fit that left me terrified. I grabbed her purse and jacket, locked a firm hand around her thin arm and pulled her toward the door. "Let's go, Moms. Which hospital are you being treated at? University of Maryland?"

"I ain't going . . . to no hospital, Tree . . . .they can check me out . . . tomorrow when I go . . . for chemo." Another coughing and gasping fit doubled her over. When she stood back up, I stared at her face. It kind of looked like the area around her mouth was turning blue.

"Moms, you're going to the hospital. Either you follow me to the car or I'll pick you up and carry you. Which is it gonna be?"

She folded her arms and glared at me. I bent over, grabbed her around the waist and was about to put her over my shoulder.

"Okay . . . " she gasped. "Girl, you . . . better be glad . . . I can't breathe . . . otherwise I'd be . . . putting you over . . . my knee. You done . . . got too grown . . . for your own good."

"Moms, that's enough. Don't try to talk anymore." I pulled her down the walk and put her in the front seat of my car. I hurried around to the driver side and got in.

"Oh, now . . . you trying . . . to shut . . . me up?" She was breathing too fast from our rush down the sidewalk to the car. I should have carried her like I threatened to.

"Moms, please. Just be quiet and breathe. Okay?" I turned to look at her while starting up the car. "Please."

She nodded and sat there gasping for air.

Thankfully, University of Maryland wasn't too far. I parked in the emergency room entrance and ran inside to get some help. "Can I get someone to help me with a wheelchair? My mom has lung cancer and she can hardly breathe," I hysterically announced to anyone who would listen.

A young, black man in scrubs grabbed a wheelchair and followed me out to the car. I didn't have to strain to see this time. Moms was definitely turning blue. She didn't have the strength to argue when he gently, but swiftly lifted her in his arms and placed her in the wheelchair. He pushed her, almost running, into the emergency room entrance. I started running after him, but he called over his shoulder, "You better move your car, ma'am. I'll take good care of her. I promise."

It seemed to take forever to get myself to the parking garage across the street, and then back over to the emergency room. When I walked in, the gentleman who had wheeled Moms in was waiting for me with a young, black woman in scrubs.

She must have seen the panic on my face and began to speak as soon I got over to where she was. "Your mother has been taken back to X-ray. Her oxygen saturation was low, but it came up some when we put the oxygen on her. We're moving quickly to figure out what happened. When the doctor listened to her, it sounded like her lungs were filled up with fluid. If that's the case, then the surgeon is standing by waiting to do a procedure to take some of the fluid off her lungs. If her oxygen saturation doesn't come up, she may need to be intubated—have a tube put down her throat—to help her breathe."

She led me over to a more private area of the waiting room and sat down with me. "I've called medical records for your mother's file, but I need to ask, do you know your mother's DNR status?"

I sat there breathing for a second, trying to catch my breath from the run from the parking lot and from all the information she had given me. "Her what?"

She frowned as if I should know what she was talking about. "Umm, with most cancer patients, early in the treatment, the oncologist—cancer doctor—discusses with them what they would want to happen in case of an emergency such as this one. If your mother were to stop breathing, do you know if she would want us to do everything to keep her alive including putting the breathing tube in, pounding on her chest, and shocking her if need be?"

My eyes widened, and my mouth seemed stuck open. I couldn't believe she was asking me all this stuff.

"Ma'am, I know that it seems like a difficult question for me to ask at such a critical time, but we wouldn't want to do anything against your mother's wishes."

I shook my head, trying to wrap my mind around what this heartless woman was asking me. "I don't know . . . we haven't talked about that at all."

She placed a hand on mine. "Ma'am, as I said, I don't mean to be cruel. With terminal patients, it's a very important discussion that needs to happen. Ideally, not during a medical crisis. Are you her next of kin?"

I nodded, shaken up by her use of the words "terminal" and "next of kin."

She squeezed my hand. "I'm sorry, but if something happens and your mother is not able to communicate with us, you're going to be the one that has to make that decision."

I furrowed my eyebrows. She couldn't be serious. "Well, why don't you get back there and help her so I don't have to make that decision."

She let out a deep breath and pulled her hand away from mine, obviously frustrated that her attempt at a "therapeutic conversation" hadn't worked.

The person sitting behind the big desk at the emergency room entrance called over to us. "Nancy, her chart is on the way down from medical records."

Nurse Nancy nodded and turned back to me. "Hopefully she and her doctor have discussed this and there's something on the chart. I'll go back and check and see what's going on with your mom. Okay?"

She got up and walked past the main desk and through a set of double doors. I fumbled through my purse for my cell phone and dialed Tiffany's number. After a few rings, it went to voice mail. She was probably still mad from our argument on Friday. She had locked herself in her room all day Saturday, and then went out that night. She wasn't back before I left for church that morning.

After the beep, I said, "Tiffany, it's Trina. I'm at the hospital in Baltimore with Moms. She's real bad sick and . . ." I almost said the doctors and nurses were acting like she was gonna die, but that would freak Tiffany out too bad. Instead, I said, "You need to get a ride and get up here as soon as you can, okay? Love you."

Next I dialed Monica's cell number. After a few rings, hers went to voicemail as well. Was the whole world mad at me? After the beep, I said, "Monnie, please call me. I just brought Moms to the emergency room. She couldn't breathe and turned blue on me. She looks really bad. I need to talk to you. Please . . ." My voice broke, and I hung up before I started crying on her voicemail.

I sat there fidgeting for a second, wiped the few tears that had slipped down my face, then flipped open the phone to make one last call. This time I got an answer. It was Zembala at the mission base in Pemba. "Zem, it's Trina. I need you to get a message to Gabriel. Tell him . . . tell him I need him."

eighteen

After about ten minutes, the nurse came back out through the double doors. I rose and rushed to meet her. She led me back over to our private corner in the waiting room. "Your mom just came out of X-ray. As we suspected, she does have a pleural effusion, or fluid on the lung. It's actually on both of her lungs. That's why she couldn't get any air. The surgeon is getting ready to tap her now, and I promise she'll be much better within minutes. As soon as they get the fluid off, her lungs will be able to expand again, and she'll be able to get air in. They'll also send the fluid to the lab to see why this happened. Okay?"

I nodded, understanding only half of what she said. "When can I see her?"

"As soon as the procedure is done. It won't take long. Trust me, she's okay. Your mom is a feisty one. She's giving everyone a fit back there."

That made me smile. To know that Moms was behind those double doors carrying on and giving people grief meant that she was okay. Tears of relief slid down my face.

Nurse Nancy reached over to squeeze my arm. "She's okay for now. All right?"

I nodded and wiped the tears away.

"Is there anyone I can call for you?"

I shook my head and wiped my face again. "I left messages for everyone already." When she left, I sank back into the chair.

Her words, "okay for now" weren't lost on me. She was making the point that although Moms had escaped immediate death, it was still imminent. How was Moms going to get healed with all her negative thoughts and with all these negative talking people around her? I didn't fault the nurse. She was speaking based on what she knew about medicine.

I must have nodded off in the waiting room chair because it seemed like only a few minutes later, and Nancy was jostling me. "Ms. Michaels? You can go in to see your mother now."

"That was quick." I grabbed my bag to make sure it was still with me and that the zipper was intact. It wasn't too smart to be falling asleep in a Baltimore ER waiting room.

Nurse Nancy glanced up at the clock over the main desk. "It's been over an hour." She frowned at me. "Are you okay?"

I nodded. "Just a little tired, apparently." I had never gotten a chance to recover from my jet lag. And I hadn't been sleeping well since I got back. The whole world was moving too fast. I wanted to stop it and get off for a week or two.

I stood and followed the nurse through the double doors. She guided me by several curtained off areas until finally she got to a little section in the back. I could hear Moms before I got to her.

"You mean to tell me you gotta leave this tube in my back? How am I supposed to go home with a tube in my back?"

Whoever was in the room with her chuckled. "Who said you were going home? No ma'am. We have a nice room with a view for you upstairs."

Moms's voice rose. "I ain't staying in the hospital. I done told my oncologist that before. You need to get this tube out my back because I'm going home."

I grabbed the curtain and slung it back. "Moms, hush. There

are other sick people in here, and you're disturbing them." I walked over to the ER bed she was sitting on. "And you're crazy if you think I'm taking you home. You almost died."

"Almost. But I'm fine now. I don't need to stay here. I can breathe now, and I can talk just fine."

I pointed to the oxygen prongs sticking in her nose. "Yeah, but you don't have one of those at home." I grimaced when I saw the tube coming out from under her gown and draining bloody looking fluid into a canister on the wall. I pointed to the canister. "And we ain't got one of those at home, either. What if I had waited to come up here tomorrow instead of today? I would have found you dead in the house."

"Tree, I ain't staying here."

I walked up closer to her bed and rubbed her leg, trying to reason with her. "You need to stop giving me and everybody else around here a hard time. For once in your life, just listen and do as you're told. We need to let the doctors figure out why the fluid built up on your lungs so they can fix it. I do *not* need for this to happen again."

"I don't need them to send those big ol' bottles of bloody fluid to no lab to see why this happened. I'm full of cancer. That's why this happened. Tree, have you heard a word I told you? I'm dying." Moms said it so forcefully that she started coughing.

"Stop saying that," I almost yelled. Tears started flowing down my face. I turned to see Nurse Nancy cleaning up the bloody gauze from the little procedure table and giving the doctor, who was still filling out his paperwork, a glance. I could almost hear their thoughts when they shared a look. "Boy, is she in denial."

I understood why Jesus put everybody out of the room before he raised the little girl from the dead. He couldn't do a miracle with so much determined doubt and unbelief around him. I wanted to throw everybody out so I could clear the atmosphere in the room and pray for my mother, but that would include throwing her out too. The nurse and doctor finally finished and left the room.

Moms reached out her hand and pulled me to her side. I didn't want to get too close because I didn't want to mess up the tubes taped to the back of her hand and coming out of her back. She ran her hand over my head and smoothed my hair back into my fake bun. "Girl, what you got going on back there?"

"Tiffy did it."

She smiled. "You let Tiffany do your hair?"

I nodded. "She was supposed to put braids in it yesterday, but we got into a little argument on Friday." I put my hand over my mouth, but it was too late to catch the words.

"Girl, ain't nothing new. What she do this time?"

No way I was going to tell her. "You know that girl can't keep a house clean to save her life. I have to fuss at her on a regular to keep her from letting her room get too nasty."

Moms's laugh turned into a cough. "That child. I don't know what's gonna happen to her when . . ."

"Moms, please . . ."

She reached up and smoothed a hand across my face. "You look tired, Tree. You ain't been sleeping since you been back? And you're looking so po'. I need to get Aunt Penny to cook you up a bunch of food to take back with you when you go."

"I forgot to call Aunt Penny." I pulled out my cell phone. "I don't even know if I have her number in my phone."

Moms grabbed the phone from me. "Please don't call that crazy old bat. You know I love my sister, but I don't need her here working my nerves. I already told her you were taking me to chemo so she won't miss me until Tuesday. Hopefully, I'll be home by then."

I laughed. "Moms, you wrong for that."

"Please. You ain't seen Aunt Penny in a couple of years. You forgot how aggravating she is."

"That would be hard to forget."

We both laughed. My cell phone rang. I was hoping it was

Tiffany or Monica. Instead, Blanche Silver's name and number showed up on my caller ID. I pressed the button on the side of my phone to silence it. Whatever it was could wait. It was Sunday and Blanche knew, unless it was dire, I didn't want to be bothered. I would call her back later and tell her I'd be working from home tomorrow.

I stood rubbing Moms' arm as she dozed off on the emergency room gurney. The nurse came to let us know they were moving her up to a room.

Moms's eyes fluttered open. "Tree, go find me some food while they get me settled. If you gon' make me stay here, I ain't eating the food."

I laughed and went searching for the cafeteria. I got one of her favorites—fried fish and French fries. I figured there wasn't any sense in making her eat healthy since she was going to . . .

I almost dropped the cafeteria carton when the thought went through my mind. What was I believing? I rebuked the thought and prayed healing scriptures all the way up to her room.

My cell phone rang again and Blanche's number came up. I silenced it again. What was her problem? I was beginning to think it was something important for her to be so persistent. I'd make sure Moms was settled and fed, and then I'd call her back.

I found Moms' hospital room. Somehow she got fixed up with a large private room at the end of the hall. It had one of those foam and vinyl chairs that let out into a bed for family members to sleep on. It would be perfect for me.

Moms' tube was going to a canister on the wall similar to the one that had been in the emergency room. She also had fluids hanging on an IV pole. I wondered what she was supposed to do when she had to go to the bathroom. I didn't think they'd be unhooking all those tubes every time she needed to go.

I pulled the rolling television cart thing in front of Moms and adjusted it to the right height, placing her dinner I'd bought on it. When I opened the carryout food tray, a huge smile broke out on Moms's face. She looked at the food, and then looked at me. "Where's yours?"

"All that food? I thought we'd share."

She pulled the food toward her and gave me a look. "You thought wrong. I can breathe now too. I'm 'bout to put a hurting on this here. You might want to get your own."

I laughed. "I'm fine."

"You need to eat, Tree. Give that man something to hold on to when he comes to see you. You know black men need something to grab." She sat up in the bed and indicated for me to prop her pillows up behind her. Instead, I pressed the button to automatically adjust the height of the bed.

She leaned back against her pillows, trying to get comfortable, but I could tell the tube was getting in her way. She seemed like she was afraid to dislodge it. I wanted to take a peek to see how it was staying in, but was afraid I'd get grossed out.

"When you gon' tell me about him?"

I pulled up a chair to her bed. "Moms, you need to eat and get some rest. You do realize you almost checked out of here a little while ago?"

"Chile, was about to bust hell wide open." She laughed to herself. "I guess ol' Satan wasn't ready for me yet."

I bit my lip. When I was about to open my mouth, Moms held up her hand. "Please, Tree, no preaching today. You know I don't believe in hell or heaven. When I close these eyes, that's it. It's over and done."

"Moms . . . what if you're wrong?" I let out a deep breath when she held up her hand and stuffed a small piece of fish into her mouth.

"You always talk about how you would do anything to make me and Tiffany happy. You know nothing would make me happier than for you to let me pray for you so God can heal you, and you can live. For you to accept Christ so I can see you in heaven one day. Years from now of course."

She swallowed her fish and asked, "If I don't believe it, but I say it just to make you happy, does it count?"

I shook my head. "You have to believe it."

She shrugged and pushed the fish around in the Styrofoam carton. "Well, I'll say the words if it makes you happy. But . . ."

I rolled my eyes and shook my head. "Moms." I reached over to grab one of her French fries, but she smacked my hand.

"I told you to go get your own." She smiled and pushed the plate over toward me. "Come on here and eat so you can put some meat back on those hips. My poor son-in-law. How old did you say he was?"

"I didn't." I grabbed a few fries and drowned them in ketchup.

"Well?" Mom took another small bite of fish and pushed a large filet toward my side of the food carton. She wasn't eating hardly anything at all, and I wondered if she'd sent me to get the food just to force me to eat. "You better get you some of this here fish before it's gone. Come on, Tree. Name, age, looks, money, give me the facts. Is he good in bed?"

"Moms!" I smacked her hand. "You know I didn't sleep with him."

She grunted. "Chile, you better test the car out before you buy it. You gotta make sure it can shift into high gear and run fast for a while without running out of gas." Moms pushed an imaginary gearshift and made some *vroom* noises.

"Moms!" I sat there with my mouth wide open.

"What? You better give me some details or I'm gonna keep embarrassing you."

I gave Moms the same basic rundown I had given Monica. She wasn't as easily satisfied. "Has he been married before?"

I nodded.

She grunted. "What happened? How long has he been divorced? How long was he married? Did he leave her? Has he ever cheated on a woman before?"

"I think I liked it better when you couldn't breathe well enough to talk."

Moms pointed a threatening finger at me.

I broke off a piece of fish and dipped it in tartar sauce. "He got married about ten years ago when he first moved to Africa. He and this girl met over there in the missionary training school and fell in love and got married within six months of being there. She couldn't handle the life, though. She wanted to move back to London where she was from, but he felt called to stay in Africa. She left, telling him she would be back, but never came back. She said she couldn't live the third world life and that she had missed God when she thought she was called to be a missionary. Broke his heart. He stayed over there all those years and hadn't met anyone else. Until me." I smiled a little when I said that.

"Well that ain't gon' work, then. It would be the same problem," Moms said. Then she stared at me, eyes narrowed. "Unless . . . Tree, you planning on going back over there?"

I shrugged and dipped another piece of fish in the tartar sauce. My stomach would give me a fit later for eating all the fried food, but it was too good.

"You are. I can see it in your eyes. Well, now . . . "

"Not anytime soon. But eventually. I feel like it's what I'm supposed to do."

"Then you do that, chile. Do whatever it is that makes you happy." She nibbled on another French fry. She looked exhausted.

I wanted to tell her to get some rest, but I knew she wouldn't leave me alone until I finished telling her about Gabe.

"So when do I get to meet him?"

"He's still in Africa."

"Then tell him to get on a plane and come meet his mother-in-law before she kicks the bucket. I'm sure he wouldn't mind." Her eyes sparkled with mischief.

"You're right. He wouldn't. In fact, I better call back and leave a message. When we got here and you looked so bad, I called over there and left a message for him to come. Since you're okay, I need to call and leave a new message."

"No, let him come. I need to lay eyes on him so I can have my peace before I die."

"Moms, please stop saying that."

"I'm just trying to help you get prepared for it. I know it hurts, but I gotta keep saying it so it won't be so bad for you when it happens. I think Tiffany is finally dealing with it. Which is why she won't come see me no more."

I looked up at Moms and started to say something in Tiffany's defense, but she held up a hand to stop me. "I know my girls, Tree. She ain't strong like you. She's dealing with it the best way she know how."

My cell phone rang again. It was Blanche again. I'd had enough. I snatched the phone open. "What Blanche?" I knew it sounded harsh, but she knew I hated intrusions on Sunday.

"Where have you been? I've been calling you all evening."

"I've had a family emergency."

"I'm sorry to hear that, but there's a work emergency that's unfolding as well. Have you watched the news at all today?"

"No."

"How can you call yourself a public relations professional and you haven't watched the news all day. Turn on a television and call me back, Trina." She hung up.

I let out an aggravated breath.

"Everything okay, Tree?" Moms leaned back against the bed. I guessed she decided not to worry about the tube.

I nodded and picked up the remote. "Yeah, just some aggravating work stuff. Apparently I need to watch the news." I turned the television on and looked at my watch. The six o'clock news would be on in ten minutes. I would keep it muted until I saw what Blanche was in an uproar about. It would've been too easy for her to tell me herself.

We sat there in silence for a few minutes, and I finished off the food. Moms wiped her hands on the towel I handed her. "By the way, I called my insurance company to try to make some payment arrangements, and they told me the account was paid in full. Thank you, baby. You know I don't like the thought of you taking care of me, but it also helps for me to have some peace about it. Part of me wants to just stay home and die to get it over with and not cost you no more money, but I feel like there's something I need to stay around a little longer for." She took a sip of the water I gave her. "Probably to meet my son-in-law." She winked at me and handed me the cup.

"I promise, though, when I do go, you'll get all your money back and more. I got a nice insurance policy set up for you girls. Of course, all the money will go to you, and you have to give Tiffany money here and there as needed. You can't give that girl no whole bunch of money at one time."

I listened to my mother make her plans out of respect, still planning on laying hands on her and praying for her after she went to sleep. I wasn't about to let her go that easy.

"One more thing, Tree. Me and my oncologist talked a few weeks ago, and I signed this paper that if something happened, I don't want them putting me on no machines or nothing to keep me alive. When my time comes, let me go. They can do things like pull off fluid and put these durn tubes in my back like today if it's a small problem that just needs a little fixing. But when something big happens, I need you to be strong and let me go. Okay?"

I nodded and squeezed her hand. "Okay, Moms. Please, enough for today. Let's make a deal. I won't talk about Jesus, and you stop talking about dying."

She patted my face. "Okay, baby. That's a good deal for the rest of today." We shook on it.

I looked up at the TV and saw Deacon Barnes face plastered on the screen. The caption read: *New evidence may lead to easy conviction.* I grabbed the remote and turned up the television to hear the report.

"A mother has come forward claiming to have hard evidence proving her son was sexually abused by Raymond Barnes, a deacon at Washington DC's Love and Faith Christian Center. Thus far, Mr. Barnes has been accused of molesting eighteen boys at Love and Faith. Several of them on church grounds. Police have not yet released specific information about this mother's claims, but we have reason to believe that if her proof is as convincing as she claims, the DA will move for a quick trial and conviction in this case."

Deacon Barnes's picture was replaced by Pastor Hines's.

"The other suspect in this church sex scandal is the pastor of Love and Faith's Alexandria, Virginia church. Clarence Hines has been accused of molesting five boys. Police and the DA's office are working around the clock to continue to uncover information about the allegations . . ."

My cell phone rang. I answered it without looking at the caller ID. "Okay, Blanche, I saw it."

"Do you know anything about this?"

"No. Doesn't sound like the press knows much about it either."

"Well, you need to get on it. See what you can find out. Talk to the Bishop, and see if he knows anything. Have you called him yet?"

"Blanche, I just finished watching the news segment when you called."

"Trina, I don't have to tell you what to do. Get to it." She hung up the phone.

I stepped out of Moms's room into the hallway to call her back. When she answered her phone, I said, "Blanche, this is not a good time. I'm in Baltimore. At the hospital with my mother. She's . . . sick."

"How sick?"

"What?" I stared at the phone. "What kind of question is that? Sick enough to be in the hospital."

"How long is she going to be in there? Trina, you know what can happen over the next few days. We don't need to let this get away from us."

"Blanche, my mother has lung cancer. She almost died today, drowning in her own fluid. The doctors had to drain almost two liters of bloody liquid off her lungs, and she has a huge tube coming from her back hooked to a suction device on the wall to keep the fluid from backing up in her lungs again. Is that sick enough for you to leave me alone for the rest of the day?"

"Sorry, Trina. I'm sorry to hear about your mother." She was silent for a second. "Don't you have a sister that can take care of all that?"

I hung up the phone.

Before I could walk back into Moms's room, my phone rang again. I didn't recognize the DC number, but answered it in case it was Tiffany calling from someone's phone.

"Hello?"

"Ms Michaels?" I recognized Bishop Walker's voice. "Blanche Silver gave me your cell phone number. Have you seen the news today?"

nineteen

I grabbed my temples. Could this day get any worse? "Hello, Bishop Walker. Yes, I just finished watching the news."

"What should I do?" He sounded nervous.

"Nothing yet. There's not enough information to even worry about making a statement. If anyone contacts you, just say you don't know what's going on."

"Can you figure out what's happening? Isn't there anyone you can talk to so you can get more information before the whole story comes out in the press? I want to be prepared."

"Is there something you need to tell me, Bishop? Something you know that you haven't bothered to share? No need to keep any secrets from me. You have no reputation to protect as far as I'm concerned." *I know you're pure evil through and through.*

He hesitated for a second, letting me know he had at least one secret he wasn't trying to share. Probably more.

"I can't help you if you don't tell me everything, Bishop. It's just like a lawyer trying to defend a criminal. If some surprise information comes out during the trial and the lawyer didn't know, he doesn't have an opportunity to prepare a defense for his client. If you know something, you should tell me. Now would be a good time, so I can prepare for it."

"No, there's nothing to tell." He said it too quickly. I knew he didn't completely trust me to keep his dirty little secrets. As well he shouldn't. One word from Monnie, and I would spill everything so fast his head would swim.

"Well, if that's all then, Bishop, I need to go. I'm in Baltimore at the hospital with my mother. I'll make some calls, but I may be out of pocket for the next few days. She was deathly ill when we arrived at the emergency room today."

"I'm sorry to hear that. Please know I'll be praying for her. You know God is faithful to heal her."

I chuckled. "Don't bother to pray, Bishop. You and I both know it wouldn't do any good." It was amazing that he was so used to saying the right thing at the right time, even though he didn't mean it. I guessed it was a preacher reflex.

"Well, then, Ms. Michaels. I'll be expecting to hear from you as soon as you know something."

It was weird, this amicable animosity we shared. Being pleasant for the sake of it, but both being willing to do whatever we had to do to take the other out at a moment's notice should the need or occasion arise.

I walked back into Moms's room. She had changed the channel. She patted the edge of the bed, and I sat down next to her. "Everything okay, Tree?"

I nodded. "I'm good."

"You took your old job back so you could pay for my health insurance and bills?"

I nodded.

"You have to make that man look good because you're trying to take care of me?" Moms grabbed my chin and forced me to look at her.

"It's not like that, Moms. It's—"

"Call the doctor to take this tube out. I'm going home to die. There's no way I'd let you do that for me. No wonder you can't sleep and you losing more weight than when you was in Africa. Tree, you know I'd never want you to do anything like that for me. I know you love me, baby, but I wouldn't want you to sell your soul to the devil when I'm gon' die anyway."

She reached around her back, trying to grab the tube. I grabbed both her hands. "Stop it, Moms. Have you lost your mind?"

"No, you have. You know I wouldn't want you to do anything like that. Let me go. When you get so grown to be manhandling me?" She tried to wrestle her hands out of mine, but I was too strong for her in her weak and tired state.

"Old lady, if you don't stop it, I'm gonna tell the nurse you're agitated and make her give you some drugs to make you behave. Is that what you want?"

She stopped struggling with me. "What I want is for my daughter to have some peace. Baby, just let me die, and you go on back to Africa and marry that angel man. Forget all this here and go where you can be happy. That's what I want."

I put my arms around her gently, so as not to disturb the tube. "Moms, I love you. I can't let you go without my best fight. I can't imagine my life without you. I need you at my wedding. I need you there when I have my first baby. And my second baby. I can't let you die." I let the tears flow down my face.

She pressed her face against my cheek, mixing her tears with mine. "Tree, baby. Death is a part of life. I'm making peace with it. I wish you could too."

"I can't, Moms. Not when I know you don't have to die. I've seen miracles. If you would just let me pray for you."

She pulled back and kissed my forehead. "Tell you what, when I die, you pray, and let God raise me from the dead. If I wake up, I promise the first words out of my mouth will be 'Jesus, save this poor black soul.'"

I laughed and kissed both her cheeks. "Deal, Moms." We shook on it. I hoped that was an indication she would soften and let me pray for her before it got to that point.

"Now you call that lady back, and tell her you're quitting that job." Moms folded her arms and stared me down.

"I can't do that. I promise I have a reason other than the money."

"Does it have anything to do with Monica?" She narrowed her eyes at me.

"Huh?"

"Don't 'huh' me. I saw Monica's face that day when we was watching it on the news, and then you jumped up and turned the television off and wrapped that skirt around my head. I ain't crazy. You got to wake up pretty early in the morning to get something over on this old bird."

I laughed.

"See, that's what I don't understand, Tree. You expect me to believe that God can heal me of cancer, but you can't believe Him to provide for you well enough that you wouldn't have to take this job that's sucking the very life out of you. I mean, if He can raise me from the dead, surely He could get you a decent job where you ain't got to shake hands with the devil every day. You Christians don't make no sense to me."

I felt like Moms punched me in the stomach. I sat there for a few minutes not knowing what to say.

My cell phone rang. I recognized Tiffany's number and answered it. "Tiffy, where are you?"

"I'm at Stacy's. I got your message. Is . . . is Moms okay?" Her voice sounded funny. Thick.

I frowned. "She's okay now, but it got crazy for a second there. Are you on your way up here?" I looked at Moms, wishing I hadn't asked Tiffany that in front of her, just in case she said no.

"I can't get no ride, Sissy. Moms is okay? Is she . . . "

The way Tiffany slurred the word Sissy let me know what was going on. "Tiffy, are you . . . what have you and Stacy been up to today? You didn't come home last night." I looked over at Moms.

I started to get up and leave the room to give Tiffany a good tongue lashing, but Moms grabbed the phone out of my hand. "Tiffany, it's your mother. I'm doing just fine, thank you so much for asking. Still alive enough to beat your tail for whatever it is that got your sister lookin' like she seen a ghost. What's wrong with you? Where were you all night? Better not be laying up under some man."

Moms listened to Tiffany for a few seconds then her eyes flew open. "You drunk? You been drinking, girl? I oughta get out this bed right now, get in the car and come down there and beat some sense into you. You done lost your mind?"

I had to push Moms back down into the bed and point to the tube to remind her she needed to be still. I tried to grab the phone away from her, but she pushed my hand away. "What is wrong with you? I didn't raise my girls to be no alcoholics or drug addicts. You think I worked hard all them years for this? Let me tell you something. You better—"

I pulled the phone away from Moms and walked out of her reach with it. I pointed to the tube and made a mean face in hopes of threatening her to stop moving around. The tube looked stretched enough to come out, and God knew I would pass out if that happened. "Tiffany, I'll call you back in a minute. You better answer, you hear me?" I closed the phone and walked back over to the bed.

Moms fussed like Tiffany was standing right in front of her. "Think I worked two jobs, working my tail to the bone so you could have everything you needed and go to college and have a good life, so you could end up being an old drunk? I didn't raise you like that—"

"Moms." I held up the phone. "She's gone. I hung up. Calm your nerves."

"Calm my nerves? Did you hear her? She sounded high as a kite."

I picked up the nurse's call button. "Either calm down, or

I'm calling the nurse to bring you some happy drugs. I mean it."
I held the button in front of her, threatening to push it.

She was still for half a second, then got herself in a flurry
again. "You knew about this, didn't you? That's what you two
got into a fight about, wasn't it? Why you keeping things from
me, Tree? You not supposed to keep things from me."

"I'm not supposed to keep things from you?" Now I was the
one almost screaming. "You get diagnosed with lung cancer and
start chemotherapy and you got me over there in Africa, having a wonderful time, falling in love, thinking everything's okay.
Don't you tell me nothing about keeping things from people."

We were both quiet, staring each other down. She finally
burst into tears. "What's wrong with my baby, Tree? Why she
getting drunk?"

I sat on the side of her bed and held both of her hands in
mine. I reached up and rubbed her arm until she stopped crying. "Moms, I think we both have to face the fact that anything
that's wrong with Tiffany is both our fault. We spoiled her, gave
her everything she wanted, overprotected her—just ruined her.
We never gave her a chance to be strong because we were too
busy being strong for her. So like you said earlier, she's dealing
with it the best way she knows how."

"My baby." Moms shook her head. "God, help my baby."

"Was that a prayer, Moms?" I chuckled. "Just like black folks.
Ain't got no use for God until you need something. Then you
want to call His name."

She pulled her hand away from mine to smack my arm. "You
need to stop playing so much, Tree." She stared out the window
for a second. "You get God to help my baby, and I'll believe."

I looked at her. "That's a promise. If God saves and fixes
Tiffany, you'll believe and accept Him for real, and not just to
make me happy?"

"If He can help my baby, He'd be worth believing."

"Okay, deal." We shook on it.

Tiffany just moved up to number two on my intercessory list—right up under Moms. I needed to pray hard and fast for Tiffany's life to turn around quick, fast, and in a hurry. I looked at the tube leading to the suction canister which was already half full.

Seemed like I didn't have much time.

twenty

I couldn't reach Tiffany for the rest of the night. I said a silent prayer, hoping she wasn't dead by the side of the road somewhere and trusted God that she was at Stacy's sleeping it off.

I was prepared to bunk in the foam chair bed in my mother's hospital room, but she insisted I go to her house to get a good night's rest. She said she wouldn't be able to rest if I weren't in a bed getting some good rest. I didn't bother to tell her I was still sleeping on the floor most nights. The thought of sleeping on the cold, hospital floor was what made me finally give in.

When I got to the house, I pulled on one of Moms's nightgowns and climbed into her bed, snuggling under her sheets and comforter. Everything smelled like her. The baby powder she drowned her body in to keep herself from sweating. The cheap, flowery perfume she insisted on wearing, no matter how much expensive stuff me and Tiffany bought her. And cigarettes. The tobacco odor infiltrated the woven fibers of her mattress and was probably embedded in the peeling wallpaper.

I pressed my face into her pillow and started to cry. The thought of losing my mother was unthinkable. Unbearable. I slid off the bed and stretched out prostrate on the floor, crying out to God to save my mother's life. I prayed for Tiffany, for Monica, and for all the violated boys of Love and Faith Christian Center. I cried out to the miraculous God I came to know in Africa, letting Him know I needed to see His hands move. Swiftly.

I awoke early the next morning to my phone ringing. The caller ID indicated the call was from the hospital. I sat up, praying nothing had happened to Moms.

"Hello?" My heart was almost beating out of my chest.

"Tree, you need to bring me some breakfast. These pancakes and sausage they done brought me taste like hockey pucks and rubber."

I laughed and picked myself up off the floor to get to the hospital. I stopped at the cafeteria to get her some pancakes, fried potatoes, bacon, sausage, and eggs, and we shared the feast together. Well, she made me eat while she only took little bites herself.

She fussed the entire meal about how many times the nurses had come in during the night to check her vital signs and the amount of fluid in the canister on the wall. "I think they thought I was gon' die or something. Kept asking me if I were resting well. How am I supposed to rest if you keep coming in here with that durn beeping machine and squeezing the life out of my arm? I tried to make a deal with her that if anything happened, I'd call her, but she wasn't buying it. Some mess about hospital policy."

After she ate a little and fussed a lot, she laid back in the bed and almost instantly fell asleep. I watched her breathing for a while, treasuring the sight of her chest rising and falling and praying that it would last forever. I thought of Hezekiah turning to the wall and petitioning God for fifteen more years. *I know forever is too much to ask, God, but can I have my mom for at least fifteen more years?* I counted in my head for a few seconds. *Well, actually twenty, God. I need her for at least twenty more years.*

After begging and pleading for my mother's life for a while, I pulled out my laptop to get some work done. It helped to get my mind off the canister on the wall, which seemed to be slowly filling up again with that awful bloody fluid.

In a few hours, I completed several press releases for some of my non-profit clients, prepared a speech for a foundation fundraiser, and made some phone calls to invite some media to an upcoming charity auction. I kept the television on mute, glancing up at it every once in awhile to make sure nothing new broke about the Love and Faith saga.

I emailed everything to Blanche so she would know I was working. She finally sent me an email back.

This isn't PR kindergarten where I need to check all your work. Stop bugging me. I haven't been able to get any info on the supposed conviction evidence. The DA's office is locked tight. You heard anything?

I typed back a quick response.

Nothing yet, but making calls all day. Will continue to try to find out something.

A few minutes later, there was a new message from her in my inbox.

Sounds good. How's your mother?

I glanced over at Moms, sleeping peacefully, breathing at a slow rhythmic pace. I typed back.

Better. Thanks for asking.

Not too much later, she responded.

No problem. Keep me updated. Sorry about last night. Take care.

After finishing a few more things, then leaving yet another message for Tiffany, I dozed off in the chair next to Moms. I woke up to the nurse who had introduced herself to me that morning as Anita shaking me. "Ms. Michaels? Wake up. Ms. Michaels! Your mother . . ."

I bolted up in the chair and looked over at Moms's bed. Someone had pulled the little curtain around her. Was she . . .

I jumped out of the chair, slung back the curtain, and immediately rushed to Moms's bedside.

She stared at me and shook her head. "I ain't dead, Tree. Lord, chile, you need to work on your faith." She rolled her eyes. "Now can you close that curtain so I can get off this bedpan? A woman can't even handle her business in private."

"Oops, sorry." I closed the curtain and chuckled at the thought of her telling me I needed to work on my faith. I turned to the nurse to see what it was that she had been trying to tell me about Moms.

Anita pointed to the canister on the wall. "As you may have noticed, it's been emptied a few times since your mother came up from the ER last night. Because of all the fluid that keeps gathering on your mother's lungs, the doctor wants to do a procedure where he puts a chemical in the small tissue space the lungs sit in to make it scar so they'll stop filling up with fluid. Then we can take the tube out."

Moms pulled the curtain back so she could see the both of us. "Then I can go home? Let's do it."

"Wait a minute, Moms." I glared at her. I turned back to Anita. "Is it dangerous? What kind of chemical? Isn't it bad to scar her lungs? Will she have problems breathing again?"

Anita smiled. "How about I have the doctor come in and answer your questions?"

I nodded, but Moms said, "The only question the doctor needs to answer is when I can go home."

About half an hour later, a fresh-faced man in scrubs entered the room and introduced himself to me and Moms as Dr. Wilkes. With his short stature, chubby cheeks and spiky hair, he looked like he was about thirteen years old. He explained the procedure in detail, but I don't think either one of us heard a word he said.

"Boy, you still got milk on your breath. You ain't injecting no chemicals in my lungs."

"Moms!" I shushed her, but had to admit that she'd said out loud what I had just thought.

He laughed. "Ma'am, I'm thirty-nine years old, and I've been a surgeon for fourteen years now. I promise you, I can do this procedure in my sleep."

"Humph," Moms grunted. "How 'bout you do this one with your eyes open?"

After they wheeled her away, I sat down to call Monica again. I couldn't imagine why she wouldn't have called me back by now. Unless she hadn't bothered to listen to my message. Could she be that mad?

When the phone beeped, I left another message explaining what was going on and begging her to call me. I tried Tiffany again, but she still didn't answer. Since Moms was so much better, I decided to call Gabe and tell him I didn't need him to come. No one answered at the mission, but I left a message for Zembala to get to him.

Moms's procedure went well, and she spent most of the rest of the day asleep. Later that evening, they were able to take her off the oxygen and said if she remained stable, they could plan to release her in the next couple of days.

I hung out with her in the hospital the next day, and we enjoyed her favorite foods from the cafeteria. At least I enjoyed them. I was going to have to do a better job of getting her to eat. If I stayed around Baltimore much longer, I was gonna put on a good deal of weight. A couple of times, Moms grabbed my hips and pinched my butt to make sure she was fattening me up enough for Gabe.

I continued to work by laptop and telephone, getting more done than I probably would have had I been in the office. Blanche and I continued to trade emails. There was still no leak on the evidence against Deacon Barnes. I left messages with all my media contacts that I knew were working as hard as I was to get the information. I knew one of them would call me back, expecting me to return the favor by letting them know as soon as Bishop Walker was prepared to open his mouth and make a statement.

Moms slept as I worked. When I shut down my laptop for the evening, I sat watching her breathing again. She lay flat on her back with her arms crossed over her stomach. It creeped me out so bad to see her in a coffin pose, I had to get up to move her arms. I leaned over to kiss her forehead, and she stirred. She smiled when she saw me standing over her. She reached up, stroked my cheek and said, "Tree, baby, I love you. Please go to the house and get some rest."

I kissed her forehead again and collected my stuff to leave.

Later that evening as I was settling into Moms's bed again, my phone rang. I looked at my caller ID, and my heart leapt.

"Monnie!"

"Trina, I'm so sorry I didn't call you back. How's your mother? Is she . . . is she okay?"

"Girl, Moms is fine. I'll probably be bringing her home from the hospital tomorrow." I explained everything that happened over the past few days as best as I understood it.

"I'm sorry I wasn't there for you, Trina."

"It's okay. I figured you were still mad at me."

"Dag, Trina. I wouldn't get that mad that if your mother was sick, I'd ignore your phone calls."

"What happened then?" I pulled up Moms's blankets around my neck and was comforted by the scent of baby powder, flowers, and stale cigarette smoke.

She hesitated for a second, then said, "I just got out of the hospital myself."

"Oh my goodness. What happened?"

"I did a little too much this weekend. Me and Kevin drove down to the beach for our friends' double wedding. Remember the ones I told you about? Khalil and Alaysia and David and Nakia had a small joint ceremony down at Tybee Island, the beach where Alaysia and Kevin got baptized and I got pregnant. With the stress of everything that's been going on with Love and Faith and maybe my trip up there, then the activities of the weddings this weekend, I think it was all too much. Then me and Kevin . . . you know . . . had a little session reliving our memories at the beach if you know what I mean . . . and I started having preterm contractions."

"Oh no." I sat up in bed. "Is the baby okay?"

"I'm fine, and the baby's fine. They gave me some medicine to stop the contractions and put me on strict bed rest."

"Why didn't you call me?"

"Kevin has been super overprotective. He had my phone and saw when you called, but . . ." Monica let out a deep breath. "He heard me screaming on the phone with you last week and thought you were calling with more about what's going on up there. He didn't want me getting upset, so he didn't tell me you called. Don't worry, I fussed him out."

"I hope not too much. He's just being a good husband and daddy. I don't blame him. So you're fine now?"

"Yeah. Just have to be still and keep myself calm the doctor says."

"Monnie, I'm so sorry about all this. You should have never come up here and I—"

"Shush, Trina. Me and the baby are fine. And I wanted to

see you. And all that stuff with Bishop Walker and Love and Faith . . . let's just not talk about it. Okay?"

"Yeah, girl. I love you, Monnie. Please take care of yourself and my nephew."

"I will. Love you too, Trina. And keep me updated on your mother. I'll be praying. Let me get off this phone before Daddy Kevin comes to check on me."

Early the next morning the phone rang. Moms was calling on her cell phone this time. "Tree, come get me. The doctor said I can go home."

"You sure?"

" 'Course I'm sure. Come get me out of this place. I don't want to be here a minute longer than I have to."

When I got to the hospital, Moms and the doctor she had introduced to me as her oncologist were in her room having what looked like a serious discussion.

I walked in, and they both suddenly went silent. "Morning, everybody. What's going on?"

Moms gave me a guilty look.

The oncologist, Dr. Miller, spoke up. "I was having a discussion with your mother about how her care should proceed from now on. As I'm sure she's told you, the cancer has spread to several places in her body. The effusions are probably the first of a number of complications we'll start to see in the coming weeks."

I sat on the edge of Moms's bed and took her hand. Dr. Miller continued, "I'm sure she's also told you that the chemotherapy at this point is what we call palliative, or just a measure to stave off the inevitable. We don't expect it to cure your mother's condition. That being said, we've had a long discussion and have decided not to proceed any further with the chemo."

My eyes widened, and I glared at Moms.

Dr. Miller held up a hand. "It's a perfectly reasonable decision. At this point, we focus on enjoyment of her last days rather than lengthening them. She'd rather be happy, feeling halfway good and eating what she wants to at home, than being sick from the chemo and spending time at the hospital. If I didn't agree and think your mother was making a rational decision, I'd go ten rounds with her. We've had plenty of fights since this all started, and she hasn't won all of them. Just most of them." He folded his arms. "And for the record, not calling you in Africa to tell you about your mother's diagnosis was a fight I lost."

Moms scowled at the doctor and pointed a threatening finger at him.

He laughed. "Anyway, your mother has also decided, and I can't disagree, that this is her last hospitalization. When it's time to go, she'd like to do so peacefully at home.

I knew my eyes had a panicky look in them because Dr. Miller said, "We can arrange for hospice care for her so you wouldn't have to handle all this by yourself. I know this can be difficult and frightening. But as I said, I think your mother is making the right decision."

Moms nodded at Dr. Miller. He reached out to shake my hand. "It's been a pleasure meeting you, albeit under such difficult circumstances. Your mother has been a blast to take care of." He put a hand on her shoulder. "She's definitely one of my favorites." Dr. Miller pressed his lips together like he was getting emotional and left the room.

I didn't see why anyone would choose a profession where their days were filled with death and dying. What kind of person was he?

"You okay, Tree?"

I nodded without saying anything.

"You understand the decisions I made?"

I nodded again. "Come on, old lady. Let's get you home."

"Actually I thought we'd stop by my house to pack my bag so I can go to Silver Spring with you."

My eyes widened.

"Tree, please. I ain't gon' die at your house. I promise. I still got some stuff left to do." She picked up her purse and paperwork the nurse left with her. "Right now, I need to see about my baby."

twenty-one

When we got to my house, of course Tiffany wasn't there. I hadn't talked to her since Sunday night when she called. I couldn't believe she hadn't even tried to contact me to see how Moms was doing.

I got Moms settled into Tiffany's room upstairs. It was still fairly clean, and I straightened up the few piles of clothes on the floor and took the dirty dishes downstairs. Tiffany could sleep on the futon in my little prayer room at the end of the hall when she came home. If she came home.

After making sure there was decent food in the house for Moms to eat, I took a long, hot bath and lay in my bed for a while. The softness of it relaxed me, and I prayed for sleep. After a few good hours of deep, dreamless sleep, my cell phone rang.

I sat up and shook myself awake, glancing down at the caller ID.

"Blanche, hey. Have you heard anything yet?" I tried to sound wide awake.

"Nothing, except that things are delicate because it involves a young boy. The DA's office is keeping things tight to protect his identity. It will probably be a day or so more before they complete the investigation, then they'll release the information. I spoke with Bishop Walker and told him to lay low, not saying anything to anybody about anything, and that we would call him when we know something. He shouldn't be bothering you."

"Thanks, Blanche. You didn't have to do that."

"I know he's not your favorite person in the world, so I figured I'd take care of it."

"Thanks." What was wrong with her? I hoped she wasn't buttering me up for some other awful client she wanted to unleash on me.

"No problem. Spend some time with your mother. I trust she's well?"

"Much better, thank you. I brought her home with me." So that was it. She was still feeling guilty about how she acted the day Moms went to the hospital.

"Good. Take a few days. You can keep doing everything from home like you have been. If anything pressing comes up, I'll call."

"Thanks, Blanche." I stared at the phone like I had just finished talking to an alien rather than my boss. I decided to thank God for the blessing and sank back into the bed.

The phone rang again with some Virginia number I didn't recognize. I didn't answer it and let it go to voicemail. I'd check it later. Even if it was Tiffany, I didn't feel like talking to her right now. If she were that worried about Moms, she could come home and find out what was going on for herself.

The cell phone rang again with the same Virginia number. Curiosity wasn't enough to make me answer. I turned the ringer off and rolled over in the bed. A few minutes later, I heard Moms's cell phone ring. I wondered if it was Tiffany. I knew it wasn't a few minutes later when I heard her cackling and talking like it was an old friend. If it was Tiffany, she'd be cussing.

A few minutes later, I heard her knocking on my door. "Tree, you sleep?"

"No, come on in." I sat up on the side of the bed. "Who was that you were talking to?"

She frowned. "What I tell you about being grown? You don't need to be all up in my business." She came over and sat down on the edge of my bed. "Why don't we get dressed up all cute and go get something to eat?"

I crossed my eyes and flopped back on the bed. "You can't be serious. Aren't you tired?"

"Tired of being cooped up inside. Tree, I went to the hospital like you asked me to and stayed there and behaved myself. I just had a good, long nap. Now I want to get dressed up and go out somewhere."

"Are you sure you're feeling up to it?" I studied her. Her breathing was pretty normal, but she looked kind of pale, and her eyes seemed more sunken than before.

"Yeah. I need some sunshine and fresh air." She grabbed my shoulder. "Come on here. You heard the doctor. The most important thing is for me to enjoy my last days. Don't you want me to be happy in my last days, baby?"

"Moms, give me a break. Don't be running no guilt trips on me. You ain't going nowhere no time soon."

She tickled my side until I sat up in the bed again. "Come on. Let's get dressed up real pretty. I'm feeling special. Don't put on no jeans either. Put on something snazzy and do something to your hair and put some make-up on."

"I don't feel like all that, lady." I was happy that she felt good enough to want to dress up and go out like we used to, but I was exhausted from the past few days. I was also concerned about what the next few days would hold. Once whatever the evidence was got released, I knew there would be a lot going on.

"Just do it, Tree. For me, okay?" She walked out my door and closed it behind her.

I threw my legs over the side of the bed to make myself get

up. I decided to be thankful that she was feeling better enough to be getting on my nerves. I pulled open my closet door, looking for something to wear. A couple of my suits that Tiffany had taken out of my closet were back. I pulled them out and looked at them. There were darts in the waistlines of the skirts and pants. I tried one on, and it fit perfectly. Somehow the jackets fit perfectly too. I didn't know what Tiffany had done, but my clothes fit like they were tailor made.

Next to the suits hung a dress I hadn't seen before. Its springy peach color would complement my skin perfectly. It was a straight shell, with darts from the breast to the waist. It was simple, yet elegant and short enough to show off my long legs. The tag in the collar said "Designs by Stacy". When I put it on and walked over to my dresser mirror, I couldn't help but smile. It was perfect. And it looked great on me.

Moms poked her head in the door just as I was turning around to look at myself in the mirror. "Well, now. Don't you look like something special. Where you get that dress?"

"Tiffany's friend Stacy made it. She and Tiffany altered some of my suits too. They came out perfect. Looks like Tiffy and Stacy may finally be on to something."

Moms walked over to me to inspect the dress. She had put on a cute, black baby doll dress that somehow hid how pitifully thin she was. "Nice." She grunted. "I'm still gon' tear her tail up when she gets here."

I rolled my eyes, knowing all Tiffany had to do was tell some pitiful lie and Moms would melt.

"Don't be rolling your eyes at me. Now go fix up your hair and your face. Hurry up. I'm almost ready."

I put a little oil on my hair and brushed it back, then fastened on the bun. I hoped Tiffany would come out of hiding long enough to braid my hair this weekend. We could fight later. I needed to get something done to my head. I took my time carefully applying make-up, keeping it as natural as possible.

When I finished, I went to find Moms. She was in the hall bathroom, putting on some bright red lipstick. She walked into the guestroom and came back with the *capelana* skirt I had bought her. She handed it to me. "Here. Make me look pretty."

I carefully tied it around her head. Just as she was admiring herself in the mirror, the doorbell rang. I looked at her. "You expecting somebody?"

She shrugged. "Might be that durn sister of yours. Maybe she lost her key. If it's her, I get first licks. You can have her when I'm done with her."

I walked down the steps, calling back up to Moms, "It's too late to beat her now. We shoulda been beating her when she was little."

I swung open the door, ready to give Tiffany a good fussing.

Instead of my baby sister, Gabriel Woods stood in my doorway.

twenty-two

I stood there frozen. "Gabe . . ."

He held his arms open, and I jumped into them. He held me tight for a few minutes, and then pulled away from me. He bent to kiss me, and I remembered how sweet his lips were. He finally stood back, holding me at arms length. "Wow, you clean up well. You look even more amazing when you're not covered with red dirt and sand."

I laughed.

He looked me up and down. "My beautiful angel."

I looked him up and down as well. "Look at you." I had never seen him clean and shaven. I was used to him with stubbly facial hair and a wild afro he couldn't seem to tame. The women of the village used to cut it with a large knife, but it never came out even. He was dressed in a pair of khaki slacks and a white, starched, button-up shirt. With his close haircut, sharp angular features, jet black skin and tall, lanky frame, he looked like a Calvin Klein model. More striking than actually handsome.

He pulled me to him again, and we both sighed and said at the same time, "You smell so good." We hung on to each other, laughing.

I laid my chin on his shoulder with my arms still around him. "Gabe," I breathed out his name. "What are you doing here?"

He pulled back and looked at me. "You called. I came." His facial expression and tone let me know he thought it was a ridiculous question.

"But I called and left a message with Zembala for you not to come."

"I was probably already on my way to Johannesburg by then."

I stared at him in wonder. "I can't believe you came."

He looked hurt. "You can't? Could you imagine anything that would keep me away if you needed me? I would have sprouted wings and flown across the ocean myself if I had to."

I laughed and traced the outline of his jaw with my finger. "But how did you get here? How did you find me? When did you get all cleaned up and fine?"

He laughed and traced my lips with his finger. "I actually got in last night. I meant to call you then, but by the time my cousin picked me up at the airport, I was so tired, I didn't even know my own name. I got up early this morning, and he took me to get clothes and get my hair cut and all that good stuff. He let me borrow his car. Driving was . . . whew."

He ran a hand over his head like he missed his wild hair. "I've been calling you all day, but you didn't answer. I had brought your emergency contact numbers with me and called your mother's cell phone. She is something else. I can't wait to meet her."

"Is that my son-in-law out there?" Moms walked over to the door where me and Gabe still stood, hanging on to each other. "Ain't you gon' invite him in?"

She reached out to hug Gabe and held on to his arm. "Come on in, baby. I promise I raised her good. I don't know why she's acting like she ain't got no home training." She led him into the house, shaking her head at me.

Moms smoothed a hand across Gabe's face. "Ain't you a fine something. You two make a beautiful couple too. Look like something out of a magazine. All tall and fashionable looking."

"Moms, please."

"Don't even start, Trina. You've known me too long to be getting embarrassed by anything I say." She led Gabe into the living room and sat him on the couch, and then indicated for me to sit next to him while she sat in the armchair. "Trina, ain't you gon' offer the man something to drink?" She rolled her eyes and shook her head at Gabe.

I didn't bother to ask what he wanted. I walked into the kitchen, grabbed a bottle of water and a tall glass of ice and brought it to him. He smiled as he accepted it, like he knew I understood what a precious gift I had just brought him.

"So you are well—Ms. Michaels, is it?" Gabe asked my mother and turned to me like he should know her name.

She reached over and squeezed his arm. "You can call me Moms, baby. I'm feeling fine. Trina made me stay in the hospital for a few days, but I'm much better now."

I narrowed my eyes at her, but didn't bother to say anything.

Gabe smiled at her. "I'm glad you're doing better. I trust that you'll let me pray for you while I'm here, yes? We wouldn't want to let that cancer continue to have any place in your body."

"Of course, baby. Anything for my son-in-law."

This time my mouth fell open.

"Close your mouth, Trina. Wouldn't want nothing flying in there. You just let me know when, Gabe. I'll be ready." Moms stood. "Well, I'm gon' get out your way so you can spend some time together." As she slowly ascended the stairs I heard her say, "Now I can die in peace."

"Not today, Moms. Okay?" I yelled after her.

When she was out of earshot, I said, "Please forgive me for my mother's behavior. I don't know where she got this habit of calling you son-in-law."

"No reason to apologize. I rather like the way it sounds." He took my hand in his. "Don't you?"

I smiled and leaned my head against his shoulder. "I'm so

sorry you came all this way and nothing's wrong. I should have called you back sooner."

"Are you not happy to see me?"

"Of course I'm happy to see you. Especially looking so good. I just feel bad that you spent so much money and went through all this trouble for nothing. Moms is fine. Well, for now anyway."

"First of all, the money means nothing if you needed me to be here. And if you were upset enough to call in the state you were in, then it's not for nothing. And what do you mean for now anyway?"

I explained our conversation with the doctor in Moms's hospital room before I brought her home. He took it all in, listening intently as I described how sick she was and that she had been released under hospice care to die. "If something happens, I can't even take her back to the hospital. I just have to watch and let her—"

"My dear, in a little while, we'll pray for your mother, and all this cancer rubbish will be finished."

"That's just the thing. Until you asked her, she hasn't been willing to let me pray for her. I think she just agreed to let you pray to make you happy. I'll be shocked if she really does." I told him about me and Moms's conversations since I'd been home.

"What does your mother have against God?"

I shrugged and shook my head, not wanting to have that conversation with Gabe. "And we haven't seen Tiffany. I don't even know where she is." I told him about Tiffany's recent behavior, the wad of money she gave me and the fact she admitted she was seeing a drug dealer. "When I talked to her when I was at the hospital, she was drunk. Moms yelled at her, and we haven't heard from her or seen her since. I hope she's okay, but who knows."

He nodded, listening to everything I said. "Tiffany is unsaved, yes?"

"She has basically the same attitude as Moms when it comes to God."

"And you don't know where either of them got it?"

I looked down and intertwined my long fingers with Gabe's.

"Or you do and you don't want to talk about it?"

I nestled my head into his neck and let out a deep breath.

"What else is bothering you?"

"Huh?"

"What was it that you were about to tell me on the phone when I called you that night, but then you decided not to tell me?"

I looked up at Gabe and smiled. I kissed his cheek. "I love you." I snuggled back against his shoulder.

He kissed the top of my head. He smoothed his fingers across my hair. "What happened?" He fingered the fake bun at the back. "What is this?"

I laughed. "Tiffany pressed it for me."

"Pressed it? So it'll go back, yes?"

"Yes. Why, you miss the afro?"

"Terribly." He stroked my arm softly with his fingertips. "Are you going to tell me the rest, Trina?"

"Do I have to? I'm enjoying being with you." I wrapped an arm around his waist.

"And you won't enjoy being with me if you tell me?" He pulled away from me a little so he could see my face.

"I'm afraid you'll be upset with me." I looked down at our hands and held his tighter.

"What could make me so upset that you wouldn't enjoy being with me anymore?" He gently lifted my chin so I would have to look at his face. "Nothing could ever make me not love you. You know that."

I got up and went to the kitchen to get him another bottle of water and a glass of ice. He followed me, asking where the bathroom was. I pointed him down the hall. "Don't forget to flush."

He laughed.

When we both came back to the couch, instead of curling up against him, I sat facing him so I could look in his eyes when I talked. I told him everything, starting with Monica's discovery two weeks before I left for Africa up until the present with my recent interactions with Bishop Walker. As he always did, Gabe listened intently without speaking.

When I finished telling him everything, Gabe got up and paced the floor. I sat there biting my lip, waiting for him to talk. My heart needed him to say what he was thinking.

"I don't understand," he finally said.

"Don't understand what?" I asked.

"Why you would think you would need to take that job when you first got back?"

I frowned. What part didn't he understand about mom's bills and mine? I started to explain again, but he held up his hand.

"Just as you called me to come, all you had to do was call and tell me about the money. You know I would have had it wired to you immediately. You never would have had to set foot in that man's office."

I shook my head. "Gabe, you know I could never ask you to—"

"And why not, Trina?" He came over to the couch where I still sat and knelt in front of me. "Why is it so difficult for you to let me love you?"

I stared at him. "Because I wouldn't call to ask you for thousands of dollars means I won't let you love me?"

He nodded. "And so many other things. You feel as if it was too much to ask for me to come here when you're carrying the weight of the world on your shoulders. Even in Mieze, for you to allow the slightest vulnerability and for me to be a man to you requires the severest conditions. Why must a child die or there be a flood or your mother almost die for you to need me? When everything is fine, you push me away. It's only when you're desperate that you're able to admit how much you love me. I can't bear this push and pull, back and forth with you any longer. I love you, Trina. I want to spend the rest of my life with you. But you're unable to believe that I could love you that much. Or unable to receive that love. Or unable to love me back."

I sat on the couch without speaking. I couldn't explain the emotions going on inside me. I wasn't sure I understood them myself. I wanted to curse him out, and I couldn't remember the last time I cursed. I wanted to scream and throw him out of my living room. And at the same time, I wanted to burst into tears.

Because everything he said was painfully true. As much as it hurt to admit it.

He looked down at himself kneeling in front of me and shook his head. "How ironic, yes? Because even if I ask you to marry me again, you'd say no. No matter how many times I asked. Wouldn't you?"

I still couldn't answer.

Gabe stood up. "I love you, Trina and I want to spend the rest of my life with you. But I can't do this what we've been doing for the last year. My heart can't take it. I want you to think about it." He picked up a pen and a piece of mail off the coffee table. He scribbled a phone number on the back of the envelope. "Here's the number where I can be reached. I'll stay in town for another few days. If I don't hear from you, I'll be on my way back to Mozambique."

He pressed the envelope into my hand and walked out the front door.

Moms must have heard the alarm beep when the door opened. A few minutes later I heard her feet on the steps. "Where's my son-in-law? He left already? What did you do?"

I rested my head back on the couch and let out a deep breath.

"Tree? What you do to run that man away?"

I glared at her. "Why does it have to be that I ran him away?"

She sat on the couch next to me. "Where did he go? He going back to Africa?

"In a few days he said. If I don't call him back."

She picked up my cell phone and thrust it in my face. "You better call that man back then."

I took the phone from her and put it back on the coffee table.

She rolled her eyes. "At this rate, I'm gon' live forever."

I laughed. "You mean to tell me all I have to do is never get married to keep you alive? That's a fair trade."

"No it's not." She squeezed my knee. "You love that man, Tree. It's written all over your face. And he loves you too. It should be simple. You love him, he loves you."

I nodded.

"So why are you on the couch looking like your dog just died, and he's on his way back to Africa?"

I shrugged.

"You refuse to let me die in peace, don't you?"

"Moms, what does my relationship with Gabe have to do with you dying in peace? Not that you're dying anytime soon."

"Everything. It has everything to do with it." She leaned back against the couch. "I'm trying to put my affairs in order. There's just some things I have to make right before I can go. The biggest one is the mistakes I made with you girls. Messed up your lives. I can't be okay until I fix that. Or at least do my best to fix it. I can only do so much. The rest is up to you."

"What are you talking about? You were a great mother. Everything I've accomplished, I owe to you." I put an arm around her thin shoulders.

"And everything you haven't accomplished you owe to me as well."

I rolled my eyes and lifted my hands to the ceiling in frustration. "What are you talking about?"

"That wonderful man you just let walk out the door."

I closed my eyes and massaged my temples. "Moms, please. I'm tired, and I have no idea what you're talking about."

"I was a great mother in many ways, but in one way, I really damaged you girls." Moms sat forward and looked me dead in my eyes. "When your father left us, I turned so bitter. Filled your hearts and heads with so much poison about men. Brought men in and out of your lives that you had no business being exposed to. Just generally gave you the wrong ideas about men, marriage, and relationships. And so for a while, you were sleeping with everyone, but still not giving your heart away. And now that you all sanctified, you just won't give your heart away. That's my fault, Tree."

I took her hand in mine and squeezed it. Her words were hurting me as much as Gabe's did.

"I taught you not to trust a man. Not to depend on no man. Not to be vulnerable or let a man anywhere near your heart. Never let a man do nothing for you. Be strong and independent and never need a man for nothing. And you learned it well. Now it's time to unlearn all that garbage I taught you so you can love that beautiful man that heaven sent you. Gabriel . . . he's an angel indeed." Moms patted my hand. "Find a way, Tree. Call on that God of yours to fix your heart. Make it right so I can have some peace. And while you're at it, pray for Him to bring Tiffany home so I can make things right with her too."

I squeezed her hand. "Thank you, Moms. I love you so much."

"I love you too, baby. Now call my son-in-law and get him back over here. That sho' is a fine looking man. Why he talk so proper though? Ain't you said he was from Detroit? How a black man from Detroit end up talking all white?"

I laughed. "He spends most of his time speaking Portuguese, Moms. When he switches back over to English, it's like a second language for him."

She grunted. "Baby, you better call that man. And you need to test drive the car while he's here." She shifted her imaginary gearshift. "Vroom, vroom!"

I swatted her legs. "Moms, you are too crazy. Shush with all that."

She took my face between her hands and kissed both my cheeks. "I love you, Tree."

"I love you too, lady."

I knew both Moms and Gabe were right. I had to find a way to overcome the pain of my father leaving and every negative word my mother had ever spoken into my soul about men. I couldn't lose him.

But I was afraid to keep him.

I would have to pray and trust God to fix my heart, before Gabe got on that plane going back home.

twenty-three

Iawoke early the next morning with Moms's and Gabe's words on my mind and prayers on my lips. I had to bite the bullet and call him. I took my cell phone downstairs and sat on the living room couch, trying to figure out what to say. As I was about to dial, I heard a key in the front door.

"Tiffy, you're home."

She looked like crap. Her eyes were swollen and red. Her cute hair style was now matted to her head and her stylish clothes were rumpled.

"You okay?"

She nodded. "Is Moms okay?"

"She's fine, Tiffany. Where have you been? We've been worried sick about you."

She held up a hand. "I don't want to talk about it. And I don't want to hear your mouth right now. Please just leave me alone."

I pressed my lips together and let her walk past me up the stairs. She had no idea what she was in for, but she told me she didn't want to hear my mouth, so I wasn't about to warn her. After she dragged herself up the stairs and into the bathroom, I tipped up the steps into my bedroom so I could hear the fireworks, and intervene if necessary.

A few minutes later, I heard the guestroom door creak open.

I heard Tiffany suck in a quick, surprised breath, then say, "Moms—you're here. I didn't know you were here."

"You didn't know I was anywhere. For all you know, I coulda been in the morgue. Did you even care if I were dead or alive, Tiffany? Huh? Did you even care that your mother was in the hospital and almost died? Huh? Have you called or answered the phone when we tried to call you? How was I supposed to know you weren't dead? Is that it? You're trying to kill me with worry? Out there drinking and smoking like you ain't got good sense."

Tiffany must have tried to leave the room because the next thing I heard was, "Get back here you little, black heifer. You ain't that grown that you can walk away when I'm talking to you. You need to answer my questions."

"I ain't got to answer nothing. You need to leave me alone."

I strode down the hall, about to put my size eleven foot up Tiffany's tail for disrespecting Moms like that.

I stopped when I heard Moms say, "I'm about to leave you alone, all right. Real alone. How alone do you think you gon' be when I die?"

I heard Tiffany burst into tears.

"I'm sorry, Tiffany. Come here, baby."

"No!" Tiffany screamed. "You and Trina keep asking me what's wrong, and you know exactly what's wrong. Just what you said. You're gonna die and leave me alone. How am I supposed to deal with that? You think I know how to deal with that?"

"Tiffany, baby—"

"And stop calling me baby. I'm tired of you and Trina treating me like a child. You two have always treated me like a baby, and then you get mad at me when I act like one. What am I supposed to do now? You trying to die and leave me here to take care of myself. We both know as soon as you go, Trina will be on a plane back to Africa. Where does that leave me? How am I supposed to take care of myself?" Tiffany sat down on the bed, holding her face in her hands.

Moms sat down next to her. I stood in the doorway, not sure what to do. Moms looked up at me. "We all right, Tree. Just need to make things right with my baby. I mean, with Tiffany."

I eased out the door and closed it behind me. I decided to leave it cracked just in case Tiffany got disrespectful again, and I needed to snatch some sense into her.

I went back downstairs and sat on the couch. I dialed the number Gabriel had left for me, but it went straight to voice-mail. When it beeped, I wasn't sure what to say. I hesitated for a second, but then the words flowed, "Gabe, it's Trina. Please don't get on a plane going back to Africa. Because if you do, you'll be taking my heart with you. And your heart will be here with me and mine will be there with you, and it would be a big mess. Please call me. I . . . I love you."

I hung up the phone and sat there, hoping he would call back soon. I decided to go back upstairs and get in the bed. I hadn't slept much the night before. I could barely hear Moms and Tiffany's voices so I trusted that they were okay.

Just before I was about to drift off, my cell phone rang. I looked at the caller ID, praying it was Gabe. Instead it was Sandra Jensen, the reporter from Fox 5 News.

"Hey, Sandy. You got something for me?"

"Boy, do I. You might want to sit down, this is pretty awful."

I sat up on the side of the bed. "Oh dear. What is it?"

"Worse than I would have ever imagined, but definitely enough to put Deacon Barnes away for a good long while. I understand why the DA's office took so long to release this. It's delicate, and to be honest, just downright sick."

My stomach sank. "Sandy, what is it?"

"This is the story I've got so far. About six months ago, one of the members of Love and Faith DC noticed a dramatic change in her ten-year-old son. He suddenly became withdrawn and quiet, staying in his room and getting sick every Sunday so he wouldn't have to go to church. Weird things started happening, like his bird died, his fish died, and his new puppy disappeared."

I frowned, but kept listening.

"When the news about the arrests broke, the mother became suspicious that her son had been molested. She confronted him and he refused to talk. She took him to a psychiatrist and he completely shut down. He hasn't spoken or eaten in the last week or so. The mother was walking through her backyard, says she was out there praying for him, and she came across the holes where he had buried his pets. One was marked with the fish's name, another with the bird's, another had the puppy's name on it, and a final grave had the boy's name on it."

I sucked in a quick breath and pulled the comforter around me, not sure I could handle the rest of what Sandy was about to tell me.

"Of course, she dug it up. In it, there was a plastic garbage bag that contained a bloody pair of his underwear. DNA testing confirms the boy's blood, and semen which was a perfect match for Deacon Barnes."

"Oh, God, Sandy." My stomach churned. "Oh dear, God. That's awful."

"The word is that his lawyer is trying for a plea."

"No way. He needs to burn for this."

"We'll see. Good luck with the Bishop today, Trina. I can't imagine what your meeting with him is gonna be like. Are you sure he didn't know anything about all this? It's just hard to believe . . . well, I know you wouldn't be anywhere near him if you thought that he had in any way known about this and done anything to cover it up."

I couldn't even say anything. I hoped my silence didn't tip Sandy off.

"Let me know if he has anything to say."

I had to make myself speak. "You'll be the first person I call."

I hung up and sank back into the bed, feeling like I could throw up at any moment. Was the boy so traumatized that he had killed his pets? What was he thinking when he dug the last grave and put his name on it? Would his life ever be normal again? He should have been playing with his puppy and instead . . .

I couldn't shake Sandy's words about believing Bishop was innocent because of me. I wondered how many others had granted him the benefit of the doubt because of my reputation.

My cell phone rang again. It was Blanche. I knew I'd get no rest for the remainder of the day.

"Blanche, I heard. I don't know if I can do this."

"Trina, I honestly have to say I was sick to death when I found out about it. Something about this boy makes the whole thing so personal."

I knew Blanche was thinking about her own twelve-year-old son.

"You honestly think he knew what was going on in his church?"

"I have factual proof that he knew, Blanche. Don't ask me how, but I do. He knew nine months ago. In enough time that he could have saved this little boy."

She was silent for a moment and finally said, "I'm gonna let this be your call. If you want out, you got it. I can't ask you to do anything I wouldn't do myself. I may be a greedy witch, but I have a heart. If this was my son, and I thought the Bishop could have prevented it, I'd take a gun and . . . let's just say he'd have a different kind of damage control to worry about. In fact, I'll be calling his office to let him know we'll be returning his check—minus payment for the services we've already provided of course."

I let out a deep sigh of relief, almost about to burst into tears. "Thanks, Blanche. Thanks so much. I can't tell you how much I appreciate this."

I sank back into my bed. *God, thank you so much. You are so good and faithful. Thanks that Moms is here with me and okay. Thanks that Tiffany came home and that she's all right. Thanks for Gabe and for the chance to make things right between us. And thank you for getting me out of this nightmare.* I laid there praying for the little boy and his mother for a while and drifted off to sleep.

I didn't bother to answer my phone for the next few hours. All the reporters calling could leave messages. I was done with Bishop Walker. His number came up on my caller ID several times, but I didn't care. The only thing that would make me answer the phone again was to see Gabe's number. Why wasn't he calling me back? There was no way he had gotten on a plane that quick.

The phone's continuous ringing kept annoying me until I finally got up. I didn't want to turn it off, though, in case Gabe called. I tiptoed down the hall to the guest room and peeked in. Moms and Tiffany were curled up next to each other asleep. I guessed they must have made their peace. I smiled and closed the door.

I went back downstairs, and the phone rang again. Instead of Gabe's number, it was Blanche's again.

"Yes, ma'am. Is everything okay?"

"I just talked to Bishop Walker. He's insisting that our firm continue to represent him. I told him we no longer felt comfortable providing services. He's such an arrogant . . . Anyway, he says if you don't call him and be in his office within the hour, he'll be forced to make good on his promise. He said you would know what that meant."

I sank into the couch, letting out a deep breath.

"Trina, do you know what he means?"

"I do."

"Well?"

"I can't talk about it. Please don't make me. Just . . . let me meet with him so we can get everything straightened out."

"You're going to meet with him?" She sounded shocked.

I thought of Monica going into preterm labor again and knew I had to. "Yes. I hope to explain later." There was no way I could tell Blanche the whole truth. Kevin's story was too juicy for her to keep quiet.

"So don't send him his fee back?"

"Not yet. I'll call you back soon. If you would, call Bishop Walker back and let him know I'll be there within the hour."

I hung up the phone and went upstairs to get dressed. I put on one of the suits Tiffany altered and headed out the door, praying the whole way. God had worked out everything so far. He would have to get me out of this nightmare with Bishop Walker.

twenty-four

When I walked into Love and Faith's administrative offices, I was surprised to see a younger woman sitting at Ms. Turner's desk.

"Good afternoon, I'm Trina Michaels. I believe Bishop Walker is waiting for me?"

She glared at me and picked up her phone. "Ms. Michaels is *finally* here, sir. . . . yes sir."

She looked at me with more disdain. "You can go right in."

Who was she and what was her problem? I entered Bishop Walker's office. "Where's Ms. Turner?" I was about to tell him about his substitute secretary's attitude issues, but he was glaring at me with similar irritation.

"Ms. Turner is no longer with us."

"Oh." I had to wonder if it had anything to do with what happened the last time I was here. Had he fired her because he was concerned she had overheard our conversation?

"Where have you been? I've been calling you all day, and when I talked to your boss, she said you were no longer representing me." He narrowed his eyes and clenched his teeth. "I thought we had an agreement, Ms. Michaels."

"So you've heard the news I take it?"

"Why else would I be calling you? The phone has been ringing all day with people wanting my statement. What am I supposed to say?"

I sank into the chair, looking up at black Jesus for an answer to Bishop's question.

"Ms. Michaels, we don't have much time. Either you tell me what to say, or my next words to the press will be that I know the source of the letter sent to the Bishop's council. And everything else that goes along with it. If I don't know how to answer their questions about this, I'll distract them with something equally as sensational."

"Could you stop talking for a minute so I can think? How am I supposed to come up with an answer with you threatening me?" I looked up at Martin Luther King, Jr. on the wall since black Jesus wasn't helping me answer Bishop's question.

Bishop continued to talk. "I have to sell him out. Say that he should be punished brutally for his crimes against children. I'll point out the fact that all his victims except one were sons of single mothers, often only children and with no older brother in the house. That he was a calculated predator who carefully studied his victims before striking. I'll finish with the fact that he himself has never been married and that it's been rumored that he's involved in a series of homosexual relationships."

Bishop Walker was one sick individual. I must have had a disgusted look on my face because he stopped talking and looked at me. "What? Not good?"

"Uhhh, noo," I said with sarcastic exaggeration. "Of course not. How does that make *you* look?"

"Oh." He drummed his fingers on his desk. "I guess I see your point."

"Tell you what, Bishop. There's no need for us to hold a press conference. You simply need to issue a general statement to the press with your answer to the new information. From what I understand, it will be released on the six o'clock news tonight. We should have a statement prepared in the next hour. I'm going to go home and work on it and I'll fax or email it to your new secretary."

"Are you sure that's the best thing to do?"

I stood and headed toward his office door. "I'm sure. I'll be in touch in the next couple of hours." At least my head could be clear if I were out of his presence. Being around him was making me sicker and sicker.

Before I walked out his office door, I turned to ask, "Where did you say Ms. Turner was again? She was such a sweet lady." I was really concerned about what might have happened to her.

"She's not at the bottom of the Potomac River if that's what you're worried about, Ms. Michaels." Bishop Walker smiled like Lucifer. I hurried out of his office.

It took me almost two hours to struggle through writing Bishop's press statement. I kept imagining the little boy's sad face, imagining the little pet graves and finally the one with the boy's name on it. Imagining his mother's face when she discovered the contents of the last grave. It was too tragic.

And not one time did Bishop mention the little boy. All he thought about was himself and maintaining his ministry. He was just as guilty as Deacon Barnes and Pastor Hines. His hands were smeared with the blood of twenty-four boys, and he needed to pay.

The more I wrote, the more I prayed. It was beyond me wanting to get out of my obligation to Bishop Walker. I wanted God to take him down. I quoted Psalm 37 over and over again in my head.

Moms and Tiffany were still snoozing last I had checked on them. Tiffany must have been exhausted from being out in the street doing whatever she was doing and Moms just from being sick. Especially with the events of the last few days.

My cell phone rang. I was tired of snatching it up and looking at the caller ID only for my heart to sink realizing it wasn't Gabe. I let it ring a couple of times and finally looked at it. My heart jumped.

"Gabe!" I exhaled all the tension I had carried all day wondering if he were on a plane to Johannesburg. "You called."

"Of course. Did you think I wouldn't?"

"I called you early this morning and left a message, and I've been waiting all day and you hadn't called back, so I thought maybe you had already gotten on a plane or that maybe you weren't going to call back or maybe you were still angry with me or—"

"Trina."

"Yes?"

"You still have no idea how much I love you. Do you?"

"I'm trying. Really hard, Gabe. I promise I am. Can you . . . maybe come over . . . and talk?"

"Of course. And I didn't call because I forgot these stupid cell phones have to be charged. I've been carrying it in my pocket all day, waiting for you to call. I finally couldn't wait to hear from you any longer and pulled it out to call you and realized it was dead. Forgive me. I don't want you to think for a moment that I would have left you. It almost killed me to drive away from you last night."

"It almost killed me when you left. Don't ever do that again."

He was silent for a second, then said, "That's what you want? For me to never leave you again?"

"Yes, Gabe," I said. "That's what I want."

"Well, all is right with the world then." I could hear his smile through the phone. "I'll be there shortly."

My heart felt light even as I faxed off the press statement to Bishop Walker. I hurried upstairs to get ready. I looked through my closet and realized that in spite of pigging out with Moms lately, all that would fit me were the altered suits and my new peach dress. I slipped it off the hanger. It was still clean since I had only worn it for an hour or so the night before. Besides, something told me Gabe would have on the same clothes as well.

I jumped in the shower. I had already bathed earlier, but I needed to wash my hair real quick. I smiled when I felt it start to sponge back into my afro. I hopped out of the shower, towel dried my hair, then grabbed Tiffany's blow dryer to finish it off. It was huge and nappy by the time I finished. I found a peach scarf that was close enough to the shade in my dress and tied it around my head to tame the afro a little.

I slathered myself in a sweet-smelling, Mango shea butter and quickly got dressed. As I finished applying my make-up, I heard Moms' voice. "Tree, where you at?"

I walked down the hall to the guest room.

When I entered the doorway, she said, "Well, now, I say. Look at you. I guess my son-in-law is on his way over?"

I laughed. "Yes, Moms."

She jostled Tiffany who was still curled up under her, asleep. "Look, Tiffany. Check out your sister."

Tiffany opened her eyes and sat up, wiping her mouth. Her eyes widened when she saw me in the dress. "Ooohhh, you found it. It fits perfect. Sissy, you look beautiful."

"Thanks, Tiffany." I spun around to model the dress. "You and Stacy are really good at this. You could start your own business."

Tiffany and Moms smiled at each other. Tiffany said, "That's exactly what we plan to do. Design clothes and do hair and make-up. It's what I've always wanted to do."

She looked back at me. "I guess I was afraid if I didn't go to college and be all professional like you, you guys wouldn't be proud of me. But it's the only thing I'm good at and the only thing I like."

"Oh, Tiffy. We'd be proud of anything you did. You know we love you, baby girl. I mean, Tiffany."

She rolled her eyes. "You can call me baby girl. Just don't treat me like one."

I wanted to say "then don't act like one" but looking at Moms and Tiffany, it seemed like they'd had a great talk with some big breakthrough, so I didn't want to mess it up with some nagging big sister comment.

"Deal, Tiffany."

Moms rubbed Tiffany's back. "Come on. Let's get up and get dressed so we can go get something to eat. Your sister has company coming."

Tiffany looked up at me. "Who?"

"Your brother-in-law." Moms pushed her toward the edge of the bed. "Come on, I'll tell you all about it over dinner."

I rolled my eyes and walked back down the hall toward my room. A few minutes later, Moms came in with the same dress she'd had on yesterday holding the *capelana* skirt in her hand. "Here, make me pretty."

"Moms, you're wearing the same thing you had on yesterday?"

"I'm trying to be an African queen like you, Tree."

I laughed and sat her on my bed. I took off her raggedy head scarf and rubbed the fine peach fuzz on her scalp.

She grunted. "Don't stop. That feels good."

I went to the bathroom to get the shea butter to give her scalp a massage. I put a small amount on her head, and then began rubbing and kneading her scalp.

"Chile, you sho' know how to treat your old mother." She sat quietly, enjoying the pampering for a second, then said, "Me and Tiffany had a good talk. I told her that she and that friend of hers need to make a plan this time instead of a get rich quick scheme that's gon' be sure to fail. She said they would get some help at the local community college putting together a real business plan. I think they could do it, Tree. Don't you?"

"Um, hmm." I put some shea butter on her neck and started massaging it.

She bowed her head for a second to enjoy it, then said, "I want you to watch them close, okay? When they finish that business plan, you check it. If it looks good, you can give them her share of my insurance money to get started. She can have my house, and I can have my peace that she won't ever end up on the street, long as she keep the taxes up. And she can drive that ol' piece of car I got until it dies. Maybe by then, her business will be working and she'll be able to get her own. You help her without babying her, okay?"

She turned her neck and pointed to a spot I had apparently missed. "And I talked to her about the smoking and drinking. And the company she's been keeping. I told her she better straighten herself out or I'd be coming back to haunt her." She chuckled to herself.

I let out a deep breath and stopped massaging my mother's neck. "You're determined to die, aren't you?"

She gently placed my hands back on her neck again. "Not determined, Tree. Just accepting. Making sure everything's in order with my girls before I go. That's all that matters to me now. I'm tired, Tree, baby."

I didn't say anything else, but planned to have Gabe pray for her before he left later. I needed to milk the whole "son-in-law" thing for all it was worth.

I finished her massage and tied the skirt around her head. "There you go, beautiful as ever."

Moms stood and reached up to me so I would bend for her to kiss my forehead. "Thank you, baby. Now you make things right with my son-in-law." She patted both my cheeks. "If you need me and Tiffany to stay away for a long time, just send me a text message that says *Vroom, vroom.*"

"Moms!" I couldn't help but laugh.

"What?"

"You know I'm not gonna do that. Not until I'm married anyway."

"If you don't test drive the car, how will you know how well it drives? Or if you even like the make and model?"

"I guess it's a matter of faith, Moms."

"Humph," she grunted and walked out of my room.

A few minutes later, I heard the doorbell ring. Both Moms and Tiffany sang out, "I'll get it."

I hurried and put on a pair of earrings and slipped on a pair of sandals so I could go rescue Gabe from my mother and sister.

By the time I got downstairs, they had already let Gabe in and had him sitting on the couch with a tall glass of ice water in his hand. He stood when I walked into the living room.

Moms grabbed Tiffany by the arm and picked my keys up off the coffee table. "Let's go, baby. We'll see you later, Tree. Don't forget to send me a text message if you need anything." She winked and they left.

Gabe pulled me into his arms and held me. "Ummm, you smell so good. What is that?" He pulled back and looked at my hair. "You fixed it." We both laughed. He kept staring at me. "You're more beautiful every time I see you."

I looked at him, now in khakis and a starched blue, button up shirt. "Hey, no fair. You changed clothes."

He laughed. "I figured you'd been back in America long enough to be offended by me wearing the same thing. Forgive me. These are the same pants, though."

We laughed and he pulled me into his arms again. He kissed my face all over, and then trailed down my neck. I had to make him stop before I did have to send my mother that text message.

We both sat down on the couch. I took his hand. "I thought about everything you said about me yesterday. Even though it hurt, it was all true. And I had to face it. I spent the evening praying about it and I realized something."

"Yes?"

"Remember what you asked me about Moms and my sister, and why they hate God so much? And then when you asked me why I'm the way I am."

He nodded. "Yes?"

I let out a deep breath and squeezed his hand. "I need to tell you about my father."

twenty-five

G abe sat forward to listen to what I had to say. He had asked about my father several times in the past year, and I had always avoided answering.

I had worked hard in my previous church to overcome issues and baggage from the past. Whenever it came time to deal with all the emotions surrounding my father, I never could push past the pain. It was like it was buried too deep to get to. And too painful and huge every time I dug it up and tried to deal with it. So I left it buried. Keeping it hidden down in my soul had worked until this moment. Staring into Gabe's earnest eyes, I knew I needed to do whatever I had to in order to get over it. Otherwise I'd lose him, or we would never be able to have a healthy marriage. Feeling his hand rubbing mine, I knew that's what I wanted. More than I had ever realized.

I set my jaw and delved into my explanation, determined to do whatever it took to heal my heart and have a future with Gabe.

"My dad . . ." I let out a deep breath. This was harder than I thought. I decided to spit it all out and try to make sense of it afterward. "My parents were never married. I honestly think my mother was one of many women my father was seeing when she got pregnant with me. When they realized I was on the way, he tried to settle down and make a family with her. I think we did okay for a while—I even have some pictures I salvaged from Moms's burning parties. The three of us at the park, or at the beach looking happy like a family should. Until Tiffany was born. Then I think the whole family thing got old to him. They started arguing and fighting all the time. He actually hit my mother a few times, but when she hit him back with a cast iron skillet, I think he got the idea that wasn't the right thing to do. He started drinking all the time and coming home at all hours of the night drunk."

Gabe squeezed my hand. "That's why it was so upsetting for you both when Tiffany did it, yes?"

I nodded and continued, not wanting to lose the momentum I had tapped into. "So he left us. Just disappeared one day and never came back. Moms had it real hard after that. She worked two and three jobs for as long as I could remember. Hard work too. Like factory and assembly line stuff where she would come home tired and sore. Then cleaning people's houses on the days she was supposed to be off.

"She tried to contact him all the time, to help out when times got real bad, but we could never find him. So she finally gave up, and he became as good as dead to us. Sometimes she had boyfriends after that, but none of them were any good either. Plus, I think she never got over my father. She really loved him."

Gabe listened intently, squeezing my hand and rubbing my back every once in awhile.

"And she didn't mean to, but in her bitterness, Moms taught us girls some bad things about men. Never depend on a man, never trust a man, never let a man do anything for you. A man will always break your heart and so on and so on. That's why I am the way I am . . ." I stopped myself, "That's why I *was* the way I was with you. And why, like you said, I have trouble realizing how much you love me and letting you love me. I know I have to work hard at unlearning all those messages. You'll be patient with me, yes?"

He smiled at me imitating his speech and leaned over to kiss my forehead. "Of course. Thanks for explaining these things to me, Trina. It makes things make much more sense. And it will help me to be patient and love you all the more to overcome those messages running around in your head." He frowned. "But that still doesn't explain why your mother and sister hate God so much."

"There's more." I leaned back against the couch and sighed. "One day, we were sitting around the table having breakfast on a Sunday morning, and we looked up at the television and there was my father. In a robe, on a stage, behind a podium . . . preaching. We all sat watching the whole program with our mouths open, unable to believe what we were seeing. At the end, they gave all the church information and it turns out that he's the pastor at this huge mega church in Florida. At the very end of the program, they flash this picture with my father and . . . 'the first family' . . . as the caption said."

Gabe's eyes widened.

I nodded. "Turns out me and Tiffany have a brother and sister we've never met. And a stepmother as well. They looked so happy and so . . . prosperous. My mother lost it, screaming about how we were really the first family. She called the number on the screen demanding to speak to him. He finally called back later that evening. She never really told me and Tiffany the particulars of their conversation. All she said was that he was happy with his new life and wanted to forget his real first family. He offered to send regular money to take care of us, but Moms said she didn't need his hush money or his guilt offering and refused. Being teenagers, of course, we wanted the money, but Moms said, 'Never let a man pay you like some whore.' She made us promise never to accept money from a man we weren't married to."

Gabriel nodded.

"Moms taught us with her words and actions to be fiercely independent and never let a man close to our hearts. Well, at least me anyway. Tiffany seemed to go in the opposite direction."

Gabe nodded like everything was making more and more sense.

"Not only was Moms convinced that all men are no good, she was also convinced that all men of God are no good as well. Because of my father, she developed a hatred for God and anything having to do with God. She's convinced that every preacher is a hypocrite and that God isn't real. And for whatever reason, that was the one lesson Tiffany decided to learn from her."

"And, so how did you find your way to God?" Gabe asked.

I shrugged. "I guess I wasn't willing to believe He wasn't real because of my mother. I kept my heart open, and one day, I heard the truth and accepted Him. How ironic that the place I got saved at was Love and Faith Christian Center."

Gabe frowned.

I explained. "I got saved after hearing a sermon Bishop Walker preached. And he's a worse hypocrite than my father ever could be. He's downright evil. I guess it goes to show that God can use whatever and whoever—His Word is more powerful than their hypocrisy."

Gabe shook his head. "Still, that doesn't mean they should be allowed to continue in their positions of leadership, misleading God's people and benefitting monetarily from it."

"I agree wholeheartedly. Speaking of . . ." I picked up the remote. I had set the TiVo to record the 6:00 news. "You're not going to believe what happened today." I forwarded through the news and commercials until I saw Deacon Barnes's face on the screen. I pressed play and turned up the volume. "Brace yourself."

twenty-six

We both sat watching the news in horror. Even though I had heard the story from Sandy Jensen earlier, it was even more terrible hearing it officially on the news. They were careful to protect the identity of the mother and son, saying only that they'd left the area to go be with family members and to get professional help for the boy. They mentioned Bishop's response, or my response, at the end, using all the right buzz words, deeply regret this tragedy . . . glad for the truth to come forward so justice could be pursued . . . will be in constant prayer for this family and all the other families that have been affected by these horrible crimes . . . immediate measures being taken to provide mental health services . . . blah, blah, blah. All rhetoric and lies. I felt sick being a part of it and prayed that God would forgive me.

Gabe stood up and paced the living room after I turned off the television. I could tell from his face that he didn't know what to say. He finally said, "We must get you out of this."

I nodded.

He paced a little more and turned back to me. "This Bishop knew and could have saved the little boy, yes?"

I nodded and bit my lip.

"God is a God of justice, and this man shall not continue to prosper in his evil." He came back and sat on the couch next to me. "We must get you out of this."

I nodded again. "Let's not talk about it anymore, okay?"

Gabe took me in his arms. "Okay, angel."

We sat there quietly on the couch, but I knew Gabe was praying—for the boy and all the other boys, for me to disentangle myself from the situation, and for God to work His righteousness against Bishop Walker. I knew with him praying, something was sure to break. Soon.

"I'm very sorry for your father leaving all of you. It seems to have had an effect on each of you in some different way, yes? Even all these years later, his memory still haunts each of you. Is that why you thought I would get on a plane and leave you to go back to Africa?"

I nodded.

"My beautiful angel, as I said, I will never leave you. In fact . . ." He leaned over to pull something out of his pocket and got into his kneeling position on the floor in front of me again. "I will never leave you, and I never want to be without you. I will ask you this again and again, as many times as you need me to ask you—"

"Yes, Gabe."

"Yes, what?"

"Yes, I'll marry you."

His face spread into a broad grin. He opened a little box he had pulled out of his pocket and slid a band onto my left ring finger.

When I looked down at a beautiful emerald cut diamond solitaire in a thick gold band, tears sprang into my eyes. "Oh, Gabe. It's beautiful." I looked up at him, wondering when he could have gotten it. "Is it—"

"Of course, dear. Conflict free, straight from Canada."

"Canada? How?" He had only been in town two days. "I mean, when did you order it?"

He grinned. "Three months ago. After the first time you said, 'I love you.'"

More tears fell, and I pressed my forehead against his. He kissed my tears away. "Do you like it?"

"It's perfect. I couldn't ask for a more beautiful ring."

"And I couldn't ask for a more beautiful wife."

He kissed me gently on the lips, and I sat there in his arms, dreaming of the day when we'd go back home, but not sure of how or when.

A little while later, we heard the door open, and Moms and Tiffany came in. Tiffany walked over and placed a carryout carton on the table in front of us. "We brought you guys something. We figured you might be hungry. Let me grab you guys some silverware and napkins." She headed for the kitchen.

Moms grunted. "They don't need no forks." She laughed at herself, but seemed to be breathing a little hard.

I stood to help her over to the armchair. "You okay, Moms?"

She waved me away. "I'm fine, Tree. Just a little tired. I shoulda known better than to go somewhere with Tiffany, running me all over the place. You young folks tire an old lady out."

Tiffany came back from the kitchen in time to hear her. I looked at her, and she raised an eyebrow and subtly shook her head to let me know she hadn't done anything to tire Moms out.

I pressed my lips together. Gabe must have noticed the worried looks on both me and Tiffany's faces and stood and put a hand on Moms's shoulder. "Mummy dear, you said you would let me pray for you, yes?" He gave her an endearing look, like he understood that he needed to milk the son-in-law thing.

Moms looked up at Gabe, looked at me, then back at him and shrugged. "I guess it ain't no harm in it."

Gabe walked behind her chair and laid both his hands on her shoulders. He said a very simple prayer releasing supernatural healing, life and forgiveness. He said a few more simple words, then bent to kiss her cheek. "Thanks, Mummy."

"Thank you, baby." She patted his face and kissed him back.

I was amused at the look on her face. She seemed surprised by the shortness of his prayer. I guess she expected him to be all long and religious. I had heard Gabe travail for hours in prayer on many occasions. I knew he could be very loud and passionate, binding demonic forces, crying out for the Kingdom of God to be established, and worshipping at the top of his lungs. I knew he understood that wasn't the way to come at Moms and appreciated his sensitivity, knowing that the simple prayer he chose to pray was equally effective.

Moms reached for Tiffany. "Help an old lady upstairs to bed, okay?"

Tiffany nodded and helped Moms up the steps.

After they were gone, I put my arms around Gabe. "Thank you for that. I can't believe she let you pray for her."

"Remember how they taught us that people may not be able to receive God's healing power if they're filled with bitterness and unforgiveness?"

I nodded, biting my lip. He had given voice to what I had been fearing all along.

"Maybe I can spend time with her tomorrow, and we can talk."

I chuckled. "Good luck with that."

He smiled. "Don't be afraid, my angel. God is still on the throne." He kissed my lips, and then my neck, then pulled himself away from me. "I should go. You're far too beautiful for me to be here this late."

I walked him to the door. He gave me one last kiss on the nose. "I'll see you tomorrow, yes?"

I nodded.

He tilted his head. "Thanks for everything that you told me. I am happy to understand you better."

"Thanks for loving me and for being patient with me. I love you, Gabe."

He kissed my lips, and I could tell he was having a difficult time leaving. "Goodnight my beautiful angel. My beautiful . . . wife."

I smiled and watched him walk down the front steps to the driveway. "Gabe," I called out to him as he was getting into the car. "Charge your cell phone tonight." He laughed and waved goodnight.

When I got back into the house, I opened the food Moms and Tiffany had brought. I should have known. Fried fish and French fries. I put the carton in the refrigerator to eat the next day and went upstairs to go to bed.

After I cleaned off my make-up and put on a T-shirt to sleep in, I slipped into my bed. A million questions ran through my mind. When would we get married? I wanted to do it as soon as possible so Moms could be there and be happy. I knew neither me or Gabe would want an extravagant, expensive wedding. It would contradict everything we believed in.

Most of the people I would want to be there were in Africa. In fact, the only people here that were essential for me were Moms, Tiffany, Monica, and Kevin. And I knew there was no way Monica could travel anywhere anytime soon. But I wasn't trying to get married in Atlanta.

There was no way I could get Moms to Africa in her current state. But maybe that was exactly what she needed to get healed, though. To be under the African skies where God was so near, you could feel His breath.

I'd talk to Gabe about it the next day and we'd get it all figured out together.

As I was about to drift off to sleep, my cell phone rang. It was becoming a regular occurrence. I squinted to see the caller ID then quickly flipped open the phone.

"Monnie, hey."

"Hey, Trina." She sounded upset.

"Is everything okay?"

"I saw the news earlier."

"Oh."

Neither of us said anything for a few moments.

"Monnie, I thought we weren't going to talk about it. I don't want you getting all upset. Remember the baby."

"How could I forget him? His head is sitting on my bladder, and he's kicking me in the ribs."

We both laughed.

"I've been thinking about what you said, Trina. About how I should trust your love for me and that you would never do anything to hurt me. And I figured it out. Because I do know how much you love me and would never let anything hurt me. Or should I say anyone?"

"Huh?"

"Don't 'huh' me, Trina. I know why you're doing this. Bishop made the same threat to you that he made to me and Kevin in the hospital, didn't he? And you agreed to continue representing him to protect us. To protect me."

I didn't say anything.

"Trina, how could you possibly believe I would want you to sell your soul for me? Just as much as you love me is how much I love you. I would never want you to do something like that for my sake."

"But what about everything you said about being happier than ever and not losing your wonderful life?"

"Trina, I was being selfish. And being my best friend that loves me, you should have been honest and told me so. I was busy protecting myself at the expense of everyone around me. Kevin really believes this is supposed to be a part of his ministry. And when he saw the news today, it confirmed it for him. The boy on the news was the same age as Kevin was when his nightmare started. He knows he's called to minister to little boys going through the same thing. He kept talking about how different his life would have been and how different our life together would have been if someone had been there to help him."

I fingered Gabe's ring and kept listening.

"It's like you said, Trina, your call is to be a missionary in Africa. Mine is to be a supportive wife for my husband. How can I do that if I won't even let him do what God is telling him to do?"

"What are you saying, Monica?"

"That tomorrow, I want you to go tell Bishop Walker that he can kiss your—"

"Monnie!"

"Sorry, girl, this cussing demon has been out of control lately. I think it's the pregnancy hormones and all this drama. Tell Bishop that you're no longer going to represent him and that you'll be helping me and Kevin with our press campaign for the expansion of his ministry—helping people struggling with their sexual identity."

"You guys are sure about this?"

"Even if it wasn't about Kevin's ministry, I couldn't ask you to represent Bishop one day longer to protect us. I want you out of this, Trina. I have a feeling it's about to get even uglier."

"Yeah, me too, girl."

"So you'll tell him tomorrow? I hope you won't lose your job."

"I won't. Me and Blanche already talked about things. She's trying to turn into a human being on me."

Monica laughed. "Call me tomorrow after you talk to him. I can't wait to hear about the look on his face when you tell him off."

"Yeah, girl. I can't wait to see it."

I decided to save my happy news for later, after the whole Bishop Walker drama was over and done with for good.

twenty-seven

The next morning, I dressed myself in my sharpest altered suit, put on some heels and make-up, but let my unruly afro fly wild with a fancy matching scarf wrapped around it. I was all about handling business that day.

I gave a quick call to Bishop's new secretary to let her know there was an urgent matter we needed to deal with and that I was on my way to his office. She had better watch her 'tude, because she didn't want to catch a piece of me.

I snuck down the hall to check on Moms before I left. She and Tiffany were curled up in the bed together again. I stood over Moms for a few seconds, making sure her chest was rising and falling at a normal pace. She cracked one eye open and said, "I'm breathing, Tree. Didn't Gabe pray last night? You *really* need to work on your faith."

I laughed and walked out the door, closing it after me.

In the car on the way to Love and Faith, I called Gabe to tell him about me and Monica's conversation the night before.

"So I'm on my way to his office right now to let him know that Silver PR services will no longer be handling his damage control campaign. I promise, I never want to see his face again, ever in this life or the next." The thought of Bishop Walker's demonic grin caused chill bumps to rise on my arms.

I heard Gabe exhale his relief. "I knew God would get you out of this. Are you sure you want to go there by yourself? This Bishop, he sounds . . . almost dangerous."

The hairs on my arms stood up even higher. I made myself calm down. "He's not dangerous in a way like he would actually physically harm me. All his dirt is done through words. And lies. He's got nothing on me, so there's nothing he can do to hurt me. And he can't hurt Kevin and Monica anymore because they're willing to go public with the secret he was holding over their heads. Everything's okay."

"Still. Are you sure you don't want to wait until I can get there? I could sit in the parking lot, and if anything goes wrong, you could call me on your cell phone and I could come to your rescue."

"Gabe." That man had a way of melting my heart. "I'll be fine. I promise. Remember that day when those banditos tried to rob me of the food I'd bought for the children?"

He laughed, remembering my encounter with some thieves on a trip back to the village from a shopping excursion in the city. "I guess I have nothing to worry about then. I guess I just feel the need to protect my wife-to-be."

"Oh, Gabe." I could hear him smiling through the phone. "I promise I'll call you the minute it's over. Maybe you can come over and we can spend the rest of the day together."

"Sounds good, my dear."

"Maybe we can talk about—"

"What?"

"Maybe we can talk about . . . you know, wedding plans and stuff."

"Oh . . . okay."

"What?"

Gabe chuckled. "One minute I'm begging you to marry me, and now that you've accepted, you're ready to plan a wedding. The next day."

"I know. I just . . ." I thought about how tired and deathly grey Moms looked.

"You're concerned about your mother?"

"Yeah."

"She's going to be fine, my angel. We're walking in faith, yes?"

"Yes, Gabe." I pulled into the parking lot at Love and Faith. "I'm here. I'll call you as soon as it's over, okay?"

"Okay. I'm praying for you. If anything happens, don't hesitate to call me."

"I won't." I hung up the phone and wondered how long it would take me to get used to being loved like I was beginning to realize Gabe loved me. It seemed almost too good to be true. I quickly rebuked the thought and reminded myself of God's faithfulness and that my relationships with men didn't have to mirror my mother's.

I sat in the car in the parking lot for a few minutes, praying. I needed God to word my mouth and end this thing without any fallout. I reminded myself of what I told Gabe. Bishop no longer had any leverage now that Monica and Kevin were willing to go public. There was nothing he could do to hurt us.

I finally got out of the car and walked into the church. When I got to the administrative suite, Bishop's secretary was halfway pleasant to me. She greeted me and asked how I was doing. Things had probably been quieter for her after our press release and she must have decided to show me a little respect. She led me into his office. I appreciated her fake smile and all, but I wasn't about to be drinking any water she might bring me.

Bishop rose to greet me. "Ms. Michaels, is everything okay? I thought the news report went reasonably well last night. As well as could be expected obviously, but I think our position came out clear, don't you think?"

"*Your* position, Bishop."

"Yes, whatever. There have been plenty of phone calls today and there were some reporters when I first got here, but for the most part, it's been quieter than I thought. Probably because we preempted with your statement yesterday. Thanks again for that. I hope we can do things that way from now on. I'm sure you'd appreciate not having to come over here to meet with me." He gave me a wry smile. "Anyway, I was thinking, perhaps now we should focus on a preemptive strike against Pastor Hines. I'm sure they're hard at work now to come up with some conclusive evidence against him. Perhaps we –"

I held up a hand to stop him. "Bishop, I came here to tell you there is no more 'we.' I can't and won't do this anymore."

Bishop Walker put on a stern paternal face. "How is it that you keep forgetting our agreement? Are you telling me I should forget about Pastor Hines and focus on releasing Kevin's story to the press?"

"If that's what you'd like to do."

Bishop frowned at me. "What do you mean, if that's what I'd like to do? You're saying you would have no problem with me holding my own press conference to tell them it was Kevin that sent the letters and that he had a past life in homosexuality? That their precious gospel star is actually a sexual deviant?"

"Would you like some of the phone numbers for my media contacts?"

He frowned again, his eyebrows appearing permanently knit. "I don't understand."

"I spoke with Monica last night. She and Kevin saw the news cast and have decided that they're not willing to be silent anymore. I'll be working on their media campaign to release the news to the public. Starting with when Deacon Barnes molested Kevin at the age of ten, and Pastor Hines molested him at the age of thirteen. Right up until the part where they told you nine months ago after Kevin's accident."

Bishop Walker turned ashen gray. And then red. He began

fuming, and I was sure he was going to blow. I was nervous for a second, wondering if I should have let Gabe sit out in the parking lot like he offered.

Just when I thought he would explode, an air of calm exuded from Bishop Walker. He narrowed his eyes and plastered on his signature demonic grin. "Okay, Ms. Michaels. I'm willing to let you out of your obligation to me. Tell Ms. Silver she can keep the payment for everything you've done so far. As I said, I appreciate your hard work." He picked up his phone, obviously dismissing me. "You take care. Give Kevin and Monica my best."

That made me more nervous. "What are you going to do?"

The Lucifer smile was in full effect. "You really expect me to tell you? I'm not foolish enough to lay all my cards on the table like you do, Ms. Michaels."

I stood there, wondering who he had picked up his phone to call. What retaliation did he have in mind?

"Ms. Michaels?" His voice pulled me out of my thoughts. "Good day." He said it firmly and finally, letting me know our amicable hate/hate relationship had come to an end.

twenty-eight

I left Bishop Walker's office slowly. I didn't feel as triumphant as I expected I would have. It wasn't enough just to quit and leave him hanging. It wasn't even enough to run Monica and Kevin's campaign and let the truth be known about him. I hoped I wasn't being vengeful. I just didn't think it was right for him to be able to continue as the Bishop of DC's largest church without having to answer to anyone. Not even God.

But I didn't know what to do to bring him down. Bishop was right. I needed to stay out of the game, because I wasn't smart enough to play it.

But I knew someone who was.

About twenty minutes later, I sat in Blanche's office, explaining the whole situation to her.

She frowned the whole time and finally said, "Do you really think so little of me, that I would 'out' your friend for the sake of a good story?"

I bit my lip and didn't answer.

"Really, Trina? I come across as that awful?"

I winced and nodded.

She shook her head. "I may need to have you work on some damage control and image improvement for me then."

We shared a smile.

"So what do you think Bishop Walker is up to?" I asked.

Blanche frowned, propped her elbow on her desk and held her forehead with her hand—her "don't bother me, I'm coming up with something brilliant" posture. She closed her eyes and sat like that for a few minutes.

She opened one eye. "How evil did you say he is?"

"More evil than you could ever imagine."

She pressed her lips together and closed her eyes again. Finally she said, "I'm not sure. He may hire another firm to run damage control, and I'm trying to think how they would frame things. How I would frame things if he came to me right now. I imagine he's not above lying about your friend and trying to twist things to make him look bad."

I thought about his plan for his statement about Deacon Barnes. "You're right. He would do that."

She blew out a frustrated breath. "I don't know, Trina. Sorry, but I'm not as evil as you thought."

We laughed. My cell phone rang. The caller ID showed Sandra Jensen's number.

"Hey, Sandy. What's up? You got something new for me?"

"I was calling to ask you the same thing. What's going on?"

I frowned at the phone. "What do you mean?"

"I just got this weird call from Bishop Walker's secretary. She says he's holding a press conference this evening and has some stunning new news to release in the case. She said it's a twist I don't want to miss. Can you believe it?"

My stomach churned. I closed my eyes for a few minutes. Just when I thought the nightmare had ended. "Yeah, Sandy. Unfortunately, I can believe it." Even though Monica and Kevin had agreed to go public, I hadn't really considered what that would look like. I wasn't sure Monica had either. Things could get really ugly in the next few days. There was no way she was prepared for that. I almost wanted to call Kevin and tell him to take her away on vacation for a while. Somewhere with no televisions and no newspapers. Just until the baby was born.

"So, Trina, what's going on? What's the twist? And why did his secretary call me instead of you?"

I stood to pace around Blanche's office. Her eyes followed my every move. She hunched her shoulders, held out her hands, and mouthed the question, "What?"

I held up a finger. "Sandy, I'm not exactly sure what's going on. I'm no longer representing Bishop Walker."

"Really?" Sandy's greedy journalist voice peeked through. "Do tell."

I figured I might as well. Everything would come out in Bishop's press conference anyway. At least this way, she would hear the truth first.

"I refused to represent Bishop anymore because I found out the truth."

Blanche's eyes widened and she waved her hands frantically. She mouthed, "What are you doing?"

I turned my back to her. "I have proof that Bishop Walker knew about the sexual abuse going on in his church for some time now."

Just as I was about to launch into my explanation, Blanche snatched my cell phone out of my hand. "Sandra, hey, it's Blanche. Trina's gotta go. A call just came in, and we gotta jump on it right away. I promise as soon as this all takes shape, you'll be the first person we call."

I stared at Blanche. "What are you doing?"

"What are *you* doing? Have you lost your mind?" She snapped my cell phone shut and thrust it toward me. "What in the world are you thinking?"

"Bishop Walker's secretary called to let her know that he's holding a press conference tonight. Some madness about a twist she can't afford to miss."

Blanche's mouth fell open. "A twist she can't afford to miss?"

She chuckled. "How corny is that? If that's the best he could come up with, his money with us was well spent."

I fell into the chair across from her desk. "Blanche, this isn't funny. He's gonna hold a press conference and destroy Kevin and Monica. I know by the time he's finished with it, he'll make Kevin look like a monster." I thought about what Bishop Walker had dreamed up to sell out Deacon Barnes. "He'll probably try to make it seem like Kevin was molesting kids in the choir or something. He'll make Kevin look awful so no one will believe Kevin when he says that he told Bishop Walker nine months ago and he didn't do anything."

Blanche slowly descended into her desk chair and assumed her thinking position again. I sat quietly, hoping she could come up with an answer to fix this whole mess. All I could think of was Monica and Kevin's little baby boy, lying in an incubator with tubes coming out of everywhere, fighting for his life because he was born prematurely.

I stood and started pacing again. What did Bishop Walker have up his sleeve? What could he possibly imagine he could say that would discredit Kevin? How many other news reporters had he called? Would anyone believe him?

"Blanche?" I sat back down in the chair.

She opened her eyes. "I'm trying to think of any way we can let the press know that Bishop Walker knew without outing your friend. Even though he and his wife are willing to go public, it shouldn't be this way. They don't want it to look like he was forced to come out because of all this craziness. When he comes forward, it needs to look like it was because he wanted to help young men with the same story. Not because he had to defend himself against Bishop Walker's lies and accusations."

I nodded. And it needed to be after the baby was born. "So what do we do?"

Blanche shrugged. "That's the problem. I don't know how we can prove he knew without telling Kevin's story."

We both sat there quiet, trying to figure out what to do next.

Sonya popped her head in Blanche's door. "Trina, there's a lady out here looking for you. A Ms. Turner?"

My eyes widened. "Ms. Turner?" I stood and held my hand up to my mid-chest, where I imagined about five feet two would be. Sonya nodded.

"Can you take her into the conference room?"

Sonya nodded and left.

I turned to Blanche. "This may be it. I'll be back."

twenty-nine

I almost ran to the conference room. There she sat. Sweet little Ms. Turner, cowering in her chair, wringing her hands.

"Ms. Turner?"

"Oh!" She jumped and grabbed the sides of her chair. When she saw my face, she put her hand on her chest and took a few deep breaths. "Ms. Michaels, I'm so sorry."

I hurried over to her and put a hand on her arm. "Are you okay?"

She nodded, but then shook her head and gripped the conference table. "I saw the news last night. It was horrible." She rocked back and forth for a few seconds, staring down at the table. "Just horrible. I know the little boy they were talking about and his mother. He was the sweetest boy in the world. Always full of hugs and kisses for everyone. Smart as a whip. Just a beautiful child." Ms. Turner dabbed at her eyes with a crumpled tissue in her hand. "And now . . ."

I sat there and waited while she rocked. Did she come just to express her sadness about the boy? If so, I'd pat her on the back a few times, and then send her on her way. I had to get back to Blanche to figure out how to save my unborn nephew's life.

Ms. Turner sniffed and dabbed her nose with the tissue. I walked over to the little snack table in the corner of the conference room and grabbed her a napkin. Her tissue didn't look like it could take many more dabs.

She accepted it and finally stopped rocking. "I didn't know what to do, who to come to. I probably shouldn't be here now, but I couldn't keep silent. Not knowing what I know. And not after what happened to that sweet, precious boy. My conscience wouldn't let me. Maybe I'm being silly to be paranoid, but I just don't know what Bishop Walker might do. I prayed about it, and I felt like God sent me to you."

Ms. Turner opened the napkin and blew her nose. She looked up at me. "You seem to have such a pure heart. That's why I couldn't understand why you were helping Bishop Walker. Until I overheard your conversation. I'm sorry for eavesdropping, but . . . nothing with this whole situation was sitting right with me. I've served and respected Bishop Walker for eleven years now. But when all this started, I started to think maybe he wasn't the man I thought him to be. That's the only reason I eavesdropped that day."

I walked over to the conference room's mini refrigerator to get Ms. Turner a bottle of water. Maybe she'd take a few sips and be able to calm down enough for me to understand what she was trying to say.

I took the top off for her and set the bottle on the table in front of her. She tried to lift it to her mouth, but her hands shook so badly, I thought she would spill it. She set it back down.

I said, "Ms. Turner, please slow down and tell me what's going on. I won't let anything happen to you, okay?"

She shook her head. "You have no idea how evil he is or what he's capable of."

I took her hand. "Has he ever killed anyone or physically harmed anyone that you're aware of?"

She shook her head again and took a deep breath. "You're

right. It's not that bad. He just makes himself scarier than he is."

She took a folded piece of paper out of her purse and fidgeted with it. "About seven years ago, a woman came to Bishop's office for an emergency counseling appointment. They talked for a while, and then she started screaming and crying. I don't know exactly what was said, but I remember her screaming over and over, even as security dragged her out, 'What if he's not the only one? What if my son is not the only one?' I'll never forget the look on that mother's face. I never forgot her name either." Ms. Turner stopped fidgeting with her paper and picked up the bottled water. Her hands were less shaky, and she was able to take a few sips.

She continued, "When all this news broke out recently, I remembered that lady and realized what she had come to tell Bishop. After he fired me, I wanted—needed to find her. It took some doing, but I located her. I called her and told her who I was and what I remembered of that day in the office. She didn't trust me at first, but then I told her that Bishop had fired me and threatened to destroy my life if I ever said anything bad about him to anyone. She believed me then because he had said the same exact words to her back then. He paid for her and her son to relocate to Dallas, and she said he gave them a nice sum of money to 'disappear.' She was ashamed that she accepted it, but she was a struggling single mother and felt like she didn't have a choice."

Ms. Turner placed the folded paper on the desk and slid it over to me. "Here's her contact information. She's ready and willing to come forward with her statement that Bishop knew about Deacon Barnes at least seven years ago and didn't do anything. I told her to hold tight and that I would have somebody call her to tell her what to do next."

I nodded and patted Ms. Turner's shoulder. "You did the right thing. Thank you so much for having the courage to come here today. God will protect you. I'm sure He will." I stood to usher her out of the office. Me and Blanche needed to get on the phone right away to counterattack Bishop's press conference.

Ms. Turner clamped onto my arm. "What about the rest of them?"

"Who? The rest of the boys? We just have to pray that—"

"No. The rest of Love and Faith." She started her rocking motion again. "The DC church has 18,000 members. The Alexandria church has 6,000. What's going to happen to all those people when they lose both their pastors?"

I had to admit I hadn't thought about that at all.

"They'll be scattered, like sheep without a shepherd," she said, quoting a scripture from the book of Isaiah. "I've been thinking about it a lot since he fired me. For something like that to happen after all these years makes you really think. I had to look at my relationship with Bishop and the way I served him, and then at my relationship with God. And I'm just not sure."

"What do you mean?"

"I mean, I love God and I know God. I've always studied the scriptures for myself. And yet I was still blind to Bishop and who he really is. What about all those people with no foundation of their own, who don't study the scriptures for themselves? I'm afraid that a lot of the people that go to Love and Faith Christian Center really don't know God. It's a terrible thing to say, but honestly, Bishop is their God."

I nodded because I completely understood. It was the reason I ended up leaving Love and Faith after having been there for three years. I had gotten saved under Bishop Walker, but after I took all the classes they offered and attended church every time the doors opened, I didn't feel like there was anything else I could learn there. Monica said the same thing after she and Kevin started attending their new church in Atlanta. They said it seemed like they hadn't been in church all their lives and had never read their Bibles.

"I hear you, Ms. Turner. We just have to pray for them. Maybe this situation is exactly what they need to find God for themselves."

"I certainly hope so. And pray so." She stood to leave. "You'll leave my name out of this, right?"

I nodded. "You have my word. Everything will be just fine."

I led Ms. Turner out the office door and made a beeline for Blanche's office.

She was waiting for me when I walked in the door.

"We got him."

thirty

I stood at the back of the multi-purpose room at Love and Faith Christian Center with Blanche, waiting for the press conference to start. I kept staring at two doors. The door leading to the administrative offices from which Bishop Walker would make his dramatic entrance. And the door from the corridor from which I hoped salvation for Monica, Kevin, and my unborn nephew would come. Soon.

I stared at my watch and scanned the crowd for Sandra Jensen. My eyes finally rested on her. My apprehension must have been written all over my face because she winked and smiled. She mouthed the words, "They'll be here."

Blanche chewed her fingernails like she did when she was nervous. It amazed me that she seemed as concerned about protecting Kevin as I did. What had gotten into her? I wasn't sure where the sudden dose of human compassion had come from, but I was grateful to have her on my side.

We had spent the entire afternoon making phone calls to everyone we knew. The multi-purpose room was packed with DC's top journalists. It seemed crazy that we were responsible for taking Bishop Walker's press conference to the next level.

Even though quite a few people we called said they had received a phone invitation from Bishop's secretary, the room wouldn't have been anywhere near as full as it was if me and Blanche hadn't pulled out her Rolodex.

I only hoped our little plan didn't backfire. I'd never forgive myself if Kevin was "outted" in front of every reporter in the DC metropolitan area because of me.

The door to Bishop's administrative suite finally opened. He emerged behind his new secretary and Pastor Duncan. He came out with his head bowed in that "I'm a victim in this whole situation" posture. When he raised his head and saw the size of the crowd, I could tell it was hard for him to keep his demon grin from erupting. He nodded his acknowledgement of the press and approached the podium.

Probably because of my height and my crazy afro, Bishop Walker spotted me at the back of the crowd. This time he couldn't keep his Lucifer grin from erupting. Even if only a little. The corners of his mouth tilted slightly and his eyes narrowed. I was probably the only one who noticed it. He nodded at me, and then stared me down for a second.

I didn't know whether he was surprised at my presence there or concerned about what I might have told the press. Did he really think I wouldn't find out about whatever stunt this was he was trying to pull? Whatever was going through that sinister mind of his, I knew my standing there, staring right back at him without flinching, was making him nervous.

As well he should be.

I glanced at the door to the corridor again, almost willing it to open. I looked down at my watch. The press conference was starting just as scheduled. Where were they? I looked back at Bishop.

Blanche cleared her throat and elbowed me in the side, breaking up the staring match between me and Bishop Walker. She looked down at her watch and pointed. I nodded and looked at the door again, giving a little shrug of my shoulders.

Bishop Walker grabbed the sides of the podium. "I would like to thank all of you for coming here today, especially on short notice. I feel that what I have to share is important enough that it garnered more than just a written statement. I wanted to meet with you face to face to share my horror over the events that have transpired in the last few days. And then to share further information that has come to my attention from the Bishop's council."

I drew in a sharp breath. That was it. He planned to release the identity of the person who wrote the letters of accusation against Deacon Barnes and Pastor Hines. I was sure he also planned to slander Kevin in whatever way his twisted mind had conjured up to do so. I stared at the door.

Please, God. Please let them hurry up and get here.

Bishop continued, "First and foremost, let me again voice my deepest regret for the tragic incidents that have taken place over the last twenty odd years in my congregation. This has been the most difficult thing I've ever had to face in my entire tenure in ministry. As I said before, as the leader of these flocks, I assume full moral responsibility for every act against every victim. This heavy burden will always weigh upon my heart. Until I go to my grave, I will experience the depth of their pain. To imagine the number of lives that have been affected is . . . unthinkable. I'm still trying to comprehend it."

He leaned over the podium for a few minutes, gripping it tightly, almost as if he didn't have the strength to stand.

Blanche leaned over to me. "You gotta be kidding me. This man is as evil as it gets." She looked around the room at the journalists scribbling on note pads, photographers snapping pictures. "And they're eating it up." She stared at the door. "Where are they? This needs to end. Now."

Bishop Walker raised his head and leaned into the microphone again. "To the family of the young boy whose life recently was so deeply affected by these tragedies, my heart goes out." His voice cracked. "As we have said of the other victims,

Love and Faith Christian Center is completely committed to your healing process. We will be providing intense psychological therapy for this young boy and all the victims that are involved." He gestured toward Pastor Duncan. "My director of pastoral counseling has already begun making arrangements for three of the victims. We hope that everyone involved will take advantage of the services being provided. That includes the actual victims and family members who have been affected by these tragedies as well. Although we can't change what's happened in the past, we hope to ensure a better future for these young men and their loved ones."

Bishop Walker accepted a handkerchief from his secretary and mopped his forehead with it. "In addition, we've taken measures to ensure a better screening process for any individual on staff at Love and Faith Christian Center. Whether it's the janitor cleaning the toilets, or my right hand men on my pastoral team, every individual currently employed or seeking employment at this church will undergo rigorous psychological testing and a criminal background check before they are hired or can continue working here."

I had to give it to him. He was brilliant. In such an evil way. I shuddered.

Blanche leaned over to whisper. "Yeah, everyone but him will be screened. I'd love to see the results of his psychological testing. Although he's such a natural liar, he'd probably come out looking like a saint."

She looked down at her watch, and we both stared at the door as if our eyes could make it miraculously open.

Bishop Walker cleared his throat. "And now finally, the news I received from the Bishop's council."

I clenched my jaw and my fists. *God, please. This can't end like this.*

Sandra Jensen raised her hand. "Excuse me, Bishop Walker. Before you move on, I'd like to ask a question if you don't mind."

Bishop Walker looked at Sandra, then looked at me, then made himself smile. "I thought I'd take questions at the end of the conference. I have one last piece of information I'd like to share, then I'll be happy to answer as many questions as time permits." He glared in my direction.

He looked down at the podium, and then up again. "As I was saying, I recently received some information from the Bishop's council as to the identity of the individual whose information started this entire investigation. Unfortunately, I have some disturbing news about that individual as well."

I bit my lip and looked from Bishop Walker to the door, to his smug face, and to the door again. He couldn't hide his sinister smile. The room was dead silent, pens poised over pads, breaths bated, greedy journalists waiting for this latest juicy nugget of church scandal gossip.

And then it happened. The door to the corridor swung open, and several men dressed in dark suits and an authoritative air strode into the room. They walked directly to the podium behind Bishop Walker. The stocky one took one of Bishop's hands. I could only see the slightest flash of silver, but the sound of the clinking metal was undeniable. The tallest one spoke with a deep voice, "Clarence Walker, you're under arrest for conspiracy to sexual misconduct, accessory after the fact, and tampering with evidence. You have the right to remain silent . . ."

thirty-one

It was over.

After shaking hands with reporters, talking to Blanche, and thanking Sandra Jensen, the whole ordeal was over, and I could finally go home to my family. I had to sit in my car for a few minutes, my whole body still shaking. My bottom lip was raw from me biting it those few seconds before that stupid door finally opened.

I picked up the phone to call Gabe. He fussed at me for not calling sooner. I had given him a brief call after I left Bishop Walker's office to let him know I had quit and was safe, but he hadn't expected me to take that long. I didn't bother to tell him everything that had just happened. I'd wait until I got there to explain.

He had gone to the house to wait for me hours ago. A scary thought. Gabe spent the entire afternoon at my house. With Moms. I needed to rescue him before something bad happened.

When I got to the house, Gabe was sitting at the kitchen table with Moms and Tiffany. When I walked into the kitchen, they seemed to be engaged in a serious conversation, so I didn't want to interrupt. I went straight upstairs to change into a pair of my new jeans I had ordered off the Internet. They fit pretty well. Might have to do all my shopping online. I went back downstairs to see what they were talking about.

When I got to the bottom of the steps, I heard Tiffany say, "I guess you're right, Gabe. If we don't forgive him, we're the ones that stay miserable while he goes on, happy with his life."

My mouth fell open. What had Gabe done? Were they actually talking about my father? Did he tell them I had told him the whole story? Moms was gonna murder me. I stayed at the bottom of the steps, listening.

I heard Moms say, "Son-in-law, I appreciate you having the courage to say all these things you said to us. It's hard, though. I'm an old bird, set in my ways. I know it's not too late for my girls to change their way of thinking, but—"

I heard Gabe's gentle voice, "Mummy, it's never too late. You just make a decision to change your heart and your mind and the rest follows. Who knows what may happen. After all the bitterness is gone, the cancer may leave your body as well."

I heard her laugh. "Baby, please. I'm just trying to make things right so I can have some peace before I go 'head and die. You and Trina and all this talk about miracles and healing—"

"We know what we've seen, Mummy. People healed from diseases just as bad as or worse than yours. Even a baby coming back from the dead. Why should we watch you die when we've seen so many healed? It simply wouldn't do."

"I love the way you talk all proper, baby. You could talk to me all day." Moms gave a nervous laugh that let me know Gabe was getting to her.

I smiled and sat down on the step to finish listening to their conversation. If I knew Gabe, he wouldn't quit until he had closed the deal and sealed their eternal future.

Gabe said, "So as I said, you cannot hold God responsible for the sins of men who claim to belong to Him. Each of us must search out God on our own to discover who He is. You cannot allow the sins of this man from your past to keep you from experiencing the most beautiful relationship of your lives. God is real and powerful and wonderful and there's no way we should have to live this harsh life without Him, experiencing His love in our lives daily. And Mummy, since you're so determined to die, shouldn't you ensure that your soul will live eternally with Christ in His paradise?"

Moms grunted.

Gabe continued, "And Tiffany, it's not a matter of what you might have to give up, or being afraid that you're not perfect enough to enter into a relationship with Jesus. You give Him your heart, and He perfects you, yes? It is only He that can make us perfect anyway."

The kitchen was quiet for a few moments. I held my breath, waiting to hear what their responses would be. I wondered just how long Gabe had been there and what all he had said before I arrived. Was he really about to get my mother and sister saved in one day after I had been trying for years? I guess the scripture about a prophet not having honor in His hometown and Jesus not being able to do any miracles in Nazareth was true.

I finally heard Tiffany's voice. "So what exactly are we supposed to do?"

Gabe said, "It's the simplest thing on earth. You simply open your heart and accept Him in."

Silence again. I was afraid to move from my perch on the steps. I didn't want to break the spell Gabe and the Holy Spirit were casting on my family.

I finally heard Tiffany's voice softly say, "Okay."

Moms only grunted. Without seeing her face, I didn't know what that meant. Her grunt could mean "I heard what you said, and I don't agree, but I'm being polite so I'm not going to tell you how I really feel." Or it could mean, "I agree with what you're saying, but I don't want to appear too enthusiastic about it." Or it could mean, "I wish you would shut up so I can go upstairs and go to bed."

Gabe didn't know Moms well enough to appreciate the art

required to decipher the meaning of her grunts. I could only pray that he would be led by the Holy Spirit in what he did next.

I heard him say, "There's no rush, Mummy. You take your time and think about it, and when you're ready, you let me know, yes?"

"Okay, baby. Deal."

I imagined they were shaking on it.

"Tiffany, you ready?" Gabe proceeded to lead Tiffany in the sinner's prayer. I almost fell off the step. I heard her voice, firmly repeating every word Gabe said.

I didn't know whether to scream or shout or cry. I felt like doing all three. But I sat there quietly, waiting to hear the end of their conversation.

When they finished their prayer, Tiffany said, "So I'm saved now?"

Gabe said, "Yes, my dear sister."

Tiffany said, "I don't feel any different."

Gabe laughed. "Trust me, you are. Completely different. And as time progresses, you'll realize just how different you are."

"So you telling me that's all Tiffany has to do to go to heaven when she die? Just say the words you just said?" Moms asked.

What had Gabe been talking about before I got home? Moms didn't believe in heaven and hell. I guess it was like she'd been saying lately though, staring death in the face made her examine all her beliefs.

"Exactly, as will be the same for you when you get saved. And should you decide not to let Jesus heal you, and you decide to 'go 'head and die,' as you say . . ."

Tiffany laughed at Gabe imitating Moms.

". . . then you're sure to go to heaven shortly thereafter."

I heard Moms' voice call out, "Tree, get off them steps and come on in here. We know you out there listening."

I laughed and almost ran into the kitchen. I hugged Tiffany, then hugged Moms, then hugged Gabe. I whispered in his ear, "Can't leave you alone for a minute. And to think I was worried about leaving you alone with Moms." I reached up and kissed him on the cheek. "I love you."

"And I love you." He kissed me on the lips. "Did you tell them?"

I shook my head. "They were sleep when I went upstairs last night and sleep when I woke up this morning."

"Tell us what?" Moms reached out for me and grabbed my left hand. "Well, now. Does this mean what I think it means?"

We both nodded.

She put her hand to her heart. "Well, now I can really die in peace." She bit her lip and grunted. "Or maybe live in peace. We just gon' have to see."

My heart swelled, and I thought I would cry.

Moms grabbed my hand and stared at my ring. "That sho is a fine ring, baby." She looked up at Gabe. "You brought this all the way from Africa?"

"Well, Mummy, actually it's from Canada."

Moms frowned. "They ain't got no diamond rings in Africa? Much diamonds and gold as they have in the Motherland?"

I slipped the ring off my finger and held it up to explain. "That's just the problem, Moms. In Africa, diamond mining is a very vicious process. Men, women, and children are often murdered or brutally attacked and enslaved to get the diamonds, so I didn't want any diamonds from Africa. And Africa has been raped for its gold, so I didn't want a gold band from there either. This ring is certified completely conflict free."

I slipped the ring back on my finger, and Gabe took my hand in his and kissed it.

Moms grunted. "Well that's all fine and good, but all I want to know is, when is the wedding? I ain't got much time left." She bit her lip. "Or maybe I do." She looked at Gabe, then looked at me. "Well, let's just have it soon just in case. You never know what might happen."

It was weird to watch her begin to struggle with the fact that she may not have to die. I silently prayed that God would continue to cause the seed of hope to grow in her heart. "I don't know yet, Moms. We haven't talked about all that. Soon, though." I smiled at Gabe. "Soon."

Tiffany asked, "Where you guys gonna get married? I know not in Africa. I ain't peeing in no holes, and I got to take a shower every day. And I definitely ain't eating with my hands, and I ain't gonna be eating no rice and beans and stuff and—"

"Tiffany, shush your mouth," Moms said. "If they decide to get married in Africa, you gon' have to learn to pee in a hole."

"So you would really travel to Africa for us to get married, Moms?"

She nodded. "I still got my passport from when me and Aunt Penny went on that cruise last year. How soon can we go?"

I looked at Gabe. "As soon as possible."

I was a little nervous about taking Moms to Africa, but then again, maybe that was just what she needed.

I looked down at my watch. "I gotta watch the news."

thirty-two

I got up from the table and started toward the living room. "What's going on?" Moms asked.

"More than I can even say." I walked into the living room and plopped down on the couch, grabbing the remote off the coffee table. I flipped through the channels until I got to Fox 5 News, Sandra Jensen's station. I sent Monica a quick text to tune into her evening news because I was sure the story would go nationwide.

Gabe sat next to me and put an arm around me.

Tiffany picked her purse up from the armchair. "Sissy, can I borrow your car to go to Stacy's house? We got some outfits to finish."

"You're coming home tonight?"

Tiffany rolled her eyes. "Of course, silly. I'm saved now. I can't be out drinking and smoking and all that stuff anymore."

Me and Gabe laughed. I tossed her the keys. Moms came in from the kitchen. "I'm going upstairs. I gotta get my rest so I'll be ready for my trip to Africa." She kissed my forehead, then Gabe's, and slowly walked toward the stairs.

I tucked myself into Gabe's side and relaxed, waiting for the news to start. "I can't believe you did that."

"Did what?"

I stared at Gabe. "Ummm, ministered to my mother and sister. You actually got my sister saved and my mother thinking. Do you know how long I've been trying to do that?"

Gabe wrapped his arms around me. "Well, you know the Bible says that some plant and some water. Let's just be thankful that God gave the increase."

I leaned back into him. "Yeah." I sighed and snuggled against him for a few minutes, wondering how much more it would take to get my mother saved.

"She'll give her heart soon, my dear. Don't even worry about it."

Just as I was about to close my eyes, enjoying the scent of Gabe's cologne, Deacon Barnes face flashed across the screen. I wondered whether when he posed for that picture if he had ever imagined it would be flashed on the news on a regular basis. For such an awful reason.

"Here it goes." I sat up and turned the volume on the television up.

"After recent conclusive evidence against Fred Barnes confirmed his guilt in at least one case of sexual misconduct against a minor, Mr. Barnes pleaded guilty today to several of the charges. Final information on the details of the sentencing with the plea are forthcoming, but it is likely that the judge in this case will want him to serve the maximum sentence because of the number and severity of his crimes."

"Wow. Looks like he's going down," I said.

"May his punishment be firm, but merciful," Gabe said.

Was my heart wrong? I wanted him to suffer for all the suffering he had caused. Maybe because it was so personal. I thought of the effect of his actions on Monica's life. On Kevin's life. I thought of the little boy scribbling his name on the index card, then setting it carefully on what he considered to be his own grave. Digging the hole and stuffing his bloody underwear in the ground. Was I not a Christian because I wanted Deacon Barnes to pay for that?

"In a related case, Walter Hines also pleaded guilty today, changing from his original not guilty plea. Although no conclusive evidence has been presented against him, it is thought that his plea hoped to provoke lighter sentencing. Once again, it is thought that the judge will have no mercy in these cases."

I clenched my fists. "Just like they had no mercy on the boys."

Gabe said, "Where is the redemption for these men? They will go to prison for a very long time, yes? But where is help? How does their deliverance come?"

I shushed Gabe when I saw Bishop Walker's face on the screen. "Listen to this." I turned the volume up a little louder.

"Breaking news today in this case. Up until this point, the Bishop presiding over the churches where the cases of sexual molestation occurred has categorically denied any knowledge of the sexual misconduct or any participation in any of the cases. News 5 today learned that Bishop Walker not only knew about at least two cases, but tried to cover them up. The U.S. Attorney's office received information from a woman in Texas today alleging that her son was molested seven years ago. She met and discussed the misconduct with Bishop Walker and gave him descriptive details of the events and circumstances surrounding her son's abuse. She alleges that Bishop Walker threatened that she should be concerned about what would happen if she were to make threats against him or any of the leadership in his church. She also states she was given money for her and her son to relocate to Dallas, Texas, where they've been living since the incident."

Gabe's eyes widened. He looked at me, then back at the television.

Bishop Walker was shown onscreen next, his head bowed and his arms behind his back between tall cop and stocky cop.

"After looking into the allegations, The U.S. Attorney's office has

charged Mr. Walker with conspiracy to sexual misconduct, accessory after the fact, and possibly tampering with evidence. Mr. Walker refused to comment on the allegations."

I let out a deep breath. I felt guilty to be so happy about what I was hearing.

My cell phone rang. I didn't have to look down at the caller ID to know it was Monica. I answered it.

"What did you do? Oh my goodness."

"Girl, it's been a day." I recounted the morning's events starting with my conversation with Bishop Walker up to my surprise visit from Ms. Turner.

"I knew he knew before Kevin told him," Monica said. "So the woman came forward?"

"Yes, Blanche and I spoke with her today, and then put her in touch with the U.S. Attorney's office. She's willing to do whatever it takes to help bring Bishop to justice along with the other men as well."

"Wow," Monica said. "So Bishop is being dethroned from his reign of terror over Love and Faith? I never thought I'd see the day. What's gonna happen to all those people, though? You know?"

I knew Monica was thinking about all our friends we'd left behind at Love and Faith. "I made a call to the Bishop's council and Bishop Walker has been officially relieved of all his duties, privileges and responsibilities as the Bishop of Love and Faith Christian Centers, Washington DC and Alexandria. The council will be sending in pastors to cover the churches while they seek new permanent leadership. If you ask me, though, they really need to look at their organization altogether. For all these things to have gone on for this long in churches under their watch, you have to wonder about them too. I just pray that the 24,000 people who've been attending both churches will find churches where true men of God with hearts of integrity are running things. I'd hate for one person to walk away from God because of Bishop Walker."

"I can't believe Bishop Walker may go to prison," Monica said. "I hate everything he did to us and everything that he let happen in his church all these years, but I never thought he'd get locked up."

"I know, but if he knew about what was going on and didn't do anything about it, he's just as guilty as Deacon Barnes and Pastor Hines."

"I know, Trina. It's just . . . this is all so serious."

"Yeah, girl. Serious isn't the word. Can you believe those two changed their plea? I think both of them were trying to get a plea bargain to get the shortest amount of time possible. But the rumor is that the judge ain't having it. The word is he's going to give them the worst possible punishment. And the two of them have the nerve to be asking for special protection. You know what happens to child molesters in prison. Especially since they're supposed to be men of God."

"Oh my God. I didn't even think of that. Crazy as it sounds, I feel like we should be praying for them. Even though what they did to Kevin and all those boys was awful, I still wouldn't want them to get raped or killed in prison, you know?"

"Yeah, girl. That would be pretty brutal."

"I can't believe all this happened. Trina, would you have even thought that two years ago when you got on the plane to go to Mozambique that all this would end up happening? It's all so much."

"It is. And you're right. I would have never guessed that any of this would have turned out this way. Like I said, what Satan means for evil, God will always turn out for good."

"Thanks, girl. For all you've done through all this. You've been the best friend I could ever ask for. Everything in my life has turned out better than I could have ever imagined. I love you, Trina."

"I love you too, Monnie." I stood and held up a finger to Gabe, letting him know I'd be right back. I stepped into my office and sat down in my desk chair. "By the way, I said yes."

"You said yes? What are you talking about?" She screeched

before I got a chance to answer. "You said yes to Gabe? You're getting married?"

"Yes, Monnie. I said yes." I told her about Gabe's surprise visit.

"Oh my goodness. I can't believe it." She was silent for a second and I knew she was realizing what I was really saying. "Oh no, that means you're going back to Africa, doesn't it?"

"Yeah, girl. Even if I weren't marrying him, though, I'd still be going back. It's where I'm supposed to be. Now going back will be even better."

"When are you going back?" Monica's voice sounded sad.

"I don't know yet. We haven't figured all that out. I guess it depends on what happens with Moms."

"Oh yeah. I forgot about that."

We were both silent for a second. "Trina, I just feel like the same thing you told me. I don't know how and when, but somehow God is going to work everything out for your good. For everyone's good. Especially Moms's. Somehow or another, she's gonna be fine."

"Thanks, Monnie. I needed to hear that." I didn't say what I was thinking. How could she be fine and she wasn't even saved? I couldn't bear the thought of my mother dying without accepting Christ into her life.

"He's gonna do it. More than you can imagine. Just like you told me."

We sat silent again, thinking about everything that was about to change in our lives.

"Oh, no. What about when the baby is born?" she asked.

"What about it?"

"You're not even going to be able to meet your nephew until your next visit. Who knows when that will be?"

"It'll be as soon as you call me and tell me he's here. I'll be on the first plane headed toward Atlanta. And I'll stay for a good long while to help out and get good and acquainted with my nephew. In other words, spoil him rotten."

"Yeah, right, Trina. You'll be a newlywed. You won't want to stay away from Gabriel more than a week, tops."

"Who said I'd be staying away from him? He'll be coming with me. You'll get to meet him."

"That would be awesome." She let out a deep breath. "Okay, I guess you can go."

"Thanks, Monnie. I appreciate having your permission and your blessing."

She laughed. "Okay, let me go. Daddy Kevin is lurking in the hallway."

We both laughed.

After I finished talking to Monica, I came back out to the couch to sit with Gabe.

He put his arm around me. "Did you guys finish talking about me?"

"Yep." I laughed.

"I trust it was all good."

"Of course. I can't think of anything bad I would say about you."

"So your mother will get on a plane and go to Africa with us?" He looked serious for a second, and I could see him planning the trip in his head.

"Do you think it's crazy, seeing the state of health that she's in?"

"I think it's the kind of crazy that gives the Father the perfect opportunity to glorify Himself."

I snuggled into his side and enjoyed the strength and love in his arms as they encircled me. His comforting touch chased away the fears about my mother's health. He kissed me on the head and we sat there quietly, thinking about what was best for Moms and our wedding. Should we just have a small wedding ceremony here, and then a big celebration when we got to go back to Africa? Since Moms's oncologist had put her on hospice care and given her up for dead, it wasn't like he would object to us taking her to Mozambique.

Really though, what was the worst that could happen? We would stay at the mission base in Pemba instead of going to our village, so she would have a real bed and access to good clean water. And I would make sure she had plenty of food and fresh fruits and vegetables every day.

In the glory-filled atmosphere there, she'd be saved in no time. If she died, she would have given her heart to Christ and would be welcomed into heaven to wait until my arrival there. It would hurt terribly, but at least I would have peace that she died saved.

In my heart of hearts though, I believed that once she got to Mozambique and soaked up the heavenly atmosphere at the mission base, it was only a matter of time before she would be miraculously healed. And she would help us take care of all the children in the village. I could see them all gathered around her, just like her Baltimore kids, talking and laughing. And she'd be passing out kisses and her magical hugs.

Maybe if she liked it, she would stay over there with us, and be there when me and Gabe started our own family. Moms could become Grandmoms. I knew my children would be loved and well cared for. And Moms would be happy. And we could all live and grow there together in our beautiful community under the African skies where the Spirit of God always hovered near.

Epilogue

"Trina, he's here." Monica sounded exhausted, but happier than I'd ever heard her sound.

"Oh my goodness." I sat up in the bed. "When?"

"At about 1:00 this morning. I wanted to call you then, but as soon as they took him to the nursery, I fell asleep. Can you believe I was in labor for eighteen hours?"

"Dag, Monnie. Are you serious? I can't imagine. How was it? As bad as they say?"

"Worse. It was horrible, girl. I can't even begin to describe it. It's true what they say, though. As soon as I looked into his beautiful, little face, all the pain was forgotten. You should see him, Trina. He looks exactly like Kevin. Head full of thick hair and all."

"Oooh," I cooed. "What's my nephew's name?"

"Kevin Andrew Day, Jr. What else?"

"Of course. Don't even know why I asked."

Gabe stirred in the bed next to me and let out a little snore. I reached over and smoothed my fingers through his wild hair.

"So I know you guys are just getting settled in and all, and even though you said you'd be here as soon as he was born, I'd understand if—"

"No way, Monnie. As soon as we get up, I'll have Gabe start looking at plane tickets. We'll give you guys a week or two to bond with baby Kevin, but after that, we'll be there."

"Yeah?" I could hear her smiling into the phone.

"Yeah." I kissed Gabe's closed eyelids and slid out of the bed so I wouldn't wake him.

"But what about . . . is Moms okay . . . you know, for you guys to leave her? We have plenty of room if you want to bring her. If she's okay to travel that far again."

I walked down the long, narrow hall of our small house in Pemba, my feet swishing on the coarse sand that always littered the smooth, stone floor, no matter how many times I swept. "Girl, please. Moms is fine. You should see her. She's eating well. She's picked up about twenty pounds in the two months since we've been here. And there's no way I could get her away from here. She ain't leaving her babies, and they ain't trying to let her go."

I peeked into Moms's room. She was fast asleep, crowded in the bed with at least four children who found a way to sneak into her room after I shooed them away every night. There were at least six more scattered on the floor around the bed. I shook my head, but couldn't help but smile.

"Is she . . ." I could tell Monica was afraid to ask the question.

"Healed? Girl, I guess so. It's not like we have a CAT scan machine or anything like that here to check." I stepped back into the hall and closed Moms's door. "All I know is she's getting stronger, fatter, and healthier every day. Her hair is growing back, her skin color is peachy again, and she can run around after the children all day long. A few days after we got here, she got rid of the oxygen tank her doctor insisted we bring after telling us how crazy we were for trying to take her halfway across the world. It's been all good ever since."

"Wow. God is . . . awesome."

I walked down the hall a little farther, into the main room with the small kitchen, eating area, and living area. "Girl, awesome ain't the word. I honestly never thought I'd see the day when my mother had anything good to say about Jesus, but she beats us to church for every service. She and the kids are on the front row every time. You should see her teaching them stories from the Bible. I still can't believe it."

I walked over to the large window and stared through the wire mesh screen out at the huge African moon. I could actually count the stars as their brightness contrasted against the pitch black sky. The thick, gnarly branches of the Baobab tree in the yard reached up to heaven, almost like it was praying.

"I may see if Tiffany wants to fly down and meet us in Atlanta while we're there," I said. "Who knows when I'll get a chance to spend some time with her again?"

"Why? What's going on with her?"

I stepped out the front door and almost tripped over the mangy dog that seemed to think he was ours. I knew it was because Moms always snuck him food because she couldn't stand seeing his ribs. "She, her friend Stacy, and Stacy's two kids moved into Moms's house in Baltimore after I rented my house out. They're really getting things going with their fashion business,and I don't know when she can get away to come over here again. Not that she'd be trying to visit. You should have seen her while she was here for the wedding. Everything was 'eeeuwww' this and 'yucky' that."

Monica laughed. "Sounds like how I would be if I came over there to visit."

"If?" I took a deep breath, inhaling the ever present, acrid odor of burning brush and trash. "Don't even try it. As soon as the baby's old enough, you have to come visit. It's only fair. Besides, you never know what might happen the first time you come. You might like it and decide to move over here too."

"No chance of that, girl. Like I said before, I like my nice big house in suburbia and my perm and my long, hot baths in my Jacuzzi, and my swimming pool, and all my favorite restaurants here in Atlanta, and the mall and my—"

"Okay, Monnie. I get it." I walked back into the house and closed the door behind me. "If I want to see you, I have to come there."

We both laughed. I walked back down the hall to my bedroom. "Okay, my friend. You get some rest and kiss my nephew for me. See you in about two weeks?"

"Yep. I can't wait. Love you, Trina."

"Love you too, Monnie."

We said our goodbyes and I crawled back into my bed. I snuggled up against my husband of two months, and pulled the mosquito net back around us.

As I fell back asleep, all I could think of was the scripture that had proven so true in both me and my best friend's lives. Everything that Satan had meant for evil, God had turned for good.

Gabe rolled over and pulled me into his arms. I nestled into his chest.

Better than good.

The end

Reader's Group Questions

1. Monica says that Trina makes her feel like she's not a real Christian because she doesn't want to go to Africa and is not concerned about helping the less fortunate. Does that make her less of a Christian?

2. When watching the news report about the molestations that occurred in Bishop Walker's church, Moms says that's why she doesn't go to church. How do church scandals, especially those involving pastors and leaders, affect the unsaved?

3. Trina mentions being afraid that Moms and Tiffany are going to talk them out of the miracle they need with their doubt and unbelief. How do people's words affect the power of God?

4. When Bishop Walker makes his threat about telling the press about Kevin's history, Trina decides that she has to continue working with him to protect Monica at all costs. Was this the right conclusion to come to?

5. How is it possible that Trina got saved under Bishop Walker's ministry, and he didn't even believe in God?

6. Trina is angry that God has let Bishop Walker get away with being an atheist while pastoring one of the largest churches in the city. She contrasts that with her mother, who is a good person, having cancer, and initially decided that God isn't fair. Is God fair?

7. Monica tells Trina she has a pride problem and that she should have asked her and Kevin to borrow money rather than work with Bishop Walker. Gabe later states that she should have called him to ask for the money rather than work with Bishop Walker. What should Trina have done about her financial situation when she returned from Mozambique?

8. Moms tells Trina that she can't understand why Trina would believe that God would heal her, but couldn't believe Him to provide for her so she wouldn't have to work with Bishop Walker. Is she right to question Trina's faith?

9. Ms. Turner states that she's worried about what will happen to all the members of Bishop Walker's church when the truth about him comes out. She says that for many of them, Bishop is their God. What does she mean by this, and what is the danger in this?

10. How did Moms' relationships with the girls' father and with other men affect Trina's and Tiffany's relationships with men?

Urban Christian His Glory Book Club!

Established January 2007, **UC His Glory Book Club** is another way to introduce **Urban Christian** and its authors. We are an online book club supporting Urban Christian authors by purchasing, reading and providing written reviews of the authors' books. *UC His Glory Book Club* welcomes both men and women of the literary world who have a passion for reading Christian-based fiction.

UC His Glory Book Club is the brainchild of Joylynn Jossel, Author and Executive Editor of Urban Christian and Kendra Norman-Bellamy, copy editor for Urban Christian. The book club will provide support, positive feedback, encouragement and a forum whereby members can openly discuss and review the literary works of Urban Christian authors. In the future, we anticipate broadening our spectrum of services to include online author chats, author spotlights, interviews with your favorite Urban Christian author(s), special online groups for *UC His Glory Book Club* members, ability to post reviews on the website and amazon.com, membership ID cards, *UC His Glory* Yahoo Group and much more.

Even though there will be no membership fees attached to becoming a member of *UC His Glory Book Club,* we do expect our members to be active, committed and to follow the guidelines of the Book Club.

UC His Glory Book Club **members pledge to:**

- Follow the guidelines of *UC His Glory Book Club*.
- Provide input, opinions, and reviews that build up, rather than tear down.

- Commit to purchasing, reading and discussing featured book(s) of the month.
- Respect the Christian beliefs of *UC His Glory Book Club*.
- Believe that Jesus is the Christ, Son of the Living God

We look forward to the online fellowship.

Many Blessings to You!

Shelia E. Lipsey
President
UC His Glory Book Club

**Visit the official Urban Christian Book Club website at www.uchisglorybookclub.net